The Trouble with Love and
COACHES

HARRIET ASHFORD

Published by Phillips House

Book Cover by My Lan Khuc

Editing by Bryn Donovan

Proofread by Ramona Mihai

Also by Harriet Ashford

The Trouble with Love and Ink

Author's Note

I'm sorry to give you a novella before the novel, but I've got a lot to say.

First of all, this book was written for the adult reader. It has come to my attention that some of my former students disregarded the warning on my first novel. I don't care that most of y'all are grown adults now. If you want to be able to look me in the eye when we bump into each other at the grocery store, you will pass on this one. If you really can't help yourself, for the love of god, skip chapters 24, 27, and 31. Same goes for my parents, siblings, and local Chick-Fil-A workers.

For detailed trigger warnings, please visit my website: www.harrietas hfordwriter.com

If you didn't know, this is book two of an interconnected series. While I suggest reading "The Trouble with Love and Ink" to get the full effect of little life updates for Emily and Beck, it's not crucial for the plot. "The Trouble with Love and Coaches" works as a standalone novel, so you should be able to enjoy the story whether you are a returning reader or new here.

One more thing, while I tried to keep the triathlon aspects of this novel realistic, I had to move the dates for the Woodlands full Ironman and

Galveston half. Sometimes the facts have to be sacrificed in the name of the plot. Like a town being named Pearville instead of Pearland, for instance . . . Just lean in and enjoy. I promise it's fine.

For my readers.

It wasn't your job to resurrect my confidence, but that's exactly what you've done.

I've got all the heart eyes for you.

Chapter 1

APRIL

I swore by all that was holy that I'd burn my running shoes as soon as I got home. I fantasized about placing them in a metal trash can along with my anti-chafe stick and running belt. My sports bottle would be used to squirt gasoline; then I'd toss in the lighter and watch them go up in flames as if they were pictures of a scorned ex.

That's how done I was. One could hardly blame me. Being a July morning in Pearville—a small town just outside of Houston—hot and humid were the words of the day *every* day, but this morning, the water gathered in the air, warning of rain. It was like running through a sauna. To make matters worse, I'd been fighting a stitch in my side since mile three. The pinch in my knee started at mile five. By mile eight, I was living on a prayer and a marshmallow-flavored gel pack. And I still had two miles to go.

The worst part? Ten miles wasn't even considered a long run in my training plan. It was just a casual Monday morning jog because my end goal was to complete an Ironman, and in one of those torture fests, you ran a marathon—twenty-six point two miles—*after* swimming for two point four miles and cycling for 112.

These races were for masochists, the insane.

They were the stupidest thing dreamed up by man. Worse than the colored ketchup in the nineties or those shutter shades everyone was wearing, thanks to Kanye.

But come hell or high humidity, I would finish one. Most people wanted to finish an Ironman to prove, to themselves or others, that they were undeniably badass. Some people completed them to stay in shape—though one might argue putting that many miles on your body is a little overkill. I, on the other hand, wanted to finish an Ironman because that's what my mom had wanted me to do. Not only that, but I felt further from her every day. It had been twelve years since she passed. I couldn't remember her scent or the sound of her laugh. I knew her eyes had been green, but I couldn't picture the exact shade. I was becoming numb to her absence, and compared to the sharp edge of grief I'd experienced at seventeen, it was almost a relief, but it made me feel horrible. I should have held onto her better.

So here I was, running to catch back up to Mom. She'd been a triathlete, an Ironman finisher. I'd become the same, even if it killed me, which I was starting to think might be a real possibility.

I tried to shove that down because I was already battling enough negativity. Specifically, the voice in my head that said, *This is a waste of time. You're just going to DNF again.*

This was my fourth shot at Ironman. Four seasons—four years of training with nothing to show for it . . . okay, my quads and shoulders looked pretty toned, and if I turned my torso in just the right light, you could almost imagine the outline of my abs. But ghost abs meant nothing to me. I wanted that Ironman title. I wanted it so freaking bad.

Wanted it enough to suffer through this run and the bike tomorrow and the swim on Wednesday and even the bike/run combination workout that would take up four hours of my limited free time on Sunday.

I would do it for Mom.

I closed out my audiobook and flipped through my music until I found a beat that could revive a corpse. Then, I readjusted my ponytail before shaking out my hands as if to physically rid myself of the doubt.

Two miles is nothing. I've got this.

That Ironman title is practically mine.

This is my year.

Freshly showered and ready for work, I stopped at the smoothie shop a few doors down from the triathlon shop my family owned. My coach, Clay, wanted to have a quick meeting. We usually communicated over a training app, but I had a local sprint triathlon next week, so I figured he wanted to go over the game plan.

He texted me to say he'd be a little late and asked if I could order him a Super Green with a shot of wheatgrass. I'd nearly finished my blueberry oat when Clay sauntered up, wearing his matching sweats from Sweat-E, his latest sponsor. It had to have a real feel of ninety-five degrees outside, and Clay still rocked the sweatpants. I didn't know if it was admirable or ridiculous to risk heat stroke to make your sponsor happy, but Clay sure was proud to be a brand rep.

I smiled and waved, but the corners of Clay's lips barely quirked—nothing new there. He had this permanent smolder, which I'm sure worked wonders for many ladies, but there was something about those puckered lips that made him resemble the kid in class who never wins bingo. That was fine. I hadn't hired him for his chipper disposition. I needed his guidance and his training plans.

"Sorry I'm late. The Triple Threat meeting took a direction I wasn't expecting." Triple Threat was the triathlon coaching company he worked for. It started drizzling outside, and Clay watched the drops splash against the window near our booth.

"Oh. Is everything okay?"

"Actually . . . " He leaned back in his seat, and from the dramatic pause, I thought he would say he'd been fired. Instead, he said, "They are giving me a shot at A-Team."

"But . . ." I stopped, confused because his words seemed to contradict his body language. "That's a good thing, right?"

I didn't know all the details, but he'd been gunning for A-Team for years—something about having the opportunity to coach world-class athletes and collect a meaty bonus while he was at it.

"It's a great thing." He took a long pull from his green smoothie. "But it's not a done deal. If I want a chance at this, I need to have a near-perfect season. They will be judging both my own performance as an athlete, as well as the athletes I'm coaching." He looked pointedly at me, and my stomach soured. "Every athlete on my roster has to perform this year. I need every single one to bring their A-game."

This conversation felt like it was dancing dangerously close to an edge, and if I didn't get a handle on it, my Ironman season would sashay off the cliff.

"Okay, well, I've been following the training plan. I haven't missed a single workout."

"I know," he said, but his expression remained somber.

"Do we need to change the plan—make the workouts more rigorous?" I thought about my morning run and how I'd barely scraped by.

But I could handle more. I *would* handle more if it meant keeping my Ironman season on track.

"I have to take you off my roster, April."

"You're dropping me?" I thought of the x's on my calendar at home. Yesterday, I'd crossed off the three-month marker until Ironman. "But Ironman is only a few months away."

"I know, and I'm sorry. If they'd told me sooner, I wouldn't have even taken you on this season."

He hadn't meant to string me along. That's what he was trying to say, but it stung. He must have seen it in the way I reeled back.

"I'm not trying to upset you, but this position is really competitive."

I put out a hand to stop him before he could crush my confidence further, which was already made of sand and built too close to the tide. "I get it." And honestly, I did. I worked hard. I put in the time and the effort, but I didn't have the competitive spirit he thought was so essential. I'd never been a podium chaser. Hell, I didn't even care what my finishing time was in a race. I just wanted to finish.

Like Mom had.

Running across the red carpet of the Ironman had been one of her proudest moments. She wanted that experience for me, so I wanted it, too. But that didn't make me the fighter Clay needed.

The ache behind my eyes warned I was in danger of crying in the middle of Frooty Tooty Smoothies, and I couldn't think of anything more pathetic. I stood suddenly, empty cup clutched in my grip. "I better go," I said. "My schedule is full. Lots of tune-ups before the sprint next week."

Clay's lips pulled into a grimace, giving me a pitying look. I thought I hated the pouty face, but pity was so much worse. "I'll keep giving you training plans until after the race next week."

"Thank you," I said, as if he was doing me a favor by providing me with only a week's worth of training when he'd already committed to the entire season. As if he hadn't completely taken the wind from my sails, leaving me stranded midseason. I could see the shore from my spot in the ocean, but I'd never make it to land on my own—not with my luck.

I walked briskly toward Just Tri. Even under the awning, the sideways rain licked at my arms, washing away my pep talk from earlier.

This was supposed to be my year.

Now, it would be the year I'd have to face an Ironman alone. And I could fight the negative self-talk all I wanted, but at that moment, the DNF looked less like a weather forecast and more like a certainty.

Chapter 2

GABRIEL

"Easy, dammit," Coach Rick growled as I made another pass at the knot in his calf.

"Sorry," I mumbled, prodding the area. "You are always so tight here. You might need to switch shoes." Most of the time, I saw Coach Rick as a father figure. He gave the advice, and I was quick to heed. This was a rare moment. When he lay on my massage table, face in the cradle, the roles were reversed, and I got to be the voice of authority. After all, I'd been doing sports massage therapy for eleven years.

"If I buy another pair of shoes this month, my wife will kill me. The number of shoes I have puts her collection to shame."

That was the life of a runner.

"Buy her a pair first. You know what? Scratch that," I said, because I couldn't imagine Rick picking out a pair of women's shoes. "Get her a gift card to go shopping."

"She doesn't need more shoes," he said, annoyed with my suggestion.

"Then don't complain when I get to the problem spots." I tried to loosen up some of that muscle again.

"Ah! Torres!"

I sighed, relenting. "I'll send you home with some stretches, but if you don't take them seriously, you'll have to let me work that knot out."

I moved onto his hamstring, which wasn't as bad.

"So, are we going to talk about your meeting with the board this morning?" Rick asked gruffly.

I slid my forearm down his hamstrings. "You already know about it. So, I'm sure you know how it went."

"Jamal told me," he grumbled. "The fact that you aren't already guaranteed my position when I retire is complete horseshit."

I huffed out a laugh.

"I'm serious, Gabe."

"I know you are." Of course, he wanted me to take his place. He'd been my coach since I was a teenager. Back then, he was a high school swim coach, but after I graduated, he quit to train triathletes, and I found myself back under his whistle and mercy. It wasn't long before he had me starting my own coaching journey as a side hustle.

I wanted the position on A-Team. I'd have access to a slew of near-professional-level athletes. Talk about making an impact. I could help some of the quickest triathletes on the planet close the difference between themselves and their podium or personal record goals. But I'd be lying if I didn't include making Coach Rick proud as a huge motivation for making the team.

"So, what will you have to do to get on A-Team?" he asked.

"Just keep doing what I'm doing." I had more years at Triple Threat than Clay and coached more athletes. The board was transparent with how the application process would work. They were taking a "holistic approach," meaning they would scrutinize everything: our own race times, athlete reviews, and athlete race times compared to their race history. In other words, they wanted to see athletes making actual progress while under our wings, which made sense. Clay's only advantage was he had an athlete who had never completed an Ironman because any time she made on the race would be considered progress as long as she finished. Even still, I wasn't too worried. My athletes always showed growth.

"We need you at peak performance for Ironman Texas. How was your last ride?"

"Fine," I said. Truth be told, I'd completed it at the targeted speed and power but just barely. Afterward, I'd collapsed on my tile floor, lying in a pool of sweat, staring at the ceiling fan and regretting all life's choices.

"Good." Then he went into full-on coach mode, talking about our plan of attack for the month in the form of training and racing schedules.

Three more months. I could hold out on this training schedule for three more months.

"I wish you hadn't taken on as many athletes this season," Coach scolded. "You need to be strong for your own race."

"When have you known me to skimp on workouts?"

He mumbled something about stretching myself too thin as I finished the session and began washing my hands in the massage room's tiny sink.

"How is Ashley doing?"

"Oh, uh—" I hadn't expected the sudden pivot to my personal life. I shut off the water. "We're not seeing each other anymore."

"I'm sorry." He said it like I told him my *abuela* passed away.

I popped my head up. "It's okay. It's not a big deal." It truly wasn't. Ashley and I hadn't really even been dating. Coach just assumed we were because he'd seen the two of us together a couple of times.

"What happened? I thought you liked Ashley." He still sounded hurt, like I'd broken up with him.

I had enjoyed Ashley's company. We had a good amount of physical compatibility, but eventually, she started catching feelings that I couldn't reciprocate—that I'd never be able to reciprocate. Breaking up with her was the humane thing to do.

She'd been upset, and I hated that. But I'd made my intentions clear in the beginning, and I wasn't going to change my mind. Love was too messy an emotion, too slippery to get a grip on, so I'd stick to casual.

"I did. It's just . . . she wanted something more serious." I toweled off my hands. "And you know I don't do that."

"Gabe, it's okay to have fun. You're in your twenties."

I bit back a smile. "I'm thirty-one."

"Christ, I'm getting old," he said, slowly lowering himself from the table.

I chuckled. "No denying that."

He shot me a glare before continuing. "My point is, you're still young, and I think you should be having fun if that's what you want. But if you've got some fear of commitment because of your dad, you need to knock that shit off. You're not him." He pointed a meaty finger at me. "And you never will be."

"I know," I said because any other answer would summon a longer conversation, and I'd rather have a fingernail extracted than navigate that topic.

"He chose to be that man," Rick said, continuing even though I knew he could sense my discomfort. That was his style. He'd always been okay with pushing his athletes past their comfort zones. "You don't have a mean bone in that freakishly tall body."

I laughed, then straightened to my full height. "I passed you in height over a decade ago. You gotta let that resentment go."

Coach Rick rolled his eyes but, to my absolute relief, started for the door.

"You're a good kid, Torres."

"Thanks, Coach." And because I couldn't stand him leaving on too serious of a note I said, "Be sure to do those stretches I'll send you, or you'll have a different outlook the next time you leave my massage table."

Chapter 3

APRIL

My hand slipped once again as I worked furiously to tighten a bolt. The workbench was usually my happy place at Just Tri—our family's store. As a one-stop triathlon shop, my focus was often split between bike repairs, shoe fittings, and the occasional question about flippers. So having a moment to be alone with the BMX on my stand should have been solace, but instead of getting lost in the puzzle of bolts, cones, and axles, I kept replaying the morning—of being fired as Clay's athlete.

With each turn of my Allen wrench, my mind circled the feeling of being lost—wondering how I'd tread the path to Ironman without guidance—and feeling hopeless.

"Every athlete on my roster has to perform this year." Clay's voice echoed and bounced in my head, then morphed into the hidden picture camouflaged by his words: *You are just going to DNF again.*

I tried to shake it off because he hadn't said that. He needed an aggressive team. I just wasn't competitive enough.

That's okay. I don't need to be fast. I just need to finish, I thought, but my fingers spun the Allen wrench faster as if racing my thoughts. It slipped from my grasp and clattered to the floor. My cousin, Trevor, got to it before I did.

"Hey, what's going on?" he asked.

I knew the conversation was coming. I'd seen the concern creased on his forehead as I'd entered the shop earlier. I'm sure I was a sight, drenched from the rain and just barely keeping the tears at bay.

Mercifully, Trevor had been inundated with customers, and Billie, one of my closest friends and Just Tri's cashier, didn't work on Mondays. I had just enough time at my workbench to gather myself—to let my emotions settle to frustration, but I still felt pressure in my chest warning me that tears were still possible.

I took the Allen wrench from Trevor's hand, then leaned back against my workbench, looking at the tool instead of Trevor.

"I uh—" I sniffed. "Clay's not going to be my coach anymore."

"What? Why?"

"He is trying to get on A-Team—It's some sort of promotion, and he needs his athletes to be competitive."

"What does that even mean?" Trevor was something like a big brother to me. In fact, many people thought we were twins. With him only being a couple of months older, we'd been in the same grade throughout school, had the same dirty-blond hair—so dark it argued as a light brown in the winter. Had the same hazel eyes, though his needed glasses. Our moms had been twins, so they'd always been delighted when people mistook us as womb-mates.

The protectiveness in his tone only made the urge to cry all the more powerful. It was having someone on my side saying my situation was fucked. Both validating and a bit soul-crushing.

"I don't know. He just needs a reliable team to give himself a real shot at the promotion. Can you blame him?"

"Yes. I can definitely blame him. You are reliable, April. Those DNFs weren't your fault, and you know it."

My eyes bore into the framed picture above the checkout counter. After eighteen years, it was still my favorite picture. My mom and a ten-year-old version of myself stood with our backs to the camera. My mom showed off her fresh Ironman tattoo on her calf. On my calf was my own crude attempt at the Ironman symbol. However, drawing it from such an odd angle made it look more like a chubby butterfly. Even still, that was one of my most potent memories of Mom—the way she'd laughed delightedly when I'd shown her my copycat leg.

The memory usually made my heart swell. Now it just hurt. I felt like my plan to be an Ironman was sitting on Jenga blocks, and Clay had taken a corner piece from the bottom.

It was going to come toppling down. It was only a matter of time.

"Maybe it's just not meant to be," I said wetly. "Maybe I'm not meant to be an Ironman."

"No, fuck that!" His exclamation was enough to rouse Johnson from his slumber in his usual spot beneath my workbench.

The one-eyed dachshund waddled out and looked at Trevor with less puppy dog eyes and more of a singular, *Pick me up, bitch,* expression. It worked and came with a side of under-the-collar scratching.

"It's fine, Trevor."

"Maybe someone else would buy that, but I know what this race means to you."

Johnson had turned his head to look at me, and I shrugged under the gaze of three eyes.

Trevor was quiet for a moment, and I could almost see him mentally grasping at straws. "Maybe this is a blessing. Maybe you'll get a better coach."

I scoffed.

"I'm serious. That guy is a prick, and what is wrong with his face, anyway? He always looks like he's in danger of shitting himself."

That had me laughing for real. "I think that face actually works on some women."

"Do you want me to talk to Gabe? See if he has any openings?"

The name sent a zing down my spine, along with a memory from nine months ago after my bike wreck during the last Ironman. Gabe had bent over me, black hair messy and sweaty. He'd been mouthing something—my name, I surmised, by reading his lips—but I couldn't hear anything after just regaining consciousness. His brows furrowed in concern, and the brutal scar that cut through one of them captivated my attention. My brain couldn't compute why I was staring at Gabriel Torres, so it locked onto one physical thing. Every time I'd seen him at the shop, I'd wondered how he'd gotten it, but it seemed rude to ask. Hazily, I'd reached up to touch it, and that's when pain electrified my collarbone, shooting all the way to my fingertips.

The rest is a blur of pain jumbled with Gabe's hand on my uninjured shoulder and his low whispering encouragements keeping me grounded until the ambulance arrived.

Though the moment towered like a monument in my memories, I really didn't know Gabe that well. I saw him occasionally at the shop, triathlon parties, and races, but we weren't anything more than acquaintances. The idea of joining his team made me feel uneasy.

The guy didn't just coach the quickest in town, but he *was* one of the quickest in town. Asking him to take me on was like giving a college baseball coach a little league player. It felt like I'd insult him just by asking to be on his team.

"I think I'm just going to try and do it on my own," I decided.

Trevor's eyes narrowed. "But you are still going to try to do it. Right?"

"Of course," I said, but the conviction in my voice had the integrity of a paper straw.

Trevor looked at Johnson and, with a *who is a good boy voice,* said, "Does that smell like bullshit to you, Johnson?" Johnson wagged his tail once as his vote in the matter.

"I'm going to try. Of course I am, but it just feels pointless."

For a moment, Trevor's eyes looked far away behind his glasses, but when they refocused, they were bright. "How about this? If you really take this season seriously, I'll finally apply for a position at *Exposure.*"

I straightened. I'd been trying to get him to apply to the nature magazine for years, but an accident after high school graduation sucked the spark right out of him and his photography career. Even though he still took the most beautiful pictures, he didn't try to pursue anything other than local gigs, race day shots, things like that. "Seriously?" I asked, unable to tamp down my reaction.

"Sure. I'll give it my best shot. But you have to give this race season your best shot, too. Deal?"

I took Johnson's grubby paw in my hand and shook. "Deal."

Chapter 4

GABRIEL

Friday was one of my days off from massage therapy. Unfortunately, in the life of a coach and an Ironman athlete, the day off from one job meant more work for the other. I'd spent the first three waking hours glued to a bike seat.

Like most other serious cyclists, I had a bike trainer—it was sort of like a treadmill for cycling. You took the back tire off your bike, hooked it up to the trainer, then binged Netflix. It was nice not having to leave the house to get a quick seventy-five miles in.

Unfortunately, the workout was one of those where the breath scraped out of my lungs. The plan called for such high power, it felt like I was going uphill the entire ride. So, I had to rewatch those episodes of Ozark. I vaguely understood Jason Bateman's character was in deeper shit in each episode, but it was hard to catch the details when I was busy working through my own hell.

After mopping up the sweat from my apartment's tile and showering, I headed over to Just Tri. Trevor had texted, letting me know they'd gotten in the new Nike Vaporfly, and I wanted to try them as my race-day runners. I had about an hour before a Zoom meeting with an athlete, and then the rest of the day would be uploading training plans for next week.

The plan was good. Get in, get out, get home so I could work on training plans for my athletes.

But then my feet stepped across the threshold of Just Tri, and it wasn't Trevor in the shoe section, but April.

For a split second, I forgot what I was even doing there. She pushed her shoulder-length, dark blonde hair behind her ears as she scanned the shoe boxes on the wall. She had a casual way about her. If her hands weren't busy fixing up a bike, they were usually in the pockets of her overalls. It was a good look on her. As a triathlete, I came in periodically, and my attention always snagged on her.

But then she turned to face a customer in the sitting area, and there was a tightness in her eyes—an expression I wasn't used to seeing.

The quirky sitting area for trying on shoes included a long bench, a rocking chair, and a full sofa. The sofa faced away from the entrance, so I didn't recognize the customer as my rival until I was close enough to hear him ask about the new Vaporflies. Then Clay's eyes fell on me, and the disdain was clear.

"Hey," I said, giving him a nod.

"Hey." He was wearing that brand of sweats he'd had on since he got the sponsorship back in winter. We'd all hoped the summer months would sweat him out of them, but no. Not even Texas in July could pry them from his body.

"Oh, hi, Gabe," April said after handing Clay a box of shoes. Her tone had its normal bubbly pitch, but her smile looked forced.

"Not used to seeing you away from your area," I said, nodding towards the empty counter. A bike was on the stand, but all the tools still hung neatly on the peg wall.

"Trevor is running a bit late. Sorry, you're stuck with me."

"I needed to talk to you anyway. You wouldn't happen to have an opening for a bike fitting, would you?" It had been over a year since I'd last had one done, and I was starting to get a light pinching in my knee.

"I don't have any availability until Monday." She frowned. "You weren't hoping to get in before the race this weekend, were you?"

"No. I'm just supporting athletes at the sprint—not participating." With a full racing schedule myself, it was rare that I could focus solely on supporting my athletes, so I was looking forward to the upcoming sprint triathlon. "Monday morning will work."

"Okay, I'll put you on the schedule." She smiled at me, and I suddenly found myself looking forward to a bike fitting, of all things.

"Where is Trevor, anyway?" Clay asked, pulling April's hazel gaze from me.

"Ned called him. Something about a dog chasing cyclists down Second Street."

"Beast is at it again, then." I didn't go down Second Street often, so I didn't know what Clay was referring to. April didn't seem to either. Clay shook his head, laughing at our blank expressions. "I see that pit bull over there all the time. Thank God he's never caught me. That thing reminds me of the dog from The Sandlot. I hope Trevor has had his rabies shot. If I were him, I'd have called animal control—let the professionals handle it."

April didn't seem concerned. "He's pretty good with animals."

As if summoned by our conversation, the door dinged, and Trevor entered the store. "Sorry," he said to April. "I got the dog to come to me easily enough, but he was nervous about getting in the Jeep."

He waved at me, but his face fell when he noticed Clay.

"I'm surprised you survived Beast," Clay said with a laugh.

"While getting chased by a dog isn't fun," Trevor said, taking a moment to clean his glasses on his T-shirt. "He's a pocket breed. Can't be more than two feet tall. Furthermore, he's really sweet. It's a natural instinct for dogs to chase, but he was all tail wags once I approached on foot. So, it's not exactly a miracle that I'm still among the living."

"Did you bring him to an animal shelter?" I asked.

"No." Trevor sighed. "He's chilling at my apartment right now. I didn't want to bring him to the shelter because pit bulls don't historically do well at those. There's a no-kill pit bull rescue not too far from here. I'll give them a call later."

Trevor's rescue didn't surprise me in the least. He was always fostering dogs. The uglier and more pitiful, the greater the chance Trevor would intervene. Case in point—Johnson.

Johnson slept, curled under April's workbench—like always. Animal control told Trevor they'd found him in the dumpster behind the Johnson Space Center. Hence the name. Or so Trevor said. But you don't name a one-eyed wiener dog "Johnson" without having a sense of humor.

"Well," April said, giving Clay and me a polite half-smile, "I'll leave you two in Trevor's much more capable hands." She turned to Trevor. I knew they were cousins, but the silent conversation between them in that two-second eye contact rivaled twin telepathy. Trevor raised a brow just slightly, and then April gave the smallest shake of her head before she was gone—off to the back.

If you weren't looking close enough, you'd miss it. I didn't know what was going on between them, but it was something that they didn't want either Clay or myself to catch—something they weren't happy about.

As April turned to go, Clay stood, testing the feel of the new shoes by leaning his weight from foot to foot.

"You trying on the Vaporfly, too?" Trevor asked me.

"Yeah. Size—"

"Fourteen," Trevor answered, then laughed. "I remember, you freaking giraffe."

Trevor disappeared into the back to get the shoes, and Clay turned to me. "How are your athletes doing, Torres?"

Had the question come from anyone else, it would have been a polite inquiry. Coming from my rival, it was a goad.

"Fine," I said, sitting on the bench across from him—not even the least bit interested in the dick-measuring contest Clay seemed to want.

"Matt looks like he's having a good season."

"He's doing okay." Matt was not doing just okay. He was my star athlete and was crushing his goals, but I didn't want to give any gasoline to the conversation.

"Wait until you see how Ned is progressing," Clay said because, of course, he wasn't finished with the conversation. "He's killing it."

"That's great," I said. "I know he's been working hard." Hard enough that he'd come to the massage clinic for sharp knee pain. I worked out some knots and suggested monster walks, side plank exercises, a strict icing regimen, and stretches to help alleviate it. Ultimately, his body needed rest—not what someone training for an Ironman wants to hear. Hopefully, he'd at least ease up on hill running. The last thing he wanted was to get IT Band Syndrome. But all that was between Ned and myself.

"My roster is deadly," Clay continued. "So don't feel bad if you don't get A-Team. There is always next year."

I was about to give him a flat-toned congratulations, but Trevor returned, plopping the shoebox next to me and giving Clay a chilly look before asking, "But how many athletes did you have to remove from your roster to make it 'deadly?'"

"Come on. Don't be like that," Clay said, jogging in place. He kept his features even, but Trevor's words had struck a chord if Clay's reddening face was any indication.

I didn't even look at the shoes Trevor had deposited. The tense exchange had my full attention. "What's he talking about?" I asked Clay.

Clay stopped jogging with a sigh and looked at Trevor. "I know she's your cousin, but it had to be done."

So, this was about April. I sat up straighter. "You dropped her?" I asked. Clay looked between the two of us, clearly unhappy to be cornered about the topic, even though he'd all but led us there. "We're three months out from Ironman," I added.

"She's not going to finish anyway."

"What do you mean?"

"She has some sort of hangup. It wouldn't matter if she was my sole athlete, and I gave her my undivided coaching. She is going to DNF like she does every year."

Not much riles me, but I could feel my pulse picking up at that statement. Because I'd been there last year.

I shouldn't have been. Wouldn't have been at that spot in the race if the zipper on one of my athlete's wetsuits hadn't jammed. I spent fifteen minutes trying to get it to go up without breaking it, delaying my start time.

But because of that delay, I was on the second mile of the bike when an athlete in front of me hit a water bottle and went over her handlebars. I was surprised when I realized the athlete lying on the asphalt was April. It took a while for her to regain consciousness and then another few minutes for the pain to wake up, but when it did, she'd clutched her collarbone—jaw clenched and pupils blown.

Something was wrong. Broken.

And she still fought me to continue. Still wanted to get back on her bike to finish the race.

"Did you expect her to keep going after breaking her collarbone?" I asked.

"Well—" Clay's face flushed deeper. "No, but that wasn't her first DNF."

"The year before last, she tested positive for the flu," Trevor supplied, crossing his arms over his chest. "Would you like her doctor's note?"

Clay sat down to untie his shoes. His cheeks were still crimson from fighting off the onslaught on two sides. I'd feel bad if I hadn't just learned the guy had abandoned an athlete in the middle of our season.

I thought back to my own races. I had a bad finishing time last year because of April's accident. The year before, I'd had a personal record. But the year before that . . . "And there was the storm," I said. I'd been pulling on my wetsuit when lightning lit up the sky. "She didn't DNF three years ago. It was canceled."

"I'm telling you," Clay said, bent out of shape. "People create their own luck, and April has created her own curse."

I searched his face, completely thrown by his rationale. After a tense moment of silence stretched between us, I said, "You don't actually believe that."

"It doesn't matter what I believe. It's what she believes. As a coach, you should know better than anyone. The mental game is half the battle with these races."

"So, you coach her through it," I said, hardly recognizing the bite in my tone. At least I didn't add the *pendejo* that I'd been thinking.

"I bet you would love that, Torres," Clay said, yanking a shoe off and slapping it down in the box. "For me to keep her on the roster. A DNF would kill my chance at A-Team, and you know it."

If A-Team was the reason he'd dropped her, he'd been an idiot. "She's never completed an Ironman," I voiced. "Any time under seventeen hours will be considered progress. She'd boost your overall score just by crossing the finish line."

Clay stopped pulling on his shoes to look at me. "If she's such an advantage, by all means—" he gestured to where April had disappeared to the back of the shop, "she's yours."

The dare hung in the air, and I had to bite my tongue to keep from snatching it up immediately. *My roster is already full,* I reminded myself. I thought back to my own coach and how he'd been irritated I'd picked up this many athletes. Adding one more to the team would give him a stroke.

"Go ahead," Clay said, still goading. "You take April, and I'll take A-Team." He stood, swinging the shoebox toward Trevor. "Do you have any of these in the black?"

Trevor didn't answer immediately, and I got the distinct feeling he was facing an internal battle—provide good customer service or tell the guy off. Eventually, the good angel on his shoulder won out. "Sorry. We're all out of black. It's a popular one."

Clay went to pay for his shoes. The cashier had been busy drawing, and she seemed irritated to have to put her pencil down to ring up Clay.

While I tried on the shoes, I fought the impulse to head to the back and offer April a spot on my team. I knew how badly she wanted to finish an Ironman, and I'd bet good money that if I looked at her training, she followed all her workouts to a T. She had a spark. She just needed guidance.

"Are you okay with the blue?" Trevor asked after I told him I'd buy the shoes.

"Yeah, blue is fine. The only other color I was looking at was the black."

"We're not out," Trevor said, waving to Clay as he left. "You two are my first customers after getting in the new stuff."

I cocked my head.

"I just told that to Clay because I couldn't stand another second of looking at that asshole."

I could relate.

"Then, yeah. I'll take them in black."

Chapter 5

APRIL

B illie surveyed a table of knickknacks with her upper lip pushed so far up, it covered her septum ring. Every item on the table was lemon-themed: lemon saltshakers, a bowl with lemons painted around the rim, and porcelain lemons of all shapes, sizes, and wedge cuts.

"What's wrong?" I asked, amused at her obvious disdain.

She scratched a line of scalp between corn rows as she decided on an answer. I noticed she had dried paint on her fingers—the pastel dots contrasting with her dark skin—and couldn't help but wonder what her latest art project was. "It's a lot of citrus for a three by four-foot surface area."

Billie was my closest friend—the most chill and hip person I knew. She found beauty in the most bizarre modern art sculptures. She never shopped on Amazon and rarely bought anything outside of consignment or farmer's markets. She only listened to indie music and read indie books—couldn't bear the idea of consuming mainstream or anything enjoyed by the masses, really. So, the fact that not even she could find beauty in the lemon table was saying something.

I picked up a framed cross stitch pattern that had *When Life Gives You Lemons, Make Lemonade* stitched across it. "What about this one?"

"Actually, we need to put that above your workbench at the shop."

"What? Why?" I asked with a laugh.

"Because," she said, moving toward a table with books, "you've been crabby ever since Clay fired you as his athlete."

I knew she had an ulterior motive when she mentioned coming to the estate sale. I was here, looking for something specific. She was here because she wanted to pull me out of my funk.

"Well, it just happened last week. I'm allowed to be moody. Aren't I?"

"You are. As long as you move on from it. Look on the bright side: you don't have to take orders from someone who looks like he's just been sent to timeout."

My hand grazed over knick-knacks and oddities of all sorts. I'd been about to pick up a dainty hand mirror with roses along the handle, but I yanked my arm back when I noticed the hairline crack along the edge. I was pretty sure the seven years of bad luck was saved for the person who actually broke the mirror, but I wasn't taking any chances. I had enough working against me, thanks.

Instead, I picked up a teacup with hand-painted monarch butterflies. My heart tugged at the sight as I instantly thought of Mom.

She hadn't been a religious person, but she was very spiritual. Always looking for little signs from the universe, careful not to disturb the cadence of nature, a believer in myths, legends, luck, and magic. Every single time she spotted a butterfly in the wild, she'd stop to point it out, "Look," she'd say, "a little bit of magic."

To her, butterflies were a sign that the universe or God or our ancestors or whoever was looking out for us. When I was little, the awe in her voice made me believe that something greater was on our side. However, the evidence as of late, had turned me into a skeptic. I wanted to do this one thing: reconnect with my mom by finishing this Ironman, and I felt like I was being punished.

I shuddered to imagine what would be thrown in my path to keep me from finishing this year. After a storm, the flu, and a broken bone, the pattern indicated something horrid waited.

The worst part? I was way too logical to believe in nonsense like fate or cosmic signs. Life was all cause and effect. You leave your bike out in the rain, and it gets rusty. You don't true a wheel, and the rim goes out of line.

But there were too many moments that didn't add up. Didn't make sense. Weren't fair. Your mom drives to work, and she never makes it back home.

I looked at the tiny butterflies fluttering along the rim.

Please give me something, I silently begged. *I just need to know the universe doesn't hate me.*

"How is training going . . . you know, without Clay?" Billie's question yanked me from my silent prayer, and I put the teacup down delicately before narrowing my eyes at her.

Despite being the cashier of a triathlon shop, she didn't have the slightest interest in the sport. To my knowledge, she'd never even been to a race. "You don't care about training."

"I don't. But I know how much this means to you. So—" She put out a hand to beckon my answer.

I shrugged. "I still have his workouts to follow until after the race tomorrow. So, things feel the same." That wasn't entirely true. The pinch in my knee was growing harder and harder to ignore. Much less like straw being added to the camel's back and more like iron beams, but I told Trevor I would give Ironman a real chance, and giving a voice to the concern felt like throwing in the towel already. So, the plan was to be positive. Fake it until I made it. I had a sprint—a shorter triathlon—the next day. I planned to show up and remind myself that I was a competitor.

Billie nodded, but even a short conversation about athletics made her smile look like a grimace. That is, until her eyes fell on a paperback. Her grin turned gremlin-like as she tossed the book to me. "Bet this is a good one to add to your porn collection." I glanced at the half-naked models on the romance cover before putting it facedown on the table. An elderly woman stopped her perusal of the teacup selection to look at us, and my cheeks flamed.

"Not porn," I corrected, louder than necessary. "Books. Literature."

"Sure." She waggled her eyebrows. "Cliterature."

I wished the game board section on my left had a Jumanji board. Maybe I could get sucked in like Robin Williams' character. Getting chased by wild animals had to be better than this humiliating conversation with Billie.

"I can't bring you anywhere," I said, straightening the stack of Nora Roberts books.

"Come on, lighten up."

"I'm light," I said through my teeth. "I just don't want strangers thinking I have an unhealthy porn obsession when, in reality, I just like to read books that are a little bit spicy."

Billie laughed. "Everyone has an unhealthy porn obsession. Nothing to be ashamed of."

Trying to put distance between Billie and her porn talk, I rounded the table and a collection of flower-printed couches, but I nearly tripped over something wedged between two pieces of furniture. My pulse picked up as I realized it was a bicycle tire. I grabbed the seat and pulled it from hiding, revealing the exact treasure I'd come to the estate for.

The paint on the bicycle was chipped and patchy. The seat was torn. Rust dusted across the white rims. But it was all cosmetic. This baby looked like it was from the sixties, perhaps even the fifties. I ran my fingers reverently over the metallic blue frame. The evening rolled out in front of me: I'd finish my sizzling audiobook while I disassembled the bike, lay out the pieces on my toweled workspace, and clean each part. I'd have to replace some parts completely. It would need new paint, but I could see the end result already. She'd be beautiful. "I'm here to rescue you," I told the Schwinn.

"Who is embarrassing who now?" Billie mumbled, but she didn't give me much shit other than that. I think she could sense the lifting of my spirit, even if just by a bit.

Chapter 6

GABRIEL

A race day buzz saturated the air at the Pearville triathlon. The sun was still just a promise on the horizon as racers scurried around the transition area, lining up their running shoes and nutrition, their bicycles racked and ready. If you've never seen a transition area for a triathlon, think of it as a parking lot. Every racer has their designated place to fit all they need to get through three sports. I checked on a few of my athletes' spaces, making sure they had everything they needed and knew the game plan. Then, I headed back over to Beck and Emily.

"That is going to take forever," Emily said, twisting her red hair into a bun while she sized up the mile-long lines to the porta-potties. Strong swimmers, my friends Emily and Beck, volunteered as unofficial lifeguards for the race. I was there to guide my athletes, so we'd rented two kayaks and decided to go together.

"You could always go in the woods," Beck said, looking at the grouping of trees outside transition.

She glared at him. "That is such a guy thing to say. I'd be inviting a snake to come bite me in the ass while I'm squatting there."

Beck put a hand on his chest. "I'm offended. Have I not protected you from all snake attacks so far?"

Emily playfully pushed him, but Beck caught her wrists and brought her in for a kiss on the nose before nodding towards the line. "Go ahead. We'll get the kayaks in the water."

She gave his cheek a pat. "Meet you at the dock."

They'd only been together for a little over a year, but it felt like forever since it was just Beck. Now, it was always the pair together in a sentence: Beck and Emily. I liked Emily, and more importantly, I liked the way Beck brightened around her, which is why, as we trekked back to my truck, I asked, "Why is her ring finger still bare? I thought the plan was to come back from that vacation engaged."

"That *was* the plan," Beck said, looking over his shoulder as if checking that Emily wasn't right behind us. "But I didn't find the perfect moment."

"You couldn't find a perfect moment in Maui?" I shook my head and mumbled, "Rich brat." When Beck didn't snap back—as in his usual way— I said, "You couldn't find the perfect moment, or you got nervous?"

I expected this one to rile a response, but Beck kept his eyes trained on the ground as our feet crossed from wet grass to the asphalt of the parking lot.

"I never thought I'd see the day," I said. "Beckett Atteridge nervous. What do you have to be afraid of? She's perfect for you."

"Exactly." Beck stopped to look at me. "She's perfect. Can you blame me if I don't want to risk messing things up with her?"

"Respectfully, you're a dumbass. How would you mess things up?"

"I don't know." He blew out a breath and looked out in the distance, and I could all but see the worst-case scenarios playing in his mind.

"What if I disappoint her with how I ask? Or she feels pressured to say yes."

"You told me you've already talked about getting married."

"We have," Beck scraped a hand down his face. "But talking about it is one thing. Taking the leap is another."

"Beck, she's in love with you. I'm surprised she's into the pretty boy thing," I said, tousling his curls. Beck smacked my arm away, as I knew he would. "But she is. So, stop messing around and put a ring on it."

"I will."

"Good, because I've already got my best-man speech prepared." I swept out a hand as if to say *imagine it.* "When I first met Beck, he was a competitor at a swim meet. Though, *competitor* might be too strong a word."

Beck's eyes narrowed. "I'm asking someone else to be my best man."

I laughed. "Whatever you say."

"See, doesn't that look fun?" I asked as another swimmer breezed past my kayak. It was nice being on this side of the race.

While you were swimming a race like that, it was all brown water below, with brief, sideways glances of the world. You worked yourself breathless but felt limited in the breaths you could take. Then there was the muddy taste of lake water and the flailing of other swimmers as you navigated around them.

But on top of the kayak, it was so peaceful, a bird's eye view of quiet splashing as schools of swimmers passed.

"This looks fine," Beck said. "It's the cycling and running that I'll pass on." I knew that response was coming. I'd been trying to get him to do a triathlon for years, and it was always the same answer. "Besides, the open water thing is more Emily's speed."

Emily dipped her hand into the lake and splashed it backward at Beck, who shielded his face with a laugh. Their kayak bobbed with the movement. Emily raised her hands as if to settle the rocking, but something in the water caught her eye.

She pointed to a pink-capped woman whose rhythm looked off. "That swimmer just got kicked by the one in front of her."

I straightened, watching to make sure the swimmer was alright. She tried to get her goggles back over her eyes but sank with the movement.

Beck lifted off his seat, ready to go in, but I put out a hand. Sure enough, the swimmer resurfaced.

"Over here!" I waved my arms, so she'd see we had a safe place for her to recalibrate.

She struggled to make it across the current of swimmers between us but eventually merged over. Once through, she hooked an arm over my kayak, sputtering as she worked to remove her goggles with her free hand.

As her hazel eyes fell on mine, I realized we weren't just dealing with any triathlete but April Baird.

The relief in her eyes was replaced with mortification.

I smiled. "You know a triathlon isn't supposed to be a contact sport, right?"

She huffed out a laugh. "Tell that to the person who kicked me. She seems to think this is The Octagon." She rubbed her head and pursed a set of full lips. "How is it that you are here to bear witness every time I get injured?"

"It's only been twice, Baird." Although, I'd had the same thought. "But let's not make a third time's the charm deal. Where did you get kicked?"

Even as I asked it, I started to make out the red blotch that went beyond the reach of her goggle imprints.

"My eye." She winced as she tested the area. "I don't know if it's good I had my goggles on or infinitely worse."

"We should probably get you looked at—make sure you don't have a concussion."

I started to dip my paddle in the water, but April grabbed it. "Stop! If you move while I'm hanging on, I'll get disqualified."

"You could have a head injury," Emily supplied.

"I'm fine," April responded, then poised to get back to swimming.

I put a hand on her shoulder. "Wait." Then I sighed. This was the same woman who broke her collarbone and still wanted to keep riding her bike. She wouldn't drop out of the race for a bump on the head, but maybe I could still help her. "You're a strong swimmer?"

Her eyebrows scrunched. "I'm no Katie Ledecky, but I'm not going to drown if that's what you are worried about."

"When you get back into the water, slowly make your way over to the left." I pointed, and April tracked the movement. "You see all that open space? It's because people love having the buoys and kayaks as a safety net. But you have a built-in safety net. If you get tired or into trouble, what can you do?"

"Float on my back?"

"Exactly."

"This," I pointed to the congested gaggle of arms, "is an injury waiting to happen." I knew Clay wasn't her coach anymore, but she'd been through triathlons while under his wing, and she acted like she'd never heard this advice before. My attention snagged on the reddening skin around her eye. "But I don't need to tell you that."

She nodded, then pulled her goggles back on.

"April." I grabbed her arm again. "If you feel dizzy or sick, wave your arms and then float on your back. I'll come get you." Before she could argue, I added, "This hometown triathlon isn't worth drowning for."

She nodded again and then was off, fighting to get across the stream of swimmers.

"Should we have let her go?" Emily asked.

"No, but I don't think we could have stopped her. *Mierda*," I cursed under my breath. It was nearly impossible to keep track of her. All the women wore pink caps. "Are you two good here? I'm going to follow her to make sure she gets out of the water."

Beck waived me off. "Yeah, go."

To my relief, I watched April slosh to shore. Or at least, I was pretty sure it was her. I didn't see any other athletes with the same purple and pink tri-suit, but I couldn't see her face to confirm.

I pulled my kayak to land and made the trek to the transition area. Jim, one of my athletes, was sitting down, pulling socks on for the bike portion. The sight of him refocused me. I wasn't at the race to keep tabs on April. I was there to support *my* athletes.

Jim got to his feet and pulled his bike off the rack, but I could see the cogs whirring, his eyes roaming over his designated area. I knew the feeling all too well. You get back on dry land, and you're dizzy from being horizontal in the water for so long. Getting to transition is a relief. One discipline checked off. But then comes the discombobulation: *What am I doing? What do I need for the bike? Which way is the transition exit?*

That's why it's critical to have everything laid out and organized. Yes, it helps with speed, but also, when your adrenaline is that high, your brain almost coasts.

I waited until he was running, guiding his bike by the handlebars to call out, "You're making good time, Jim!"

His head snapped up, and I saw the usual light of recognition that an athlete gets from hearing his name called during a race. The '*I'm not alone. People are on my side'* feeling.

"Thanks, Coach!" he called before hopping onto his bike.

The bike course stretched for miles, and the athletes zipped by, making spectating pointless. So, I stayed until my last athlete made it out of the water and then journeyed to the one-and-a-half-mile marker of the run. It was a great position. The run course looped, so I could see athletes at the halfway point and then watch them cross the finish line.

Trevor must have had the same idea because I spotted him sitting on the curb with a cartoonishly large camera. He often took pictures for races and sold them, but it would be a while before the first runners reached the three-mile mark. Trevor passed the time by scrolling on his phone. Johnson lay in the grass next to him, looking bored. It was like someone stuffed a sixty-year-old man's personality into a wiener dog. There was just no impressing him.

"Hey, Trev," I said.

"Hey, man." Then, "You're not racing today?"

"Nope. Just here for my athletes."

Trevor nodded. "Have you tried out the new shoes yet?"

"I did a five miler in them yesterday. I flew."

"I knew you'd like them."

Johnson shifted his eye between us without picking his head off the ground. I thought of the pit bull Trevor had rescued and wondered how Johnson reacted to sharing his home and human with someone else.

"Were you able to get the pit bull to that no-kill rescue?"

"No." Trevor sighed. "They don't have space right now, so he's going to stay with me until they find someone to foster. The only problem is that pit bulls aren't allowed at my apartment complex. So, I have to be sneaky when I take him out for walks."

I considered offering to take the dog off Trevor's hands, but I honestly didn't know the first thing about dogs. I'd had one pet as a kid—a goldfish I'd won from a carnival game—and he died within his first week at our home. The dog would be better off waiting for a more suitable home.

Eventually, a runner made his way down the course, and Trevor settled his camera in front of his face. It made a constant shutter sound as the athlete passed. When my athletes came by, one at a time, I high-fived and offered encouragement.

"Keep it up, Sandra! Looking strong!"

Red-faced, she still found the energy to beam at me. "Thanks, Gabe!"

Trevor chuckled quietly.

"What?"

"Can you just cheer like that for everyone that passes?" He shifted the lens to a more comfortable position. "These runners all look like they are close to death. Then, you call their name, and they look like anime characters with stars for eyes." He paused, a crease forming between his brows. "Speaking of, see if you can pull your magic on my cousin."

I snapped my head up to see April coming down the path. Her jog was a deflated shuffle. "Trev, if you take my picture," she panted, "I'll shove that camera up your ass."

He moved the camera away from his face. "You don't look so good. You okay?"

"Peachy," she said, dragging her feet past us. I followed her. My stride was long, so I could have kept up with just a brisk walk, but that felt insulting. Instead, I jogged next to her.

"What's going on?"

"Suffering. Suffering is going on." Her breathing was jagged. "If I pay you twenty bucks," she said, stopping to gulp in air, "will you carry my bib to the finish line?"

"When's the last time you had nutrition?"

"Uhhh . . ." By the judge of her pause, I knew I wasn't going to like her answer. "I had eggs, toast, and a banana at like five a.m."

I looked at my watch. She hadn't eaten anything in three hours. "April—"

"Clay never worried about nutrition plans for sprints."

"I could see skipping nutrition if this was a 5k." Still jogging, I pulled my backpack around and dug in it until I found a water bottle and a package of chews. "But you've been racing for an hour. You need to refuel. Have you ever tried these?" I asked, handing her the package.

"I'm more of a gel girl, but yeah. Chews are fine." I slowed down to untwist the cap off the water bottle and handed that over, too. "Here, drink first."

"Yes, Coach," she mumbled as if answering a nagging parent.

I smiled. "See you at the finish line."

"Your cousin is pretty resilient," I said to Trevor after rejoining him and Johnson.

"Yeah," he agreed. The camera shuttered as he captured another wave of runners.

"Did you know she got kicked in the face this morning?"

That got his attention. He looked up from the viewfinder, effectively missing the last three runners in the group.

"It was the swim," I said, realizing I needed to clarify so Trevor didn't picture a karate brawl in transition. "I tried to get her to stop the race and get checked out by a medic, but—"

"She's stubborn."

I hesitated but then finally asked what had been gnawing at me ever since the day she'd broken her collarbone and had still wanted to re-mount her bike.

"Why is racing so important to her?"

"Her mom dreamed of them completing an Ironman together. So she feels like she needs to fulfill what she can. I think it's also a way for her to feel connected to her."

I knew about her mom, Tiffany. As the person who'd opened the town's first and only tri-shop, she'd been somewhat of a legend in our triathlon community. It had been a while since she'd passed, but people still talked about her.

An ache grew behind my ribs as his words settled—the kind of pain that throbs when you recognize the hurt in someone else, which was ironic because April's drive was the direct opposite of mine. If her goal had been a sketch made in ink, mine was the whitespace around it.

She desired to hold a connection with her mom, and I was coming at the tether to my dad with diamond cutters. Still, we shared a likeness in having a parent drive our decisions even long after they were out of the picture.

And I felt that likeness acutely, enough so that I knew that if she was willing, I'd have one more athlete to create a training plan for when I got home.

Chapter 7

APRIL

I'd scheduled Gabe for his bike fitting before I'd known he'd watch me getting my face kicked (literally) and my ass kicked (metaphorically) at a race the day before.

The funny thing was, we really hadn't had any availability for a fitting, but I was trying to be nice by opening the shop early for him because I knew his training was a huge chunk of his career.

No good deed goes unpunished, I thought as I unlocked the door for his hulking frame. He put my five foot three to shame with his six foot something ridiculous. Honestly, he should have been a basketball player. At least then, he wouldn't be standing in my shop resembling an Olympic cyclist in his tri-suit. He looked like a force to be reckoned with, a machine, a pro. With some people, training for triathlons made them lose muscle tone. With all that cardio, you'd blaze through calories, so it was no surprise seeing triathletes with willowy frames. Not Gabe. He was lean, but you could see the contour of muscle under the thin fabric of his suit, which meant he had to be adding weight training to his workout routine and carefully planning out his nutrition—all of this on top of his jobs as a massage therapist and a coach.

"Good morning," I said, but he'd been the first person I'd talked to that day, so my voice sounded like rocks in a blender. I cleared my throat for a softer, "Morning."

"Morning," he said, his voice smooth as butter. Like he'd been up for five hours. Then I considered that. He probably had. I bet he got in a brisk fifty-mile ride long before the first rooster had a cup of coffee. His eyes roamed to my left eye, and he winced.

It had been quite the shocker this morning when I woke up to the plum shading there. I tried my best to cover it with concealer, but it only did so much. I'd considered wearing sunglasses inside, but working with shades on seemed annoying and would probably warrant as many questions as the shiner would.

"Does it hurt?" he asked.

"Only every time I blink." His face fell, and I had to laugh. "I'm kidding. It's fine." Gabe let me guide his bike from him to the trainer we had at the shop. "My legs, however, feel like they are only one hundred signatures away from the petition they need to leave."

Gabe laughed—a low thing that reminded me of distant thunder.

I bent over to take the back tire off his bike, but he stopped me. "I know how to take a tire off. Rest your legs. We can't give them any more reason to hate you."

"Thanks," I said, watching him quickly hook his Quintana Roo up to the trainer. Trainers were great for indoor bike riding. In fact, I probably did ninety percent of my cycling on a trainer. However, they were great at the shop too. I could see exactly how an athlete rode while the bike stayed stationary.

After he finished, I jotted down some quick measurements before I had him mount.

"Is there anything specific you want me to look at today? Any problems?"

"Can you make me go faster?" he asked, smiling cheekily.

I laughed. "Possibly."

"Actually, I'm here because my knee has been pinching."

We were knee-pain twins, then. However, with some luck, Gabe's issue would be a quick fix.

"Okay. Just pedal nice and easy for me."

He leaned onto his bars into the aero position and took long, effortless strides. Right away, I could see the problem.

"Your seat is low. Can you hop off?"

I raised the saddle a bit and had him get back on. It took a few attempts to get the adjustment just right, his torso and legs hitting that forty-five-degree angle sweet spot. When I finally had it where I wanted, I told him to keep pedaling to make sure it felt right for him.

It was honestly a little bit of a fight to keep my professionalism at this point. I kept having to remind myself that I had a job to do and that my eyes did not have permission to roam freely up and down the length of Gabe. After all, we were a respectable establishment. Still, I couldn't help but think I had the best job in the world, a front-row seat watching this beast of an athlete work.

I particularly liked how his calf muscles worked under the red M-dot tattoo. A lot of athletes who completed an Ironman got the symbol tattooed there. It showed that the person with the ink was an absolute badass, albeit slightly insane. I hadn't decided if I wanted the Ironman symbol tatted on me or not, but I figured I needed to finish the damn thing before I worried too much about that.

"You'll have to let me know when you're available for an FTP," he said as if he was having a nice stroll instead of pedaling at podium chasing speed.

FTP? I couldn't remember exactly what it stood for. Functional Training Purposes? Or something to that effect. Clay used to have me complete one every so often. Basically, for twenty minutes, you increased effort until you reached an I-never-want-to-sit-my-cheeks-on-a-bike-again point. There were some practical uses for the test—besides the serotonin boost coaches received from torturing their athletes—such as establishing target training zones.

"We don't do that here," I said, keeping my eyes on his form, wondering if we needed to move the stem to extend his reach for the handlebar.

"I'm talking about measuring *your* FTP."

"Why would I do that?" I laughed, but it was short. "I don't even have a coach."

"That's what I'm saying, April." We locked eyes. "You do now."

He stunned me. I let the prattling and whooshing of Gabe's pedaling fill the space for a moment. "You're offering to be my coach?" I asked dumbly.

"Yes."

"But don't you only coach . . . pros?" He worked for Triple Threat like Clay, but certainly, they were on different levels. Gabe's athletes were the Monstars from Space Jam, and I was Daffy Duck getting smacked with an anvil at every turn. I assumed he was already on the A-Team that Clay was gunning for.

Gabe laughed, then seemed to weigh my question. "I've got some great athletes this year, but I don't only coach pros."

"You don't think I'd be a waste of time?" I was grateful for his offer, I really was, but I couldn't just accept without making sure he knew exactly what he was getting into by bringing me on the team. "I'm not going to help your coaching portfolio. I'll never come close to a podium."

"Honestly, you would look great on my portfolio."

A second of flattery flourished before logic snuffed it out. "You've never coached an Ironman virgin?" I guessed.

"No," he agreed. "I haven't." His nose crinkled. "But let's call it something else."

"Pedal faster for me," I prompted. I'd honestly seen enough, but I needed a moment to think. At this point, Gabe was booking it, and I finally got to see a little bit of perspiration drip from that thick, black hair of his. One drop fell from the scar that sliced through his eyebrow. He wasn't ugly breathing yet, but his nostrils flared. The pure power in each pedal astonished me.

In all our interactions, he seemed gentle, but judging by his standards, I could imagine him being a nightmare of a coach, a total hard ass.

"What do you think?" Gabe asked, finally breathless.

"We might need to adjust the stem. You can stop."

He clicked out of his pedals and planted his feet. "I mean about you being my athlete."

I crossed my arms and chewed my bottom lip, still debating as he dismounted. "I don't know if you are in my budget. I'm assuming you charge more than Clay."

He shook his head. "We have to keep the same rates—company policy."

I frowned for his sake. That didn't seem right. Gabe coached on a whole other level, didn't he? I thought Triple Threat had different tiers of coaching.

"But, before you decide," Gabe continued, "I want to be completely upfront with you." He paused to wipe sweat from his brow with the back of his arm. "I expect a lot from my athletes. I won't go easy on you."

My throat went dry at that statement, which was silly. There was nothing sexual about it. He was setting expectations. But my perverted, spicy-literature-loving mind drew up an entirely different connotation. I broke eye contact and, out of habit, looked at the picture above the counter: my mom with her Ironman tattoo and me with my knockoff design.

I'd asked the universe to send me something, and it had sent me a coach. This could still be my year.

I extended my hand. "You've got yourself a deal, Coach."

Gabe smiled, his large hand swallowing mine whole.

Chapter 8

APRIL

For all that talk about not being easy on me, Gabe mercifully gave me a week to recover from the sprint triathlon before asking me to complete the FTP.

When the time eventually came, I set up my tri-bike on the trainer in my garage, just like I usually would for indoor rides sanctioned by Clay. But this time, I hung Mom's Ironman medal on the wall, so when I looked up from pedaling, it's what I saw.

This was it. I could feel it. Those 140.6 miles were mine. With a new coach, I wanted to put forth my best effort. Maybe because I knew Gabe was going out of his way to take me under his wing, but I felt this strong drive. I wasn't delusional enough to think I'd ever make him proud, but I thought I could manage not letting him down if I worked hard enough, which is how I ended up in a pool of sweat on my garage floor, heaving breaths. I'd completed the FTP, putting out more watts than I ever had.

Still lying on the floor, I sent Gabe my results. He immediately replied.

Gabe: We can work with that. Could you stop by the rec on Friday? I want to get a look at your form in the water and have you run a magic mile.

A magic mile? I let my hands fall back against the cold concrete. A magic mile was similar to an FTP in that you ran a mile as fast as you could to get a baseline for pace. My body wept in the form of sweat.

Me: I don't get off until 6 Friday.

Gabe: Meet you at the Rec at 7?

Me: I'll be there.

I finally coaxed myself off the floor with the idea of dinner, a shower, and hours of tinkering with the old Schwinn while engaging in my most beloved guilty pleasure—listening to a romance audiobook. The evening laid out like a treat for surviving a day of customer service and physical exertion.

I had a long "everything" shave and shower and even topped it off with exfoliation. I was obsessed with my new raspberry vanilla sugar scrub. I imagined it rubbing away all the stress from the day along with the grime. Clean, and slightly pink from all the scrubbing, I padded down the hall in an oversized T-shirt and crew socks.

One of the baseboards near the kitchen looked a little warped. I nudged it with my socked foot—another item to add to the growing list of things to fix around the house. But I'd do it, put every broken piece back together to keep the house I grew up in whole.

About five years ago, my dad declared he was putting the house and the store on the market. While I looked at our home as endless memories with Mom, I think he only saw the places she should still be: in the back garden planting squash, on the couch with an arm over my shoulder, at the table with a deck of cards smiling mischievously because she'd bested the both of us.

He wanted to start new. Scrap the store. Sell the house. The only path was forward for him. I respected his choice to move on, encouraged it even, but I begged him to sell me the house and pass the business onto me. He agreed and even offered me a generous, flexible payment plan. He got his new life in Alabama with his long-term girlfriend, Cindy. And I got to hold onto the house and the store.

That's where I'd found Mom's vision board. She probably wouldn't have called it that, but that's basically what it was. I'd been digging through old files in the office and found a folder sectioned into two columns: short-term goals and long-term goals. And under long-term goals, my name caught my attention.

Cross the red carpet with April for her first Ironman.

I'd sat on the tile floor of the office and cried my eyes out, broken by all the things she'd been excited about. Then, still wiping away tears, I'd registered for my first Ironman. Maybe she couldn't be here to race it, but I could cross the red carpet for her.

Starving and excited to get back to work on the old bike Billie and I found at the estate sale, I didn't bother heating my leftover ravioli. I ate it cold right out of the container as I laid out the necessary tools. The goal of the day was to finish disassembling the bike and then start stripping the frame of the paint.

After taking the last bite, I put on my over-the-ear headphones and started up the new audiobook I'd just purchased that morning based on a Bookstagram review. Within the first chapter, the love interest was described as tall with thick black hair, and instantly, I pictured Gabe. I tried to imagine someone else. It was a bad idea to cast my coach as the male main character in a book whose readers rated it as three spicy peppers, but as the story unraveled, my diligence kept slipping, and Gabe always ended up being the one to lean against the door frame or smile without it reaching his eyes or tuck a lock of hair behind the heroine's ear.

Needless to say, I stayed up two hours past my bedtime, completely enraptured.

At the rec on Friday, I found Gabe on the upstairs track, looking down at the contents of a binder. He wore his usual: a racing T-shirt and basketball shorts, but I felt a little dazed by his appearance, because though he'd spent the night rent-free in my head, he looked better than what my memories could even draw up, with his black hair artfully messy and that wicked scar at his eyebrow. I wondered, again, how he'd gotten it. With all the falls we took cycling, it was easy to imagine that it was a sports-related injury.

He looked up and interrupted my curiosity with a smile bracketed by dimples. "Hey, Speed Racer." That made me pause. "Your FTP was better than I anticipated. You sure you're not chasing podiums?"

I barked out a laugh. "Don't patronize me."

"I'm not. Start stretching, Baird. I want to see that energy in person." Why did the way he used my last name make my insides turn to goop? Clay had called me Baird all the time but, to be fair, I also never pictured Clay as a lead role in a romance novel. That was only one of the two fatal errors I had made the day before, because after pushing myself during that FTP, Gabe expected that same level of athleticism (if you could even call it that) in my magic mile.

Unfortunately, that was a text that couldn't be retracted, so I lowered into a runner's stretch with a, "Yes, Coach."

Something sparked in Gabe's eye at that, but before I could appreciate the full effect, someone slammed their locker directly behind Gabe. Anyone would have been startled by such an abrupt bang in an otherwise quiet room, but Gabe seemed frozen in place, eyes wide, knuckle-white grip on his binder.

I straightened, concerned. "You . . . okay?"

He blinked and then shook his head, the human form of rebooting. "Fine." He pointed at a nearby bench, back to business. "Use the side to get a good calf stretch."

Just as I feared, the stretching ended way too quickly, and it was time to get to brass tacks. Gabe had me do a couple of warm-up laps before I started the dreaded magic mile. Just like the FTP, I was expected to give my all. To finish with no gas left in the tank. At least this one was only a mile, so my suffering would be short-lived.

Four laps. I gazed out at the loop. We were on the second level of the gym, and the track stretched above two neighboring basketball courts. Four laps was nothing compared to the literal marathon I was set to run, but there was a big difference between endurance running and going as hard and fast as possible.

"Okay, Baird," Gabe said, thumb poised over his phone to start the stopwatch. "Let's see what you've got."

Before I could let apprehension settle too deep, I took off. On the first lap, my feet pounded on the slightly squishy track, and I felt unstoppable. In those few minutes, I wondered if that was how my mom felt, tearing up a racecourse. Light, airy, a bird in flight, but as I rounded the second corner of my second lap, I realized that I was Icarus, flying too close to the sun. The pace was going to kill me. My lungs could have turned to lead for the effort it took to breathe. I probably should have slowed, but Gabe would notice, and the thought of disappointing him was enough to force my legs to keep the beat of the crazy song I'd already started.

At the end of the second lap, Gabe called, "That's it, Baird! Halfway there." The praise powered me well enough through the first half of the lap, but I was ugly breathing by the end of it, and my knee gave a warning pinch. "Come on," Gabe encouraged. "Pick the pace back up."

When I didn't, Gabe joined me on the track, effortlessly keeping up with my strained stride. "That's it. Match my pace," he said, having no problem hitting my fastest speed and coaching me through it. I realized I'd never once worked out with Clay. He'd always been more of a sideline coach, which was fine. However, there was something equally irritating and motivating about Gabe staying just a foot ahead of me, saying, "Keep up. Come on. Just a little further."

If nothing else, his beautiful form, which could block out the freaking overhead lights from his height, was enough to distract me from my abused lungs, chest, and legs.

"Eight minutes, nineteen seconds," Gabe announced proudly as we reached the end of the loop, and I would have been impressed if every cell in my body hadn't been thrown into survival mode.

Gabe led me through some cooldown exercises and stretching, and ultimately, I was satisfied until he asked the dreaded question. "What kind of core work did Clay have you doing?"

As soon as the question left his lips, I knew I wouldn't like this turn of the conversation. I wondered if this was what Johnson felt like whenever Trevor said the words "bath" or "vet."

"You mean, other than the swimming, cycling, and running?" I asked. My abs got used enough, thank you. I might not have had a visible six-pack, but the muscles lurked somewhere below the surface.

"I'm talking about targeted core exercises."

I scratched the back of my neck.

He lowered his binder. "April?"

"Gabriel," I said, meeting his disappointed gaze with an exasperated one.

"He didn't have you doing any core work?"

I shrugged.

Gabriel was unimpressed by my indifference. "A strong core will improve balance, stability, endurance—"

"Okay, okay." I put my hands out to stop the gush. The lecture reminded me of trips to the dentist when I didn't floss well enough. "I get it."

He squinted at me. "I'm going to give you core exercises. I need you to commit to five minutes a day."

Five minutes didn't seem like much to ask, but I was no fool. Time doing ab workouts was like dog years. Multiply the time by seven to get the real feel. I wanted to complain, but Gabe was sacrificing his time to coach me. If five minutes of suffering a day was my penance, I supposed I could pay it. "Okay. I can do five minutes."

"How long can you hold a plank?"

I should have made up a freaking number. Instead, I blurted out, "I wouldn't know. I haven't done one since high school gym."

Gabe reached back and pulled a mat off the wall. It slapped against the floor between us.

"No time like the present. Let's see how long you can last."

I knew it was an innocent comment, but I'd pictured Gabe saying that exact line last night as the audiobook had entered a steamy scene. I kneeled, ready to give my face a reason for reddening.

"Okay," I said, arms braced. "But be ready for disappointment."

Gabe knelt in front of me. "Whenever you're ready."

After a generous inhale, I lowered to my elbows and stretched my legs out behind me.

It was embarrassing how quickly the burn ripped down my stomach, how fast my arms started to shake.

"Lower your hips," Gabe's deep voice rumbled with the merciless demand.

I did as I was told but had to bite back a gasp.

"You aren't going to last if you don't give your body oxygen," he said. "Breathe."

I inhaled, but even that hurt. "I'm not—" I tried but had to pause. "Lasting much . . . longer . . . anyway," I said, voice strained.

"You've gone thirty seconds. All you have to do is hold."

Oh. Is that all?

The pain blazed through my core, up my chest, down my arms.

"I can't—" I gasped at the pressure. I wanted to say I couldn't hold it any longer, but it was too much effort.

"You're going for a minute," Gabe said—a low, calm command. "You can take it." And once again, I pictured a scene from the book. Gabe towering over me in bed.

The image took up the entire frame that was my mind.

"Time," Gabe said, and I flopped down, trying to recover both from my burning abs and the fantasy.

"Not bad for someone who hasn't planked in a decade." Thank God he didn't call me a good girl. I would have melted onto the mat. "I'll let you rest for a minute, and we'll hit it again."

"Again?" I asked, not able to keep the anguish out of the question.

Gabe gave a rumbly laugh. "I told you I wouldn't go easy on you." And I wondered if the cleaning crew at the gym had a protocol for cleaning human-turned-oobleck out of the training mats.

Chapter 9

GABRIEL

Moths dove and swooped under the parking lot lights as I stepped into the night air. After cooking its citizens during the day, you'd think Texas would give us a break at night. But no. It was still hot, still humid. Even with the temperature, I caught my reflection in a car window and realized I'd been smiling to myself.

I'd just started as April's coach, and I liked it—a little more than I suspected was normal. It had a lot to do with her drive. If I could bottle up her determination and add it to my other athletes' electrolytes, my team would be unstoppable. There was this raw potential just waiting to be sculpted. April had been fighting through her triathlons with, what seemed like, the minimal guidance Clay had given her. With some support and actual coaching, she could fly.

After her magic mile and planking, I'd had her change into her swimsuit, and we went over to the natatorium side of the rec. I'd used my GoPro to get footage of her doing a few laps. Once I got home, I'd analyze her form and see what drills she'd benefit most from. When I asked her what kind of drills Clay prescribed for her, she'd said he just gave her an amount of time to swim for each workout.

There was no way he was pulling that shit with some of his more competitive athletes, but he'd done it with April because he knew he could get away with it. Her days of having half-assed coaching were over. She'd have targeted workouts for training and actual nutrition plans for races, as well as a carefully crafted weight training plan—nothing intensive, but a little would go a long way to increase her power and endurance.

I was excited about the untapped potential of a new athlete. But I couldn't pretend that was the only reason for my smile. There was also something about how she called me Coach—with a mischievous glint to those hazel eyes. Those eyes sparkled. They dared.

Most of my athletes called me Gabe, but the ones who called me Coach certainly didn't send a current down my spine like she did. I shouldn't have had any such reaction to an athlete. Ever. It was unprofessional and not at all the reason why I'd asked her to join my team. I was there to help her achieve her goal of crossing the red carpet. That was it.

I sat in my truck but didn't start it. I was only switching out my shoes—an older pair of Brooks with too many miles for running—to the newest pair of Nikes I bought at Just Tri. Though excited to have April on the team, meeting with her cut into my training time. I had seven miles to get in. Luckily, the street in front of the rec had a sizable hill, so I'd get in some incline work.

After twenty minutes on said hill, I treated myself by turning into a residential neighborhood. There were longer stretches without lamps, but I'd take a potential ankle twist over going back up the hill to see if the other side provided better lighting.

As if to punish me for that decision, a form in the dark moved when I rounded a corner. I ripped out a headphone to hear a, "What the fuck?" I willed my eyes to adjust in the dark as the human-shaped silhouette moved away.

"Hey!" I put out a hand. "Sorry! I'm just a runner. Forgot my light at home."

There was a pause before I heard, "*Gabe*?"

I squinted, trying to put a face to the voice. "Trevor? Is that you?"

"Yes! Jesus, man! Do you know how horrifying it is to come across your tall ass in the dark? I thought a fucking Dementor had turned the corner." Something clinked. "And some protector you are. You didn't even bark."

It took me a moment to realize he was talking to his dog. I chuckled. "Are you seriously relying on Johnson for protection?"

"This isn't Johnson. It's the pit bull . . . Can we move to a lit area?"

"Good idea."

We bumped into each other several times before finding our rhythm toward the streetlight.

"So you're still trying to hide the dog from your landlord?" I guessed.

"She caught me sneaking him in this morning." He sighed. "I have three days to get rid of him, and I'm not allowed to walk him at our apartment complex."

"I didn't realize some apartments had that rule. My landlord has two pit bulls: Sonny and Cher." They seemed to smile widely at everyone who passed by the office.

Trevor's shrug became visible as we neared the light. "Every place is different."

We stopped under the lamp. The dog in question sat and looked up at me. His head was entirely too large for his body, but he was kind of adorable in a he's-so-ugly-he's-cute kind of way. I knelt and let him sniff my hand, which he promptly licked.

"It's not your fault you're a pit bull. Is it?" I asked him. Lines of missing fur crossed over his muzzle, and there was another long line above his eye, just like my own scar. My thumb brushed over it as I rubbed his head.

"I wish I could keep him longer. He could use someone kind," Trevor said. "He ducks every time I lift my hand."

Someone had been beating him. My blood ran cold. A ghost of my dad's yelling wisped through my mind, and I had to fight to keep from flinching even at just the memory.

"I'll take him in." The words were out of my mouth before I had time to consider what having a dog would even look like for me.

"What?" Trevor asked, just as thrown by my response.

"Just until the no-kill shelter has an opening," I clarified. "I'll take him."

"That's—thank you. I really appreciate it."

I stood, suddenly nervous about becoming responsible for something other than myself. "What does he need? I've never had a dog before."

Trevor laughed. "I've got extra dog bowls and toys he can have. How about you give yourself a couple of days to think about it? If you are still up to it, you can bring him home."

"Okay."

"Is this your first pet?" Trevor asked, and I could tell he was trying very hard to hide the amusement in his expression.

"Does the goldfish I kept alive for less than a week count?"

Trevor nodded once. "You know what? I'll send lots of articles on dog care."

"I'll read them," I promised the dog sitting at my feet. "For both our sakes."

Chapter 10

APRIL

My hand was wrapped around a wrench, and my body was in front of the bike I was supposed to be working on, but my eyes were on Billie's phone as she showed me the eleventh Bookstagram video in a row. She'd sent all these videos to me, but she wanted to see my reactions live.

It was funny. Billie read, but she wasn't into romances like I was. However, she'd started sending me funny smut videos, and now that's all the algorithm gave her. I'd had to hold my side the last three videos. I thought I'd burst at the seams laughing about shadow daddies and dark romance references.

Then, the lighting in the room dimmed as a tall figure partially blocked the natural lighting. Gabriel Torres ducked his head ever so slightly as he entered like he was used to hitting it on door frames. Our fluorescent lighting washed out most skin tones. Not Gabe's. His bronze skin looked radiant. At some point, I had to stop drinking him in every time he entered a room.

I straightened from the reel Billie had been showing me, and my abs and ass simultaneously protested at the movement. It had only been two days since my magic mile/plank/swim test nightmare with Gabe, and my entire body felt like a piece of gum that had been chewed well past recognition and flavor.

Gabe nodded towards us. "Billie. Baird."

"Coach," I answered.

And he smiled, so I smiled, which, in turn, made Billie's head snap my way so she could openly search my face.

"Hey, Gabe!" Trevor called, entering from the back, his arms full of boxes. "Can you give me one second? I'm working on inventory."

"No rush," Gabe answered, eyeing the nutrition display.

"What?" I asked Billie because she was smiling as she walked backward to the checkout counter, her thumbs moving like crazy over her phone.

My phone vibrated.

I sighed, pulling up the message I knew would be from her.

Billie: You've got a thing for your coach.

My cheeks flamed, and I put my phone face down, signaling I wouldn't entertain the conversation.

Gabe turned to me, holding up an empty box. "You wouldn't happen to have any more of these in the back, would you?"

"No, sorry. Those are the only chews we have."

"Might as well not even show up to the race this weekend. Salted watermelon is my good luck flavor." The pout on his face was playful, but I could tell he was a little disappointed.

"Which race are you doing? The one in Sugarland?"

Gabe nodded.

"Mandarin is pretty good," I suggested.

"I like the blackberry flavor, myself," Billie said.

That got Gabe's attention. "I didn't know you raced."

"Oh, I don't. I just like snacking on the chews."

Gabe made a face at that but met Billie at the counter with several chew packets. "Would you like to check your coach out?" she asked me with a faux innocent expression.

"No." I turned to our mini fridge to give myself a reason to hide my face. I let the cool air kiss my cheeks, which felt as hot as a summer sidewalk. I pretended to contemplate the contents when my only option—a container with spaghetti—sat directly in front of me.

Once my cheeks felt cool enough, I dove into my lunch. Gabe looked over, nose scrunching. "Are you eating . . . cold spaghetti?"

My mouth was full, so Billie answered for me. "She eats all her meals like that."

I slurped up a noodle. "I do not."

"Yes, you do," Trevor called from the back.

"Do you guys not have a microwave?" Gabe asked.

"We do," Billie answered. "It's in the office."

"I'm too busy for that," I said defensively.

Gabe made a show of looking around. He was the only customer.

"Okay, it's empty now, but it could change like—" I snapped my fingers, "—that."

The door dinged with a customer.

"You'd think you'd be better at not jinxing things this far into working retail," Billie said, an annoyed expression on her face.

The customer, whose name escaped both Billie and me, had been secretly nicknamed The Viking because he looked like a bearded Norse god in running shorts.

"Gabe!" The Viking called. "I wasn't expecting to see you here."

Gabe leaned back against the counter. "Hey, Steve! How's it going?"

Steve? Yeah, *The Viking* fit him better.

"You've healed me. I haven't had a problem with my shoulder since I was on your massage table." Viking Steve waggled a finger between Billie and me. "Have either of you had a session with Gabe?"

"No," Billie said. "But I've heard enough stories."

"Here we go," Gabe said, shaking his head and looking at the ground.

"He had me sweating and crying two minutes in. Longest half hour of my life." I eyed Gabe. The idea of him making someone as muscular as Viking Steve suffer . . . *Remind me to take care of myself, so I never end up on Gabe's table.*

"Not my idea of a massage," Billie mumbled.

"It was worth it, though. It's like he tore up the muscle so it could form back properly. Honestly, I'm a new man."

"I'll stick with my old muscles, thanks," Billie said.

Viking Steve laughed, then turned to me. "I'm actually here because my headlight gave out. Do you have anything in stock?"

"Yeah!" I came around the corner, the spaghetti container still in my hand. "Were you wanting something for your handlebars or your helmet?"

A clamber of nails on tile made us swivel around. The pit bull, or Beast, was on a leash, pulling Trevor behind him.

Beast cowered as he approached Gabe, but when Gabe knelt and spoke softly to him, his tail wagged so fast that his entire body shook. Trevor told me he was bringing the pit bull to the shop because he'd found someone to give him a temporary home, but I hadn't known that someone was Gabe.

"Wait," I said. "You're the one taking Beast in?"

"Yeah," Gabe answered, still smiling at the dog. "He's going to crash at my place until someone can find a better home for him."

Gabe laughed as Beast made a valiant effort to lick his face, which, in turn, only made Beast try even harder. I couldn't help but think Beast didn't need a better home if he was with Gabe. He'd taken me under his wing, and my plans were starkly different, more in-depth, almost holistic. I couldn't imagine he half-assed anything: triathlon training, coaching, dog ownership. Whatever he decided to do, he was in it. One hundred percent.

I didn't know what had gotten into Gabe that he was suddenly taking in strays, or maybe he was just always like this, but I had the distinct feeling that both Beast and I were in good hands.

Chapter 11

GABRIEL

The Sugarland Tri started promptly at sunrise, so athletes organized their gear under floodlights. Some athletes looked jittery, laying out their things. This wasn't my first rodeo, nor was it a big race, so I felt calm as I ran through my mental checklist of items. Just as I finished, I heard a familiar, "Coach!"

No doubt, there were plenty of coaches in attendance at this sprint, but I recognized April's voice. Sure enough, I looked up into hazel eyes. Her hair was braided into two short pigtails. She looked happy to see me, but not more than I was to see her. I had no idea she'd be at the race, and I certainly couldn't conjure a reason for her to be here so early. We still had about thirty minutes until the start.

"What are you doing here?" I wasn't able to keep the delight out of the question.

"Trevor is taking pictures. So, I asked him if I could tag along." She offered something to me. "Besides, I couldn't let you lose a race due to the wrong flavor." I took the chews from her. My smile brightened even further as I saw the flavor: salted watermelon.

"I thought you were out!"

"We got a shipment in yesterday."

"You didn't have to bring it all this way."

She shrugged. "It's no big deal."

It shouldn't have been a big deal. She'd just brought me chews, but the small gesture felt grand.

Trevor appeared at April's side. "Hey, good luck today, man."

"Thanks."

I eyed the camera, thinking of the next race I'd be volunteering at. "You wouldn't happen to be working the Waco race next month, would you?"

"Yeah, actually, we both are."

"I'll be doing bike repairs at the technical tent," April supplied.

"I'm volunteering at the massage tent," I said. "Do you guys want to ride together and split a room?"

Trevor and April looked at each other, doing that twin-like thing where they read each other's minds, but they didn't leave me in suspense for long.

"Yeah," Trevor said.

"That sounds great," April answered.

A megaphone crackled in transition. I couldn't make out everything, but it was something about the swim start.

"We'll hash out the details later," Trevor said. "Go get ready for your race."

"Thanks again," I said, holding up the packet of chews.

"Just do me a favor," April replied, backing away from the fence. "Kick this race's ass."

Having April at my race had a profound effect on me in that I wanted to ignore my own coach and the plan he'd explicitly crafted for the race. There were certain target zones I was supposed to adhere to, and going faster than said zones was as much of a punishable offense as going under them because I risked not only burning out but injuring myself, which put my training in jeopardy for future races.

We had to be selective when choosing peak races; we only got one or two races a season where we had permission to put everything on the line.

I tried to remind myself that this was just a glorified training day—that I needed to keep my designated pace to keep my body in peak condition for optimal training. But then I'd see April in the crowd, jumping and cheering, and some caveman part of my brain was activated. Part of it was that I wanted to show off, but more than that, I felt ignited.

So, eventually, I ignored the voice in my head that told me to slow down and the buzzing of my watch that said I was going too fast, and I just went for it, fully embracing the sweat in my eyes and the ache in my muscles.

As I stood on the top step of the podium, first place plaque in my hand for my age group and a new personal record for that distance, I found the lens of Trevor's camera winking in the sunlight and next to that April. She smiled so brilliantly that her eyes crinkled, and I realized I didn't need salted watermelon chews for good luck. I needed her.

I didn't fully grasp the consequences of my rebellious speed until I stood in my swim trunks in Coach Rick's garage while he filled up an ice bath.

"I'm just trying to figure out what part of the race plan was confusing to you," he said, dumping another bucket of ice into the tub.

I had to fight an eye-roll. Sometimes, I felt like a teenager back in Rick's lanes, getting scolded for poor form.

"Nothing was confusing, Rick. You've said it yourself. Sometimes we have to reevaluate the plan on race day. Deviations are expected."

"Not that much of a deviation, Gabe." The faucet squeaked as he shut it off roughly. "You bordered on reckless."

I decided to opt for humor to try and lighten the mood. "You know, most coaches would be happy with their athlete getting first place."

Humor was the wrong move. He looked like he was a second from popping a blood vessel. "Is that your goal? To beat the hometown little guy? Or do you want to hang with the top athletes in the world? Let me know now. I'll change your training plan."

I let the scolding seep deep as I looked down at the concrete floor. He was right. What's worse, I knew the effort and care that went into each training plan because I made them for my own athletes. "You're right," I said, then forced myself to meet his gaze, which was no easy feat considering my childhood had taught me to avoid the eye contact of an angry man, but Rick had been the one to teach me men can be upset without being hurtful—that you can have hard conversations without involving fists. I think that's why his disappointment stung even more. He was the father mine didn't know how to be. "It won't happen again. I'm sorry."

Something softened in Rick at that, but he fixed it, grunting out, "I know it won't. Now, get your ass in the water before it warms up too much."

I padded to the metal tub, eyes trained on the ice islands. This would not be pleasant, but I forced my expression to remain neutral. My choices had led me here, I wasn't going to bitch about it.

As I lowered myself in, my movements were jarred—my body fighting my mind over each inch of submersion. I had to bite back a noise as I slid down to my stomach, thinking healing had never felt so punishing. Briefly, I wondered if that's how my clients felt on my massage table.

Submerged to my shoulders, my knuckles were white with the effort to hold myself there instead of popping up like I wanted to. I sat, painfully rigid. Then I thought of what had gotten me into that mess.

April and her smile.

Ay, aquella sonrisa.

I drew a full breath at the memory, my muscles relaxing, even if just by a bit.

Chapter 12

APRIL

I'd just finished taping a handlebar when Gabe entered the shop. I stepped from around the stand so we wouldn't have a bike between us. "Hey, it's Pearville's fastest citizen." I hiked a thumb toward the clipping hanging behind the counter. Gabe's first-place finish had earned him a spot in the local paper.

I might have been the one to submit the story and picture. After that race, Gabe deserved a little hometown fame. The hardest part of the submission was picking out a picture from the shots Trevor got. In every single one, Gabe looked like a towering statue standing on the podium.

Gabe laughed. "I don't know about fastest—" His gaze and smile dropped. "What the hell is that?"

"What? Where?" I whirled around, searching the floor. The week before, Billie had squished a giant spider, only for hundreds of tiny spiders to scatter. It was horrific. So, I just knew Gabe had spotted a baby spider back to enact its revenge.

The tile was a little scuffed but ultimately arachnid-free, so I turned back to Gabe and realized he was looking a few inches below the hemline of my overall shorts—right at my icepack-wrapped knee. I'd been wearing it off and on for a week and had honestly forgotten it was there.

"Oh." I waved off his concern. "It's nothing."

"If it were nothing, you wouldn't have your knee on ice."

"It's just runner's knee." I shrugged. "I'm training for an Ironman. Aches and pains are part of the game."

Gabe wasn't satisfied with my answer. "When did it start?"

I put my hands on my hips. "You're the customer right now, Coach. What did you come in for?"

"Baird." Gabriel stepped closer, and I soon found myself in his shadow. "How long has it been hurting?"

Gabe was such a friendly guy—all bright-eyed and dimpled, but towering over me, sans smile, made the scar running through his eyebrow look more severe. I could picture him as a romantasy character. He may as well have asked, *"Who did this to you?"*

"I—" I swallowed. "Uh, for a few weeks."

His face fell. "April—"

"I promise, it's not that bad."

"That's what they all say." He tipped his head back and closed his eyes. "You've been doing every workout. Your running hasn't slowed."

"I didn't want to disappoint you." And even though that seemed like a normal admission to tell my coach, the tips of my ears burned with the words. I couldn't put a name to it yet, but it was more than just not wanting to let my coach down.

There was a long pause. "Why didn't you come to me? I'm a massage therapist, specifically sports massage. Helping injured athletes is that other thing I do."

"I know," I answered sheepishly. "But I didn't want to bother you with this. You're already sacrificing a lot by taking me on as an athlete."

"That's why you should have said something. Because you're my athlete." There was nothing romantic in that statement, but the possessiveness of the "*my*" made me feel tingly.

"Okay," I conceded. "I'm sorry."

His eyes lingered on mine for a moment before he asked, in a softer tone, "Where exactly does it hurt?"

I bent down to the point where the pinching occurred each time I ran. Gabe surveyed the store. We were only ten minutes from closing. It had been dead all day, so Billie left early. Trevor was working on online orders in the back. Other than that, it was just us.

Gabe nodded to a bench in the shoe section. "Okay, lie down."

If I'd been drinking, I would have done a spit take. "What?"

"I'm going to see if the problem is what I think it is."

"Right now?" I asked, sounding scandalized.

"I'm not going to give you a full-body massage. Just a quick assessment."

My brain snagged on the words *"full-body massage."* The idea of Gabe's hands all over me made my tongue feel too big for my mouth.

"Unless, if you feel uncomfortable . . ." He scratched the back of his neck. "I don't have to be the one to do it. There are plenty of capable therapists at our clinic."

I should have told him I wanted that option. It would have kept clear boundaries between coach and athlete. But that felt weird—sexualizing something Gabe did professionally to help people feel better. I fixed bikes. He fixed people. Same difference. Besides, no one was here to witness it. Even if someone walked by the store, the sofa blocked the bench.

"No," I finally answered, untying my work apron, removing the icepack from my leg, and crossing over to the bench. "I'm not uncomfortable."

"Lie flat on your stomach. Runner's knee could be from a tight Achilles, but it's usually a hamstring."

I did as he asked, trying not to think about how many asses had sat where my cheek touched the bench.

"Now, bend the leg that's bothering you and try to get it to touch your glutes." Again, I obeyed, which prompted an, "As close as you can get it."

I pulled it in, maybe half an inch further.

"That's as far as you can go?" Gabe asked.

"Yeah. Is that bad?"

"Flip over," he said instead of answering.

I turned to find Gabe kneeling next to me. He brandished his hands. "If it's okay, I'm going to feel along your quad—see how tight you are."

Those words, while looking at his long fingers, were doing a number on my spicy literature connoisseur mind. Heat licked across my chest. "Okay," I squeaked. And then, to try and show how fine I was with his hands on me, said, "Yeah, cool."

If I'd been a turtle, I would have ducked into my shell. Fortunately, Gabe seemed unaffected by my awkwardness. He was all business.

His fingers skated over my knee, and goosebumps immediately sprang up. *He's trying to find the root of the problem,* I told myself, *like running diagnostics on a bicycle.*

But then he made a slow, gentle sweep up my leg. And no. It was not like working on a fucking bicycle because a bicycle didn't have to bite back a moan.

He slowed down—his fingers catching at my upper thigh. He made another sweep and got snagged on the same spot. His eyes looked far away as if picturing the muscle in his mind. His index and middle fingers made small circles, and his brows furrowed. "I think we found our problem spot." His deep voice did nothing to douse the flames his touch had ignited. Gabe's dark eyes met mine. "A little pressure. Okay?"

I nodded, but his warning hardly registered because he'd started back at my knee, and I was distracted by the bulge in his biceps as he pressed down harder. It wasn't until he was at my thigh that I realized by a "little pressure," he meant pain.

I thought of Viking Steve and how he'd said Gabe had him sweating and crying on his massage table. I could see how. He wasn't even leaning his entire body weight on me, and I still couldn't contain the groan when he reached my upper thigh.

He opened his mouth to say something but was interrupted by a, "Hey, April, can you—Oh!" My head whipped around to find Trevor frozen at the opening to the back. As if I were a guilty teenager found canoodling on the couch, I jolted upright.

Trevor slapped a hand over his eyes. His face turned crimson around his hand. I felt my skin color match his.

Gabe's hand had been up my overall shorts, his body nearly on top of mine. And that groan could have easily been mistaken for a moan.

I felt my soul leave my body.

"Trevor—" I started, wanting to hurry up and explain so my cousin didn't think he'd just walked in on something.

"I didn't see anything!" He pivoted for the office, but with a hand still over his eyes, he smacked into the door frame. "Ow! Fuck!"

His glasses clattered to the ground, and he reached for them, eyes on the floor as if making eye contact with one of us would turn him to stone.

"Trevor, we weren't—he was just giving me a massage."

He closed his eyes. "For fuck's sake, April. Do *not* give me details!" Then he snatched up his glasses and disappeared into the back.

Gabe sat back on his haunches, staring at where Trevor had exited. He ran a hand through his hair from front to back, making it stand up wildly. "Does Trevor think we were—"

"Yep," I answered before he could finish. Silence stretched for the longest, most awkward moment of my pathetic existence, and then Gabe tipped his head back and released loud, unbridled laughter.

I stared at Gabe, mouth agape, until laughter erupted out of me, too. Just like that, the embarrassment took on a lighter shade. Something was solidifying about sharing the weight of a mortifying moment with someone else.

"Good news," Gabe said after our laughter settled down. "I think I can help you with your knee pain."

"And the bad news?" I asked, sensing it lingering.

"I came here to get Trevor's advice on dog food." He looked at where Trevor had retreated, a scowl on his face. "He's not going to attack me in defense of your honor, is he?"

I laughed. "That doesn't seem like his style, but he's average in height—so like half your size. Push comes to shove, you could take him."

He rolled his eyes as he stood. "Thanks for the pep talk, Baird."

I hadn't been to a massage parlor often, maybe twice in my life, but Gabe's room seemed different. No soft flute music, scent diffuser, or mood lighting.

That was because most massages were to help you relax—chase the stress away with deft and sure fingers. Gabe didn't need low lighting because he was in the business of fixing. Even still, I decided to mess with him a bit.

"Where is the menu? I think I'll start with hot stones or a facial."

Gabe shook his head, but he was fighting a smile. "Get on the table, Baird."

"And how much will this massage set me back?" I asked, not meaning to sound cheap, but I was a small business owner with a large Audible bill.

"I'm not charging you."

"Yes, you are. I'm not letting you spend your time and . . ." the word *service* escaped me, so I settled on, "*talents* without you getting payment. That's not fair."

"You are already paying me for coaching. This is me doing my job, making sure my athlete performs well."

"But—" I started.

"On the table," he said, cutting me off with a tone that brooked no argument.

Okay. Well. Him being bossy had no reason to make my stomach feel like a lava lamp, but here we were.

As I lay down, Gabe emptied his pockets. When he went to put his phone on the counter, he stopped to smile at it. I pictured him reading a text from a girlfriend and felt an unwarranted wash of jealousy.

"Sorry," he mumbled. "One of my friends sent my mom the picture from the paper. She's a little pissed to be the last to find out about my race."

"Why didn't you tell her? You two aren't close?"

"What?" He stopped washing his hands to look over his shoulder at me. "No. We are. I just didn't think this race was that big of a deal, but I should have known better, considering she comes to all my races—the big ones and the hometown sprints. She would have been at this one, but she's spending a few months in Mexico—visiting family."

So what? He's close to his mom and doesn't think making first place is a big deal.

Fuck me. Why was that hot?

Gabe approached the table, and I used humor to battle the nerves. "Do you have patient confidentiality?"

His head cocked.

"I just want to make sure my crying isn't going to become a party story."

Gabe laughed. "What are you talking about?"

"Just thinking about Viking Steve's warning."

"*Viking* Steve?"

"Sorry. Inside joke. Just thinking about what *Steve* said about you making him cry."

He searched my face with an amused expression. "I'm not planning on making you cry today, April."

"Is that what you told Steve?"

"He was being dramatic, but I will say—" he said, stopping to point at me, "—and if you repeat this, I will deny it. But women, generally, have a higher pain tolerance than men. In fact, the burlier the man, the harder time they have on my table."

"More muscle to get through?" I guessed.

"Sure," Gabe said. "Let's go with that."

I wanted to hear more about beefed-up men being babies, but Gabe pumped some oil into his hands, and the application on his long fingers transfixed me.

"Let's get you feeling better," he said. And for one long, dumb-ass second, my brain glitched, and I thought he'd read my dirty little thoughts. Then I rebooted and remembered what I was there for: knee pain.

I managed a nod, and as Gabe's fingers ran gently up my shin, I prayed I'd stay solid instead of liquifying beneath his touch.

Soft laughter broke my concentration. "Try to relax."

I realized I'd had my legs locked. Releasing a slow breath, I willed myself to act normal.

"Much better," he praised.

Minutes into the massage, I forgot all about my nerves. Every cell released an exhale. I was putty on his table.

As he rubbed and leaned and smoothed, I watched him get lost in his work, a slight furrow to his brow as he concentrated. My attention was drawn to the scar that sliced there.

Finally, my curiosity won out. I pointed at the mirrored spot on my own brow. "How'd you get that?"

Gabe's hand slipped on my leg, and his eyes met mine. They were so dark, it was hard to tell where pupil ended and iris began.

"Sorry," I offered. "That was rude. You don't have to say."

"No. It's okay." He went back to watching his hands work. "I fell when I was a kid—hit my head on the corner of a coffee table."

"Ouch."

Gabe shrugged. "One perk of blacking out is that you don't feel any pain."

I was about to ask him more about it when he made a pass at my upper thigh. It twinged in protest at Gabe's touch. His hand made another sweep, and he gave a sympathetic wince. "That's definitely the problem spot."

"What's the protocol? Do I scream into a pillow? Or are the other clients used to hearing crying from your room?"

"April." I had him going again, and I didn't know what was better, the sound of his laughter or those dimples. "It's just going to be some pressure."

"Bamboo under the fingernails—just some pressure," I said because I was addicted to his laugh. "Burned at the stake—just some heat. Water-boarding—just some hydration."

He fixed his features into a neutral expression, but he couldn't keep the laughter from his eyes. "Are you finished?"

"Unfortunately, yes."

He positioned himself so that his forearm rested against my outer thigh. "Then take a deep breath."

After some hesitation, I finally obliged, and on the exhale, Gabe pressed down, sliding his forearm against tense muscle. At first, it wasn't too bad, but then he leaned more of his weight into it, and my breath snagged.

"Keep breathing, Baird," he said without letting up.

It was work, exhaling without groaning, but I did it. I focused on my breathing, let it ground me through the pain—sorry, *pressure*—as he worked mercilessly.

"That's it," he encouraged. "You are going to feel so much better when I'm done."

By the time Gabe finished the massage, my eyes were dry, but my fingers were sore from gripping the table's edge so hard. Viking Steve had not been kidding. My thigh muscles felt like they had been rolled out like dough.

Gabe washed the massage oil off his hands, then came around to the table to help me down, which was appreciated. I wasn't sure my legs would work anymore.

"How does it feel?" Gabe asked, his hand still holding mine as I tested putting weight onto that leg.

"Tender." He released my hand as I took a few steps. "But also like I have new legs."

Gabe nodded. "You're going to want to drink lots of water and stretch over the next few days. I'll change your plan to swimming and walking this week. By your next run, you should feel much better."

"Thank you," I said. And I meant it. He didn't have to spend his time and his talent, but he had.

"You're welcome." Then he ducked his head, his dark eyes searching mine.

"What?"

"Just making sure I didn't make you cry."

I pretended to check by prodding under my eyes. "Would you look at that? Now I can rub it in Viking Steve's face."

Gabe laughed. "Go home, Baird. And I'm serious about the water and stretching."

"Yes, Coach," I said, saluting with my exit.

Chapter 13

APRIL

It was a gorgeous day for a trip to the farmer's market. Well, it looked gorgeous. The sun shone, the sky was blue, and vibrant green leaves decorated the trees. The September breeze, however, felt like a hair dryer. That was to be expected this time of year. Our area wouldn't see any relief until about mid-October, and even then, those days were few and far between.

At any rate, I was excited to be out with Billie, even if that meant shopping in an air fryer. Everyone else in Pearville was, too. The parking lot was packed. I zeroed in on the lone spot within a mile radius. I was so focused that I almost didn't see the flash of black dashing across the parking lot.

Billie screamed, "Cat!" right as I slammed on the brakes. We bounced to a stop, frozen by the close call, and the black feline disappeared into the bushes.

As our breathing slowed, I pulled my Subaru into the spot, this time at a crawl. When I put it in park, Billie looked at me and said, "You're not going to be weird about that black cat, right?"

"Of course not," I replied, but my stomach felt slightly nauseous as I pondered what the universe had in store for me today.

"Because you know bad luck isn't real."

"I know. That's why I don't believe in it," I lied as I exited the car.

Billie gave an unconvinced, "Sure you don't," which I ignored, forcing myself to focus on the cute booths instead of my impending doom.

Ten minutes into shopping, Billie picked up a little horseshoe charm from a vendor. "Why don't you get this to offset the bad chi."

"I thought you said luck isn't real."

"It's not. But the problem is that it's real to you. So why not make your own good luck to battle the bad? Fight magic with magic."

"That's actually—" I eyed the adorable array of charms. "Not the worst idea." I picked through the options. There was also a rainbow and a four-leaf clover, but then my fingers grazed the smooth surface of a tiny butterfly.

I could almost hear my mom say, *Look, a little bit of magic.*

I purchased the charm, along with a silver chain, to make a necklace. Now, I'd always have a bit of magic with me.

With the little butterfly on my chest, I stopped worrying about the black cat and just enjoyed shopping. Billie found some mushroom jerky. I bought a box of intricately painted cookies in the shape of flowers. We oohed and ahhed at a booth with braids you could clip into your hair.

Billie stopped to point a carrot at me as we picked our way through a vegetable stand. "Oh, before I forget. I've got you down for bringing the artichoke dip to the party." She was hosting a triathlon party the next day, which was laughable. If there was an Olympic sport for disinterest in sports, Billie would bring home gold every time. She once wore a T-shirt to a Superbowl party that read: *I hope both teams lose.*

Billie pretended to be offended when I asked her why she was hosting it. "I'm obviously passionate about the sport. I'm a cashier for a triathlon store." Then she'd straightened her septum ring. "And women who do triathlons have the most spectacular thighs." And finally, the truth had entered the chat.

I frowned. I always brought artichoke dip. "What if I want to bring something else?"

"No."

"No?"

"No means no. You're bringing the artichoke dip."

"We'll see."

She looked ready to argue further when her eyes shifted to the left of my face. "I think I see your coach."

I swiveled, shamefully fast, at the mention of Gabe. I'd had a hard time getting him out of my head since he'd had his hands all over my leg for that massage. Honestly, I kept having to restart audiobook chapters because it would get to a spicy scene, and I would insert my own fantasy—Gabe running his hand from my thigh to my center. Those long fingers exploring me.

"Stop staring at him like a weirdo and say hi," Billie said, breaking me from the perverted images my mind liked to torment me with.

Leading Gabe was the pit bull Trevor had given him. The dog's tongue lolled out of his mouth, and he pulled against his leash so hard the harness went sideways, giving him an awkward gait as he pushed forward. He wasn't the apprehensive dog Trevor had found. He had the confidence of a dog who knew he'd have a place to sleep at night.

Busy reading the nutritional facts on a bag of dog treats, Gabe probably wouldn't have noticed us if I hadn't said, "He's looking so much better."

Gabe looked up, and I watched the question in his eyes turn to recognition. Then his smile stole the show. It was so genuine; my knees felt like noodles cooked al dente. I was pretty sure I had never paid attention to dimples before, and now I was waiting for his to appear.

"Oh, hey!" He looked down at the dog, seeming to slowly piece together what I'd said. "Yeah, he's coming around. I probably shouldn't let him pull when I walk him, though."

"Man," Billie said. "Don't stress about shit like that. Rules aren't even real."

Gabe tilted his head, and I realized that not everyone was used to the free spirit that was Billie. Finally, he settled on, "I thought it would be a good idea to get Chuck around people—to socialize him a bit."

"Chuck? Didn't Trevor name him Beast?" Billie asked.

"He needed a real name. Beast makes it sound like he's a wild animal. Chuck is dignified."

"You *re*named him? That's worse than naming him." Billie laughed. "There's no way you will give him up now."

"Trust me. This is a limited-time deal."

I knelt to offer *Chuck* a hand to sniff. He did a nervous half-circle, head low but tail wagging like crazy. Then he nudged my hand with his snout and started licking. I looked at his too-big-head paired with his stubby legs. "Don't ask me to explain it, but he does look like a Chuck," I said.

"Is he already sleeping in your room?" Billie asked.

"Well . . ." Gabe hesitated like he knew his answer was an admission of guilt. "Yes, but not in my bed."

Billie laughed. "Dude. You are so fucked."

Gabe, clearly looking for a change in subject from his impending permanent dog ownership, turned to me. "How are you feeling?"

"My knee is so much better. I haven't had a problem since I was on your table." I gave Chuck a scratch around his scruff, getting under his harness before standing. "You've got magic fingers."

I heard myself say that and inwardly cringed. Billie's head snapped my way, and I didn't dare look at her. Still, I could feel her smirk. My cheeks warmed.

Gabe's gaze dipped to my cheeks, a bemused smile playing at his lips, but being the saint he was, he didn't comment on the blush. "Glad you're feeling better," he said. "I'll give you another week before I put running and cycling back on the training plan. Have you been doing the stretches?"

"The stretches, the walking, the swimming." I made a face. "The ab routine."

Gabe laughed. "Good."

Billie's gaze bounced between us, her eyes narrowing, and I felt like I was under an X-ray machine. Finally, she smiled and settled her attention on Gabe. "Are you coming to the tri-party?"

"That's tomorrow, right?"

"Yeah. April is bringing her artichoke dip." I gave her a side-eye, but my glare was cut short by Gabe's answer.

"I'll be there." And just like that, I was looking forward to the party.

Chuck had begun sniffing and pulling on the leash—like a kid tired of mom socializing at the grocery store. "I better get him moving. But I'll see you tomorrow." Gabe gave me one last smile, and I took a mental picture to hold me over.

When he was out of earshot, Billie grabbed my elbow and pulled me close. "Are we going to talk about your coach giving you a massage?"

I knew she'd make a big deal of it, so I hadn't told her anything. "Listen. It isn't a sexy thing. That's what he does for a living."

Her lips pressed into a knowing grin. "Look me in the eyes and tell me having his hands all over your body didn't make you hot and bothered." I looked away, and I swear, it felt like even my hair blushed. "You *are* into him. I knew it!"

I shrugged, trying to play it cool, even though we both knew I was past that point. "He's cute. So what if I have a tiny crush?"

"*So* you should get you some, girl." She swatted at my butt, but I dodged.

"He's my coach, Billie."

"Okay, that would be gross if he was older, but I assume he's about your age. You are both adults."

"The coaching company he works for might see that differently." My eyes followed the edge of the grass as we walked along the concrete path. "Besides, what if it's one-sided?"

Billie snorted a laugh. "Did you see the way he smiled when he saw you?"

Her words made my own grin appear, but I tried to shove it down. "He's like that with everyone. He's just a friendly guy."

"Mmmhm," Billie hummed, not entertaining any of my logic. After a stretch of silence, she sighed and then said, "There's just one thing."

"What?" I asked.

"For the record, I think you should climb Gabe like a tree."

"Billie!" I laughed.

"But I heard from Ashley that he doesn't do commitment." I kept waiting for her to continue—to get to the problem, but she stopped there.

"Okay. Well, I'm not exactly looking for someone to grow old with right now."

"I know. But you've only had sex with people you were serious with, right?" She was correct. There was Aiden, who I dated for the first two years of college, and then Wyatt. We'd been together for a year, and I'd wondered if he was the one.

"I could do casual," I said, but the uncertainty in my voice gave me away. I really didn't know if I could be intimate with someone and not catch feelings.

"Again, I think you should go for it. You've been so stressed about this race. You could use a release. Casual sex might be exactly what you need."

A teenage boy looked our way and smiled.

"Why don't you say *sex* louder?" I said out of the side of my mouth. "I don't think enough people heard you."

"I'm just saying—" Billie pulled me off the path. "Get it out of your system, but be careful. Gabe is the kind of guy who gives a dog a name and still plans to get rid of him. I don't want to see you get your heart broken."

I appreciated her warning, and it gave me a lot to think about, but unable to be serious with her for long, I said, "Thanks, Mom. I'll be careful."

"Yeah," she said, matching my energy. "Use protection on your nethers and your heart." She jabbed a finger at my chest, then she looked past me at a row of vendors we hadn't been to yet. "Are you ready to leave? My bank account weeps every time I step into a booth."

"Yeah, I need to get home anyway. I've got artichoke dip to make."

Chapter 14

GABRIEL

After the market, I went home and worked on training plans while Chuck slept at my feet. All the sights and smells at the market must have worn him out. Occasionally, he'd distract my work with a man-like snore. He was pretty cute for a bobblehead.

When it was time for my swim, I moved slowly, not wanting to wake him. His head popped up anyway. "It's okay, bud. You can sleep," I tried to tell him, but Chuck followed me around the apartment while I got on my swim trunks and checked the items in my duffle. I nearly tripped over him because he stayed right under my feet.

He must have realized I was leaving because he sat back on his haunches, big eyes on me as I twisted the door handle. "I'll be back soon."

He gave one wag, but it looked sad. As I locked up the apartment, I had a nagging feeling in my chest that I realized was guilt. I felt bad for leaving Chuck. Billie's skepticism over me being able to give up Chuck when the shelter had a vacancy started to solidify. I pushed away those thoughts as I started the truck. *He's just crashing with me for a while. There's a better home out there for him.*

But my thoughts didn't quiet over the matter until I spotted a certain bike mechanic slapping the vending machine in the hallway of the natatorium.

"You have got to be kidding me," she growled, trying and failing to shake the machine.

I stepped closer, biting back a laugh. A bag of chips lay horizontally—caught on the inner lock of the machine. Then, even more humorous, was the dangling beef jerky. It had gotten stuck on the B5 sticker.

"What are the odds?"

April whirled around. Her eyes hit my chest first, then rolled up to my face. She smiled, then forced her full lips back into a neutral line. "That God hates me? Pretty high."

"I mean, two stuck snacks?" I let out a low whistle. "We certainly can't rule out that possibility."

Her gaze left mine. "It was that damn black cat," she mumbled.

"What?" I asked.

"Never mind." She turned back to the machine. "If I had a screwdriver, I could get them out."

I reached around her to shake the machine, arms on either side of her, which I hadn't thought would be a big deal. But suddenly, I wasn't thinking about shaking a snack free. It was all too easy to picture her between my arms, enjoying a different cardio than what we'd both come to the natatorium for. The thought sent a jolt down my spine.

It was getting harder to fight off my attraction to her. Case in point, when I'd had her on my table at the clinic. At first, I wasn't worried about losing my professionalism with her. Not until she'd made this little moan of pleasure. I started salivating instantly. My mind could be professional all it wanted, but my body didn't know the word. From then on, the entire massage had been a battle to keep my composure.

I shook the vending machine probably a little harder than the situation warranted, trying to jostle myself out of the hold April had over me. The snacks broke free, and I stepped back to let April dig out her prizes.

"Thank you! I'm so hungry."

I noticed a swimsuit strap poking out from the neck of her oversized shirt. "Well, can't swim on an empty stomach."

"Are you swimming, too?"

"I came here to swim, but now coaching sounds more fun." Honestly, I'd have to get my laps in after, but that took the back burner.

April's shoulders dropped. "I don't know if I like the sound of that."

"Fuel up, Baird. I wanna see those quicker swim times in action." That pouty lip was out, and I'd never loved messing with someone more. Adding gasoline to the fire, I asked, "How's the core work going?"

"Great," she said, the tone and word not matching the way she plopped her duffle bag onto the bleachers.

"I'm glad—"

"If—" she interrupted me, "—*great* was a code-word for *feels like what I'd imagine the seventh circle of hell to be.*"

I threw my head back and laughed.

"Seriously." She paused to chew some jerky. "Every time I get on the floor to do a plank, I feel like I'm offering a little piece of my soul to Satan."

"Hey, whatever it takes to finish that Ironman, right?"

She snorted, folding the jerky bag closed and sticking it in her duffle. "I bet hell is just a bunch of triathletes talking about their PR."

She had me laughing again. Until she took off her shirt.

It was a perfectly normal, expected activity. I *knew* she wasn't going to swim in a T-shirt and sweats. But *fuck*. Her curves in that swimsuit.

Speaking of making an offering to the devil. That body was doing unholy things to me.

I realized, a beat too late, that I was staring at my athlete's breasts. I tore my eyes away, making myself busy with my phone while she continued to undress. My thumbs scrolled aimlessly over training plans. My eyes roamed over the screen, but I couldn't tell you one thing I looked at even if I'd had a gun to my head. The afterimage of April's curves was burning a hole behind my eyes.

I didn't dare look up until I heard a splash. With that body safely submerged in the water, I finally approached.

Luckily, coaching at this point was something I could do on autopilot, which was enough to get her through warm-ups. Then, I gave her some drills, and I was truly captivated by the change in her form. She was no longer fighting against water but working with it. My chest swelled with pride. She'd already made so much progress.

I started my watch to time one hundred yards. She flew down the lane with strong, even pulls. Someone's flip-flops smacked on the deck near me, but I was too enraptured by April to look. She hit the other side of the pool for her first seventy-five yards, and I pushed the lap button on my watch.

"Who is that?"

Clay's voice made me glance over. He was watching April with interest.

It gave me great pleasure to say, "That's Baird."

"No, it's not." He laughed, then looked down at my watch. "Baird isn't that fast."

I wasn't usually one for confrontation. The world was harmful enough without me adding to it, but a bit of my self-control snapped.

"Maybe she just needed some targeted workouts instead of an amount of time in the water."

His head swiveled like an owl's, but April had made it back to our side, ending the conversation as far as I was concerned. I stopped my watch as she popped out of the water. Eager to hear her time, she ripped off her goggles and looked up at me.

"You crushed it," I called. "One forty-five." Her fist pumped in celebration until she noticed Clay. Having him around for our conversation felt like having the enemy in our camp. "Go ahead and do a cooldown lap. We'll talk after."

I turned from Clay, ready to strip down to my swim shorts so I could get my own workout in.

"Unbelievable," Clay said. "You put her on your roster."

"You insisted I take her on," I said without turning around.

"I didn't think you would actually do it," he spat.

"I'm confused." I pulled off my shirt and laid it out on the bleachers. "Are you mad that she's on my roster, or are you mad that she's doing well?"

"I'm not mad," he said, voice rising contradictorily. He got right up to the bleachers to put himself in my periphery. "I would just think that as a fellow coach, you would take my warning seriously. There's a reason I dropped her."

I'd had my hands in my swim cap, spreading them apart to put it on, but his words stole my full attention. I looked him in the eye. "And there's a reason I picked her up."

Clay sucked his teeth. "Whatever, man. I guess I should be thanking you. You've pretty much made sure the promotion is mine. The girl is a DNF risk. This will make two years in a row that she costs you A-Team."

When he realized I wasn't going to entertain that with a response, he stomped off, his sandals making his tantrum all the more comical, until I turned and saw a dripping April standing there. Her swim cap was off, and her hair had been finger-combed back. She was beautiful, even with goggle lines around her eyes, but she also looked upset, and I realized she'd just heard Clay call her a DNF risk.

"Hey, don't listen to him."

"What did he mean?" She swallowed, and water rolled down her throat. "About me costing you A-Team?"

"Nothing. He's an asshole."

"You are his competition? For A-Team?"

"I—" I stopped. I'd figured Clay had told her. "Yes."

"I thought you were already on A-Team." She put a hand on her mouth, then dropped it. "You were supposed to get on it last year, weren't you? But then you stopped to help me." She looked like she was about to cry.

I took a step in her direction. "It's not your fault."

My words looked like they bounced right off her. "And if I don't finish this year, it could stop you from getting the promotion again?"

"I'm not worried about that because you are going to finish, April."

She took a step backward. "You don't know that."

"The past few years weren't your fault. You just had some bad luck."

"I can't—" Her eyes brimmed with tears, and the sight made my chest throb. "I just need a minute." She sniffed, then pivoted, rushing to grab her bag and towel.

"April, wait—"

But she was already padding down the deck.

I sat on the bleachers, eyes on the swim cap still in my hand. I knew she'd feel better with time, but I wanted to fix the doubt and the hurt now.

I watched the water lap against the rope barrier as a swimmer in a different lane torpedoed past. The idea of swimming made me sick. If I couldn't make my athletes feel confident in their abilities, I didn't deserve a spot on A-Team anyway.

I thought about going back to the truck and calling it a day, but then I thought of my own coach counting on me to perform for his last year.

Feeling heavy, I pulled my swim cap on and headed for the water.

Chapter 15

GABRIEL

In the twenty-four hours between seeing April at the pool and Billie's party, I think I typed out a message only to delete it roughly fifty times. Ultimately, I decided it would be best to just talk to her in person.

What I hadn't accounted for was a call from Rick, wanting to do an in-depth recap of my athletes and their training. It was all going fine until we reached the last name on my roster.

"And how's the new athlete?"

"She's great." Unfortunately, I had a hard time making myself sound convincing after what happened the day before.

"I wish you hadn't picked her up. Sometimes you are too nice."

"She's a hard worker."

"She's a wildcard," he countered.

"She just needs better guidance than what Clay was giving her. Besides, she hasn't completed an Ironman before, so any time she gets will be considered progress."

"*If* she makes it across the red carpet. If she doesn't, she could cost you A-Team. She doesn't exactly have the best track record."

"She's had some bad luck," I conceded.

Rick answered in a softer tone, "You know, I would normally never advise you to do this when we're in the middle of the season, but . . . it's not too late to drop her."

"Rick—" I sighed.

"You have until the middle of Oct—"

"Rick," I said firmly, "I'm not dropping her." She'd completed every workout I'd thrown at her. Even when her knee hurt, she hit the times I designated. April had been under my direction for only a month, and she'd made leaps and bounds. When I looked at her, I didn't see a DNF risk. I saw an advantage. "I'm telling you, this is her year. You've done a great job mentoring me. Trust that your training has paid off."

There was a long pause. "Okay. Alright. Fine. It's just the idea of that little bastard, Clay, taking over my spot is making me lose sleep."

I thought of the half-assed coaching Clay had done for April and how he'd upset her at the pool by calling her a DNF risk. I felt my pulse pick up. "Don't worry. He's not making A-Team."

Billie's apartment was packed by the time I arrived. I weaved past the normal groupings of friends because cliques assembled even in a niche group of triathletes. There were the diamond runners—who left the group and their shirts behind on long runs, the chill group—they didn't care about times, just having fun completing triathlons, and the elitists—who spent most of their time arguing about form, shoes, nutrition, and which training methods had the best impact. I noticed Clay's absence from that usual grouping. Good. I didn't know if I could be civil to him after what happened at the pool.

I said some quick greetings to a couple of my athletes, but I kept pushing through the crowd. I had a specific one in mind. My height had many advantages, one of which was that I could look over heads when searching for someone. I found April sipping a margarita with Billie in the kitchen. She had on an olive-colored jumpsuit, and usually, I would have seen that kind of outfit as industrial. Something worn in a factory. Not on April. It cinched at her waist, showing off her curves even under the dark fabric. She topped off the outfit with gold earrings, dressy sandals, and even curled her short hair in waves. The sight of her made my intentions turn fuzzy.

I am her coach, I reminded myself as I refocused on the goal at hand—making sure that asshole, Clay, hadn't gotten to her.

I stepped in her direction but was intercepted by someone who'd heard I was a massage therapist and wanted to know what I thought he should do for hip pain. By the time I had him booked with me for a Tuesday afternoon, Blake, a new guy in the tri group, had saddled up to April.

They laughed together, and I felt a sharp edge of jealousy that didn't make any sense. Other people were allowed to make her laugh, even if those other people were guys who had ulterior motives.

So, I joined a conversation about bike bags and pretended to be interested, even though I watched April out of my peripheral. Billie poured them both another drink. With generous giggles, heavy blinks, and a sway to her stance, April was looking less and less tipsy and more drunk. I knew April was just having fun, and she deserved that, but it took quite a bit of self-control to keep my feet planted instead of pouring all of Billie's tequila down the drain.

My plan to be a casual observer dissolved when April slid past our group for the restroom. Blake's eyes were glued to April's ass. I could hardly blame him. She looked killer in that jumpsuit, but I excused myself from Ned and Jessica's conversation about bike modifications to head to the kitchen.

"Hey." I nodded at Blake.

"Hey, man."

I dipped a chip into the artichoke dip and tried a bite. Pretty damn good coming from a woman who ate cold spaghetti for lunch. "Listen," I said, leaning on my elbows, trying to look as least threatening as possible, which I learned was hard to achieve at six foot, four inches. "You know nothing is happening between you two tonight, right?"

"What?" Blake asked.

I nodded at the direction April had gone. "You and April. I'm not saying you can't shoot your shot with her some other time." It was physically challenging to get those words out, but she was my athlete, not my girlfriend. I had no right to play gatekeeper. "But she's had too much to drink tonight."

Blake's eyes widened. "Oh, yeah." He straightened, but he smiled good-naturedly. "No, man. Of course. We were just having fun."

"Great."

"I'm actually about to head out. Early run tomorrow." *Even better.* "You know how that goes."

"Sure do." I huffed out a laugh, thinking of my own early morning run.

When he was gone, I looked at Billie, who had been drinking at the same rate as April but seemed unaffected. She rested a hip against the counter and smiled mischievously at me over her drink. "Scaring off the competition?"

"Just making sure April isn't taken advantage of."

"Hmm," she said, then took a sip of her drink. "What a gentleman."

She was definitely onto me, so I decided to switch the subject. "Is your goal to ensure she can't walk in a straight line?"

"Oh, let her have some fun. She's having a bad day, which I know you already know about." She crossed her arms, resting the margarita glass against her shoulder. "And why haven't you called her—talked to her?"

"I thought it would be better to talk in person, but that was before I knew you'd have her drunk by the time I got here."

She waved me off. "She'll forget about her problems for the night and be good as new tomorrow." Then Billie laughed, her dark fingers prodding even darker braids. "But goddamn, she is such a lightweight."

A loud laugh near the restroom stole our attention. April leaned her hands on her thighs as she belly laughed. Ned and Eddie looked at her like she'd grown another head. "I'm sorry," she said, wiping at her eyes and smearing her makeup a bit. "It's just—" She erupted into laughter again. "You boys think you know everything about bikes." Her laughter continued as she entered the kitchen. "Where is Blake?"

"He had to go," I said. "Early morning run."

"Oh." April shrugged, and it pleased me that she didn't seem bothered he'd left. "I should go too. I open the store tomorrow." Some loose salt from the chip bowl had fallen onto the counter. I watched April push several grains together before pinching them between her fingers and tossing them over her shoulder.

I cocked my head but focused on the task at hand—encouraging April to leave before she had to be carried out. "That's probably for the best."

April's attention snapped to me. She had plump lips to begin with, but they really looked full when she pursed them in contemplation. I didn't get to enjoy them for long, however. She narrowed her eyes and turned to Billie, exclaiming, "Let's do one last shot!"

Billie laughed. "Atta girl!"

"I think you've had enough," I said.

April put her hands on her hips, trying to look tough—which was hilarious, seeing as I towered over her—and I realized I was making the situation worse.

"You might be the boss on the track, and in the pool, and even on my bike." She poked a finger into my chest. "But you have no power here."

I leaned back against the counter, biting the inside of my cheek as April threw back the shot Billie handed her. "You feel in charge now?" I asked as her face pinched.

"Shhhh, Gabe. Just let me have this." She giggled. The action threw her off kilter. I straightened her and realized Billie was right; she was definitely a lightweight. Not that I had room to judge. I could have been one, too, but I'd never know. My dad's habits had turned me off alcohol for life. "Now I've had my nightcap. I can go." April gave Billie a clumsy peck on the cheek and started for the door.

"She can't drive like that." I looked to Billie for help. Then, I scanned the crowd and realized I hadn't seen Trevor at the party.

"You're right," she said, eyeing Jessica as she bent over the ice chest to get a beer. "I have a party to host, so go get her, Coach." She winked and then went back to pouring shots.

"I—" My argument died when I realized April was already out the door. I left Billie with her shots and snaked around people to get to the exit. I feared I'd make it outside and April would be gone, so I was equally annoyed and relieved to find her mounting her bike on the sidewalk.

"What are you doing?" I asked as I approached. Under the twitchy lamplight, I got a look at her commuter bike. It was mint-colored and had a basket. Of course, it would. This woman was equal parts grime and glitter. She'd wear makeup but have a grease smear on her cheek. Her job was rusted gears, but she made repairs with bubble-gum pink nails.

Her ass slipped off the seat, but she recovered. "Uh . . . riding my bike?"

"You can't ride like that. You're drunk."

"Pshhhh," April said, unimpressed by my concern. "Could a drunk person do this?" She took off down the sidewalk before I could intervene, then removed her hands from the handlebars, raising them in the air but remaining surprisingly balanced.

I was impressed she could do that in her state, but I kept my expression neutral as she jerked the bike around. She stopped right in front of me and had to put both feet out to keep from falling. "Yeah. That's pretty good. Still can't let you ride home like that."

"Hey, Coach, listen." Lots of people called me coach. That's what I was. But for whatever reason, when she did, it seemed to awaken every cell in my body. "I'm not taking this thing down 288. I'm just going down that—" She waved a finger in one direction, squinted, then shifted so she pointed in a different direction. "That trail. My house is on the other side."

I peered into the darkness, looking for said trail. Then my eyes popped open wide as I realized she referred to the barely there path eaten by thick darkness as it wound into the tree line. "Through serial killer woods? I don't think so. I'll get you an Uber."

"And wait thirty minutes for a two-minute ride?" April shook her head, and it made her entire body sway. "No way." She meant to push off again, but I grabbed the handlebars. She looked at my hands gripped there for a long moment before meeting my gaze.

"I cannot, in good conscience, let you ride home like this."

She leaned her butt on the seat. "You don't have to do this."

"Do what?"

April huffed out a breath and gestured vaguely at me. "The whole chivalerous—" April narrowed her eyes as she quietly tested out the word. "Chivalrous. You don't have to be chivalrous. I know that's your thing—that's why you stopped when I wrecked last year. But you don't have to worry about me riding my bike home. And you don't have to worry about me being a DNF risk because I'm bowing out."

"Come again?"

"I . . . am . . . quitting," she said it slowly like I was the one inebriated. "Now, you don't have to worry about me ruining your chance at the dream team." She made jazz hands at the end of the sentence, then tried to push off again, but I held onto the handlebars tight. I wanted, more than anything, to discuss her decision to quit Ironman, but I knew she wasn't in the right headspace for that conversation. Instead, I focused on the most important thing—getting her home safely.

"We can talk about your race tomorrow, but please, for my sanity, let me bring you home. Or, if you'd prefer, I can get Billie or call Trevor."

She rolled her eyes and let her hands fall to her sides. "Fine. Where's your car?"

I led her to my Silverado, which she leaned against while I loaded her bike. When I closed the tailgate, I realized she was staring at me. I thought maybe she had a problem with the way I'd positioned her bike. "What?"

"Nothing." She shrugged heavily. "It's just—I picture you as the love interest in every audiobook I listen to. Tall, dark hair, the scar—" She reached over and pinched my bicep. "Muscular."

"Hey, hands to yourself," I said with a laugh, but I could feel my neck flush.

"It's okay," April said, teetering toward the passenger side. "I can call you hot. You won't remember this tomorrow."

She was drunk. She hardly knew what she was saying, but the compliment still had me grinning. Then, she tried to get in, only to slip back onto the curb, which was entertaining considering my truck wasn't raised. "Let me—" I got behind her to serve as a guide right as she lost her footing again. I caught her by the hips, but her ass still fell into me.

The world narrowed to the press of her body against mine, and I imagined us in the same position doing something very different.

She. Is. Your. Athlete.

My hands jumped up to a safer spot—her ribs—and I held her at a distance as I helped her into the seat. Closing her door, I thought the worst was behind us, but as I started the truck, April's hand roamed aimlessly over her shoulder, trying to find the seatbelt.

I reached across her to help. *¡Dios mío!* She smelled vanilla and fruity. As if she needed anything else to make her enticing. Between her curves and those lips—the color of strawberry sorbet, she always looked delectable.

"Thank you," she mumbled drowsily as I clicked it into place.

"No problem," I answered, my voice strained.

We were quiet as we exited the apartment complex. At the street, I stopped the car, waiting for her direction, but she just stared out the window. "April?"

"Hmm?"

"Which way am I going?"

"Take a right," she answered. Then, "Do you think my mom would be disappointed in me?"

My eyes flashed to her. "What? No!" Her head lolled against the seat. She looked on the verge of tears. "It's not your fault you haven't finished an Ironman yet. You've had some bad luck, that's all."

"But that's the problem. I'm always unlucky."

"I really think this year is your year."

"You *think*, but you don't know." She closed her eyes. "Anything could happen."

"You're right. I can't guarantee it, but all you can do is worry about the things within your control."

"That's such a coach-y thing to say," she said, her sassy tone back momentarily before turning somber again. "I wanted to do an Ironman to feel closer to Mom, but I feel further every day." Her admission was so raw and vulnerable. It felt like someone had dropped a rock in my stomach. She wiped at her tears hastily. "Shit. You were supposed to turn there," she said, pointing at a street as we passed it.

"You know your mom would be proud of you, right?" I said as I hooked a U-turn.

"Yeah," she said, still looking miserable.

"April?"

"Yeah, I know. I just miss her, is all."

We finished the drive silently, save for April's directions, which all came a beat too late. I parked my truck in front of a cozy house. I could make out the light-yellow paint even in the dim streetlight. There was something so welcoming about the enclosed porch, the way the bay windows looked out to a wild garden. It reminded me of the homes I'd always see on TV as a kid, where the mom weeded the flowerbed, and the dad grilled. A home where families looked happy and whole.

"Nice place," I said.

"Thanks," April answered as I helped her step down from the truck. "It used to be my parents'."

She looked more balanced as I walked her and her bike to the front door, but I had to ask. "Are you going to be okay on your own? You won't choke on your own tongue in your sleep, will you?"

She laughed as she fought to fit the key into the hole. "That's not a thing." She finally got it in. "I'm fine."

"Okay," I said. "Lock the door when I leave. Okay?"

"Yes, Coach."

And as I walked to my truck, I was already making plans because I wasn't done hearing her call me that.

Chapter 16

APRIL

I had my head pressed against my workbench when a knock sounded at Just Tri's door. The sound made me wince. It had been a while since I'd had a hangover, and I forgot what a sensory nightmare it was.

"We're closed," I half mumbled, half whined into the wood. When the knocking came again, I forced myself to straighten. I'd make this potential customer leave, and then I'd have thirty minutes to gather myself before I had to put on my best customer service smile, even if it felt like an elementary's recorder band played freestyle in my skull.

My intention of shooing away the eager customer was quelled when I realized Gabriel Torres' tall frame filled the glass door. He waggled fingers at me in greeting, and I tried to muster a smile, but it ended as a grimace.

When I unlocked the door and pulled it open, Gabe said, "Can we talk?"

I tried to remember if I said something that crossed the line the night before. I vaguely remembered being sassy, him helping me into his truck, his large, warm body around mine. And, oh yeah, telling him I was quitting Ironman. Which, I figured, was why he was there.

I may have said and done some crazy things the night before, but I was still sticking with that decision. Clay was right; I was a DNF risk. The universe played goalie to this plan of mine, and it would always win, would always find some way to knock me down before I reached that finish line. I was done wasting my time, and I certainly wasn't going to drag Gabe down with me, but I still owed him more than a drunk explanation.

"Hurry," I said, squinting against the sun's assault on my corneas. "Before it follows you inside."

He turned around, checking to ensure nothing was behind him. "What follows me inside?"

"The sunshine."

His eyes roamed my face, and I was sure I looked like shit. I hadn't had time for makeup—not when I'd wasted half an hour kneeling in front of my toilet, puking until I was dry retching. "That bad, huh?" he asked, voice soft.

"It feels like every light, sound, and smell has a personal vendetta against me," I answered.

"I brought you this." He held up a brown paper bag with a greasy outline coating the bottom half.

I gagged.

"I'm so sorry," he said, pulling the bag to his chest wide-eyed. "Greasy food always helps my friends get over their hangovers."

I fanned my face and wiped the tears out of my eyes. "Thank you. Yes. Greasy food . . ." I had to pause to keep from gagging again. "Usually does help. I just wasn't ready for the . . . smell."

"Here, is it okay if I set it on your workbench?"

I nodded and closed my eyes, working to take slow, deep breaths. When I felt like I wouldn't throw up in front of Gabe, I opened my eyes again and found him pulling the blinds, blocking out the strong, natural light.

"Thank you," I said, feeling brave enough to approach the Whataburger bag. The thought of food made my stomach roil, but I knew I'd feel better after a few bites. "So, you wanted to talk?" I asked, bracing myself for a coach-like scolding.

Gabe leaned against the counter next to me. I noticed he did a lot of leaning. I wondered if keeping that height upright was difficult or if he did it to be more on level with the rest of the population. If so, mission unaccomplished, he still had me beat by half a head.

"So last night, what you said about Ironman . . . was that just the alcohol talking?"

I unwrapped the greasy breakfast sandwich to give me something to look at rather than the disappointment on Gabe's face.

"What gives you the impression alcohol did any talking last night?" I asked, then nibbled a bite of sausage, egg, and cheese biscuit.

Gabe smiled at the floor as if he remembered something specific. My face flamed. *Good Lord.* What had I said to the man? I wracked my brain, but it felt as though too-tight screws held my skull together.

Finally, Gabe shrugged a single shoulder. "Just a hunch." Then he put his hands in his pockets. "But I'm specifically interested in the part where you said you were quitting." His eyes lasered onto mine.

"Oh, that." I took another bite, giving myself enough time to plot a course while I slowly chewed and swallowed. I decided on ripping the Band-Aid off. "I meant what I said, Gabe."

I waited for him to show some emotion—anger that he'd wasted so much time on me or relief that I wouldn't weigh him down anymore. Something, anything, but he didn't let an ounce of feeling show. "Because of what Clay said about you being a DNF risk?"

"He's right," I said by way of answering.

"Do you control the weather?" I squinted at him, not at all sure where he was going with that question. "Because the race was canceled three years ago because of a storm."

"Yeah, well—" I started, but Gabe interrupted me.

"Were you faking the flu a couple of years ago?"

"What? No!"

"And I know you didn't fake last year's injury. I was there." I rubbed the phantom wound at my collarbone. "It's not your fault you couldn't finish the past three races. You aren't a DNF risk. You've just had some bad luck."

I lowered the sandwich. "That's the problem, though, Gabe. I think I'll always have bad luck when it comes to Ironman."

He cocked his head, and strands of dark hair shifted above his brows. "What do you mean?"

I tried to think of a way to explain how I thought the universe didn't want me to finish this race without sounding insane, but I ultimately decided on a different path. "Just that I have a mental block. I don't think it's going to happen for me."

My eyes drifted up to my favorite picture—the one of my mom and me. My heart throbbed. I tore my gaze away, but judging how Gabe's eyes studied mine, he'd clocked my internal struggle.

"Let me help you. What are you most worried about?"

Looking at the order of plagues that had kept me from reaching the finish line: weather, illness, and injury. What was the most logical thing the universe could throw in my path? A hurricane? A meteor? A busload of toads invading Ironman Village? Anything was possible. However, the idea of Gabe losing A-Team was at the forefront of my concern. "I don't want to drag you down with me," I said. "I would have never agreed to be your athlete if I'd known your career hinges on this race."

"That sounds more dramatic than what it is."

"Is it? Because wouldn't you already be on A-Team if you hadn't stopped after my wreck?"

He held my gaze. "I don't regret helping you."

"You are dodging the question."

"And you are missing the point," he volleyed back.

"The point is that if you don't get on A-Team this year, it won't be my fault because I quit." I turned around, straightening a row of Allen wrenches.

"That's your right, just like it's my right to keep you on my roster anyway."

It took a moment to process his implication, but once it clicked, I turned around so quickly that I had to pause to keep the two bites of breakfast sandwich from making a reappearance. Was he threatening to throw away A-Team if I quit? "You can't do that."

"I can." He straightened to his full height and then stepped toward me. "And I will."

"Don't be ridiculous, Gabe. Just take me off your roster."

"I'm not going to do that. I'm not giving up on you."

I looked for a shred of bluff in his dark eyes, but I couldn't find anything to contradict his threat. "I know you think you can help me, but you can't. We're both going to end up losing."

He shrugged. "Win or lose, we do it together."

His declaration made me breathless. "Why? Why would you risk it?" I whispered.

"Because I know how badly you want this, and I can help you." His features softened. "So, let me."

The idea made me nauseous—more than I already felt. Because wasn't I sucking Gabe into my own misfortune? It was like having strep throat and coughing in someone's face. He would catch the bad luck that hovered over me like a black cloud.

No. I argued with myself. *I don't have bad luck because luck isn't real.* I swallowed. "Okay."

He backed toward the door. "I will let you recover today, but we hit it hard tomorrow." He was halfway out the door when he called back, "We're going to make Clay eat his words."

Chapter 17

GABRIEL

It was still dark when a large group of runners talked and stretched outside the high school track where we'd agreed to meet. The group was diverse in every way imaginable. Runners of varying builds, ethnicities, and ages chatted, yawned, and stretched.

The cool thing about these large group runs is that you will always find someone who runs close to your pace. No one ended up alone. However, I was only interested in one running buddy. I started to feel a sense of dread as I scanned above the heads of the crowd and still hadn't found my favorite bike mechanic.

April had completed all the prescribed workouts this week, but her confidence was brittle. Building it back up felt like nursing a baby bird. It was going to take time and balance. Her workouts needed to be strong enough to build her strength without being so harsh that they shattered her self-esteem.

All week, I waited for a phone call from her telling me she was done and couldn't do it. She'd kept the faith, but could she hold until race day?

Then, I strode past the bathrooms and found her stretching by the bleachers. I stopped. April stood on one leg, an ankle in her lap. She held onto the chain-link fence to get a deep hamstring stretch. And, *¡Dios me ayude!* her ass in those running shorts.

I forced my eyes away. The last thing she needed was for me to make things messy between us.

I'm her coach.

With that mantra, I approached. She released the stretch and used the fence to prop her foot up, stretching her calf. As she did, she looked up at the sky, her eyes locked on a robust full moon.

"It looks closer this morning."

April's head whipped around. Her gaze met my chest before she tilted her chin to look at me. Her smile was slight—still guarded. That was okay. I would win her over. I just needed time. "I was just thinking that."

A sharp banging noise assaulted the air. For a moment, my nerves froze, like I was back in Coach Rick's ice bath. A primal instinct told me to duck and hide: *he's mad again.*

It took me a moment to realize April had asked me a question. "*Gabe?*" she said in a way that told me it wasn't her first time trying to get my attention. "Are you okay?" Her eyebrows were scrunched with concern.

I forced a smile. "Fine."

I turned to find Clay smirking on the bleachers, a metal water bottle (the mallet he'd used to bang on the bleachers) in hand.

"Sorry," he said. "Forgot you don't like loud noises."

¡Pinche pendejo!

"Listen up," Clay addressed the group now. "We've got a lot of runners today, which is great for visibility, but it also makes it harder to notice someone lagging. So, we're going to do the buddy system. Pick someone close to your pace and stick with them the entire run."

I raised my eyebrows at April, but she gave me an exasperated look. "We cannot be buddies."

"And why's that?"

"Did you not just hear Clay say to pick someone close in pace? I'm not fast, Gabe."

"How dare you bad mouth one of my athletes. I have access to your training data, and I wrote your plan. I know how fast you are supposed to take this run."

April crossed her arms over her chest. "Here's the thing: eighteen miles is a long distance to be pushed to the max. So, if this is going to turn into some blare-Rocky-music-and-push-me-to-the-limit training, I'm gonna have to pass."

I put my hands in the air. "No Rocky music, deal?"

She eyed me warily but made no further protests as we joined the others in jogging toward the street.

Ten miles with my running buddy told me she could hold her own in a run. I kept up conversation as a way to make sure I wasn't pushing too hard. If she could talk without getting winded, she was good.

Chatting with her felt natural as if we'd known each other for ages. We laughed about dumb athletic trends and talked about music tastes and favorite movies. I didn't second-guess myself with her—didn't feel as though I needed to use a filter.

We'd just started a conversation about Chuck's snoring when I saw something scurry across the street not too far ahead of us. In the dark, it was hard to determine what kind of animal it was. I put out an arm to stop April. She must have seen the animal too because she didn't question me.

We stayed frozen, watching the shadowy figure lope around. Then, the animal scampered under the orange glow of a streetlight, and a white stripe became visible.

April released a breath. "It's just a skunk," she said, obviously relieved. The animal disappeared into the bushes, and we started jogging again.

"Just a skunk?" I repeated. Because, to me, that was one of the worst things you could encounter on a morning run. "What were you expecting, a mountain lion down Magnolia?" Magnolia being the endless street we were running down. In suburbs that rested just outside of Houston's circumference, there wasn't much of a threat from wildlife.

"No." She gave a breathless laugh. "But it looked like a black cat for a second."

My brows furrowed as I tried to follow why a cat would be worse than a skunk. Then I thought of how she'd thrown the salt over her shoulder at the party, and it clicked into place.

"You're superstitious."

Our heavy breathing filled the space. When it became apparent that April wouldn't comment on my observation, I continued. "It's okay. Lots of people are."

"Not like I am." She looked over at me. "I'm legitimately terrified of bad luck, and I hate that about me. I'm too logical for that shit, but I can't stop. I feel like an atheist who constantly prays. I tell myself I don't believe, but I do."

"Have you always felt this way?"

"No. My mom was the superstitious one. My dad and I always poked fun at her for it."

"What changed?"

"After she died, I kept seeing signs of luck everywhere, making me think of her. At first, it had been like finding little Easter eggs of Mom.

I'd see a broken mirror, and I could picture her reaction. It was a way to stay connected, to make it feel like she was still here. And then, somewhere along the way, I internalized it. Now I'm always watching out for signs—warnings." She looked at me briefly and then stared ahead again. "Which is why I'm a little worried about this race. I feel like the universe is trying to tell me that it's not going to happen."

I felt the urge to spew some coach wisdom, then clamped it down with a, "Hmm."

Unfortunately, she could sense it. "What?"

"I just—" I pondered how to put my thoughts into words without sounding dismissive of her concerns. "If you believe in something as magical as luck, why not choose to believe the universe is on your side?"

Her gaze snapped up, and I worried I'd said something to make her angry by the intense way she scrutinized my face, but she very calmly answered, "I would love to believe that someone in the great beyond is looking out for me, but I've had a hard time since my mom passed."

I thought about my own mom: her strength, her warmth. "If something happened to my mom, I'd have a hard time seeing the positive too."

"You know how my mom died, right?"

I remembered someone in the triathlon community mentioning it, though it had happened several years before. "A car wreck?"

"Did you know she'd just rung the bell for her last chemotherapy treatment?"

"I—No." I found myself at a loss for words. To have watched her mom fight for her life and win, only to lose her to something else. "I'm so sorry."

"For months, I thought breast cancer was going to take my mom. Then she rang that bell, and I thought, 'We made it. Mom is going to live.'" April paused, and the air felt thick in the silence. "Her hair hadn't even grown back to chin-length when we lost her to a texting driver. So, I have difficulty believing that the universe is on my side."

"I'm sorry. I had no idea."

"It's okay. I just want you to understand. I've been fighting this pessimism since I was seventeen. And if I seem weird about superstitions, it's because I am."

I stared ahead, my mind racing as I looked for a way past the hurt, to find a solution to her problem. Completing an Ironman on its own was a huge mental battle. Trying to finish when you thought God himself didn't want you to—near impossible. "I don't think it's weird," I answered honestly. "But it's good to know." And then, because she seemed withdrawn, I added, "I'll make a note in your file: no pointing out black cats on rides."

She laughed. "Be sure to do that."

We completed the rest of mile eleven in silence, but then April revived the conversation with her own question. "How did you get into massage?"

"My mom worked at a massage clinic—not as a therapist but as part of the cleaning crew. I used to hang out there after school. I'd do my homework at the front desk. Then, one summer, I worked scheduling appointments. I liked the idea of people coming in with aches and pains and leaving feeling new. So after high school, I got certified in it. It's perfect for me. I enjoy helping people, but I'd never have the patience or attention span for medical school."

"How long have you been doing it?"

"A little more than ten years," I said, feeling ancient.

"And do you still enjoy it?"

"I do. If I had to pick between coaching and massage therapy, I'd pick coaching, but that might be because I'm relatively new to coaching. I like the fresh challenge."

"It's cool. You get to help people in different ways."

"Yeah."

We fell back into silence as I worked up the nerve to speak again. "At the risk of offending you, can I ask a question?"

She nodded, little drops of sweat releasing with the movement and rolling down her hairline.

"The Ironman stuff—You're not that into it. Are you?"

"That obvious, huh?"

I lifted a shoulder.

"I don't hate running and swimming, but I don't get the same rush as when I cycle. And even when I am riding my bike, it doesn't come close to the way I feel when I'm fixing one." She sighed. "As far as an Ironman, I think the 140.6 miles is admirable. Completing one makes you a badass, but I only want to finish for my mom."

"There's nothing wrong with that. Actually, I can't think of a better reason to suffer for sixteen hours."

"Sixteen?" She pretended to look hurt. "I was thinking I could finish in under fifteen."

I pretended to look pensive. "We might be able to swing that if you'll let me push you a bit."

"Absolutely not. You do enough pushing." Her smile waned a little. "My turn. Why did you decide to take me on as a client?" April's lips pursed. "And don't say it's good for your portfolio. I'm not falling for that, Gabe."

"I don't know." I thought back to that race. The misery was obvious, but she still wanted to keep going. "I just . . . I could tell this race was important to you. I wanted to help."

For a long while, she looked ahead as we jogged, as if letting the words soak in. "You already helped me. I'll never forget how you stopped your race that day, and now that I know it cost you A-Team . . ."

"It's not a big deal."

"It is, though."

The crash flashed behind my eyes, how still she'd lain on the asphalt. "I couldn't just leave you there."

"Upwards of two thousand people racing that day. I still can't believe you were the one to find me. That you'd had problems that morning that caused a late start—that you'd even been behind me."

"It is crazy," I said, but it felt larger than coincidence, jogging side-by-side on a quiet road, pink hues promising a sunrise on the horizon. I felt like I could almost see the world through April's eyes, that everything was on purpose, that someone was up there pulling the strings. Only, I did think fate was on our side. Maybe we were brought together to help each other.

But first, I needed a strategy to help April overcome her mental block. The idea of a plan was hatching. I just needed a little help from a friend.

Chapter 18

GABRIEL

"I'm going to need you to man up." I had the phone pinched between my head and shoulder as I simultaneously scolded my friend and wiped down my massage table. "I thought you were over your issue with oceans."

"It's not an ocean issue," he said, laughing. "I just don't see the appeal in getting thrown into a body of water with thousands of other swimmers so we can all fight our way forward."

"Beck, you'll be fine. You are one of the strongest swimmers I know." As soon as the words were out of my mouth, I regretted them. I visualized his smirk on the other end of the phone.

"What was that? I didn't quite hear you."

"You know what, never mind. I'll ask someone else."

"Why does this even matter to you? You don't need me for a relay. Isn't this race like a half version of the bullshit you normally do?"

"Yes, but this isn't about me." I paused, not wanting to overshare April's problems.

"I'm listening."

"I have an athlete," I said, hand-picking my sentence. "And she's having a hard time with the mental game of an Ironman. I think this will be the confidence boost she needs." I could nearly hear the gears churning as Beck considered. "Please. I'll buy you a double meat from Whataburger," I offered, thinking about how he'd offered me the same when we were just kids, and he was looking for pointers after a swim meet.

There was a long pause and then a groan. "Fine. Make it a triple, and you have a deal."

I laughed. "Sure."

"I gotta go. Emily wants me to help her plant the fall garden today."

"Tell her I said hi."

"Alright. Later, man."

I looked at the time as I hung up. I had an hour until my next massage appointment. I could have just called April about my idea, but the thought of seeing her reaction in person made me pull my keys out of my pocket.

"Welcome to Just Tri!" Billie called without looking up from her phone. "Where you can suck at three sports instead of one," she said with mock enthusiasm.

I was pretty sure that was not the designated tagline for their store, but Trevor and April were a little too occupied to notice. Trevor was mid-conversation with a customer in the shoe section, and April's eyes were locked onto the chain she was threading. Not wanting to break her concentration, I waited until she had it on to say, "I think I found a loophole."

She jumped, and her hand knocked against a tire, shaking the entire frame.

"Woah, sorry!" I said, grabbing the stem to steady the bike. "I didn't mean to startle you."

"No, it's okay." She put a hand to her chest, and I could only imagine the hummingbird of a heart beneath her palm. "I'm just a little jumpy today." She closed her eyes and breathed deeply before continuing. "Now, what about a loophole?"

I carefully released my grip on the bike stem. "You said something is holding you back from finishing an Ironman. What if we did a relay for the Galveston half? All you have to do is focus on one discipline—your favorite—cycling. My friend will do the swim. I'll do the run. We finish and break your Ironman curse."

April's eyebrows pinched. "That feels like cheating fate."

I shrugged. "Maybe it is. But if the universe has been playing dirty, I don't see why we can't."

April's hand reached up to the little butterfly necklace she wore. She rolled it between her thumb and pointer finger for a moment before her features relaxed into a smile. "Let's do it."

"Yeah?"

"Yeah."

"Okay, great!" I noticed an open container of fettuccini alfredo on the counter, which, by the clumpy appearance, looked like it hadn't been microwaved. I was eating into her limited lunch time. "I'll let you get back to work. Will I see you for the ride later?"

"Later, as in tomorrow, right?"

"No. Did you not get the group message?"

She sighed. "I haven't gotten any messages. My phone is in rice." She put up a hand to stop the question on my lips. "Don't ask. It's a long story."

"Okay. Well, they moved the ride to later today because tomorrow's weather looks bad." In fact, it looked bad all week. I was excited about the cold front, but the idea of indoor exercise for a week gave me cabin fever. "Tell me you don't have to work late," I said. "This is our last chance to get outside for the foreseeable future."

"I—can't, today." How she said it made me think she had plans she didn't want me to know about, but that didn't make any sense. I was her coach, not her boyfriend. If she was going out, that was her business. Still, the idea did make me feel hollow. "I'll do the workout," she continued. "I just can't make the group ride."

"Okay." I tried not to sound deflated. "If you change your mind, let me know. I'll save your spot as my riding buddy."

She gave me a half-hearted smile, making me mentally replay the entire conversation about the upcoming ride. On the drive to the clinic and while with clients, I kept trying to figure out what I'd said wrong. Then, I checked the calendar to reschedule an appointment for a customer. The date may as well have been luminescent for how my vision locked onto it. No wonder why April wasn't going on any outdoor rides.

It was Friday the Thirteenth.

Chapter 19

APRIL

I had a coffee stain on my jumpsuit, a new scratch on my watch, and a cut on my hand. Those were just the afflictions you could see. Lady Luck had landed other punches, like when one of the screws holding the basket on my commuter bike had spontaneously come loose, and my bag fell into a puddle. Hence, my phone's spa day in rice. Billie was also running late, which left me fumbling through the register. Later, when I'd finally made it to my workbench, I realized I'd ordered an entire box of the wrong product.

So, when the doorbell rang, you can understand my apprehension to open it. I ran through the catalog of possibilities: a Jehovah's Witness who wouldn't take no for an answer, a member of the HOA letting me know the type of roses I had violated neighborhood policy, the Grim Reaper himself here to take my weary soul. The possibilities were endless.

Which is why I was equally surprised and happy when I looked through the peephole and found Gabe looming over my doorstep.

"Hey?" I said, but the greeting came out like a question. Gabe had his bike resting against his hip and his tri-suit on. I worried he was there to convince me to join the group ride.

"Hey, sorry for the unannounced visit. I tried to call."

"But my phone is still healing," I offered.

He nodded and was quiet for an uncomfortably long moment. When he spoke, his voice rumbled low. "I pieced together why you don't want to ride with the group." His gaze smoldered. "It's Friday the Thirteenth."

I waited for the verbal lashing, for him to tell me I was being ridiculous. I thought, for sure, he'd tell me to go get my bike so we could join the group ride. Instead, he said, "I'm sorry. If I had realized the date, I never would have asked you to come on an outdoor ride."

"You don't need to—" I shook my head. "I'm the one who should be sorry. I should have said something at the shop, but it's . . . embarrassing. I hate that I'm like this. But believe me, today definitely felt like Friday the Thirteenth."

His brows drew in. "Why? What happened?"

I waved him off. "It's a long story."

"Well, maybe we could talk about it on our ride." I frowned, but Gabe continued. "I thought we could do our own group ride—just make it indoor. I have my trainer in the truck, and I packed my laptop so we could watch movies."

My mouth fell open. I couldn't believe he'd want to spend the ride with me when he could be out in the fresh air with the group.

"Unless . . ." He ran a hand through his hair, making it stick up wildly. "You definitely don't have to. If you have other plans—"

"No." I stepped aside to let him in. "That sounds amazing. We can set you up in the garage."

As Gabe's body filled my doorframe, his eyes trailed across the living room. It's not like my house was a mess, but I had a cardigan on the back of the couch, the bookshelf could have used dusting, and I would have moved my shoes to my room if I'd known someone was coming over.

"You said this used to be your parents'. Was this the house you grew up in?"

It felt kind of personal, letting Gabe see into a window of my life that ran all the way to the beginning. "It's the only home I've ever known," I said by way of answering. Then I thought that sounded a little pathetic. A twenty-nine-year-old living in the house her parents had brought her home to from the hospital. "It needs a lot of work," I admitted, eyeing the damn baseboards I still hadn't had a chance to replace.

But Gabe said, "It's really nice." And there was a hint of something there, so light I'm sure I would have missed it if I didn't know him better—maybe a little bit of longing, but he covered it quickly. "Where should I put this thing?" He nodded toward his bike.

I led him to the garage, and after his bike was set up, he walked over to the old Schwinn that was looking less and less like junkyard pieces by the day.

"Do you bring your work home?"

"No," I said, looking at the scattered pieces on a towel. "This is a side project."

He appraised me. "You work on bicycles all day, then come home and work on them for fun?"

I shrugged, my cheeks heating as I realized how boring I sounded. "I really enjoy it. Each one is like a puzzle."

"Did you start working on bikes after your mom opened the store? Or is it something you've always done?"

I shook my head. "It wasn't until after my mom died that I became interested."

"You picked it up to be closer to her," he guessed. "Like the Ironman."

"Not exactly." I put a screwdriver back on the wall to give my hands something to do, a place for my eyes to look instead of at Gabe. "You know the stages of grief?" I could feel the intensity of his gaze, the way you know someone is drinking in your every word. "Well, I was somewhere between denial and anger. I saw my mom's bike in the garage. I wasn't allowed to touch it normally. You understand. Our bikes are our babies."

Gabe huffed out a laugh and nodded.

"Well, I thought if I took apart her bike, she'd have to come back. If I messed up her bike, she'd be mad, but I'd have her home. At seventeen, I was way too old to actually believe that, but denial can be overwhelming." Tools and parts straightened in front of me. I finally found the courage to look back at Gabe. A little crease had formed between his brows. "Anyway, my dad found me on the garage floor," I gestured to the exact place it had happened, just a few feet away, "fingers bloody, parts everywhere."

"Was he angry?" he asked, eyes searching mine.

"No. He sat with me on the concrete for the longest time, just holding me. Then he said, 'It's okay to fall apart. But now we have to put the pieces back together.' That was the first time I assembled a bike."

"He sounds like a good dad," he said, looking relieved.

"He is," I agreed. "I don't see him too much now that he lives in a different state, but he still video calls me on holidays and texts me to make sure I vote each election—you know, typical dad stuff."

Something indeterminable crossed Gabe's features, but it passed before I could read it. "I'll go get my trainer," he said, hiking a thumb back towards the door.

"Right, and I'd better go change." We did have forty miles to get through.

By the time I'd come back, Gabe had his bike and laptop set up. He let me pick what we watched. I went with a highly acclaimed action movie I'd been wanting to see, but I didn't catch any of the plot points.

We got too busy talking as we pedaled. I asked Gabe about Chuck, and when I told him he should have brought him, Gabe replied with, "Next time." Only to shake his head and say, "There I go inviting myself again." I pressed my lips together to avoid suggesting we make these buddy rides a regular event.

The movie switched to a jungle scene. "That looks just like Costa Rica," Gabe commented.

"Have you been?"

The question prompted a story about a crazy bachelor party where he'd had to share a bed with a man named Koontz and didn't sleep a wink because the guy tried to spoon with Gabe in his sleep. Gabe had moved to the floor, but he kept waking to things crawling on him because they had been in a jungle, after all.

He had me hanging on every word. That is, until the workout grew too intense. Our bike machines had our preloaded workouts. The gears would match the desired resistance to act like hills, and at intense stretches, our focus narrowed to breathing and pedaling.

While my intervals were horrid, Gabe's seemed like absolute hell. I never saw the man winded, and now he was fighting for his life through the sets. Sweat rolled off him at a steady rate. Where I had sprinkles of perspiration under my bike, he had a pool.

"I can't tell if your coach really likes you or sort of hates you," I said as the set ended.

"Yeah." Gabe laughed, but it sounded pained. He was still in aero position and hung his head as his back rose and fell with quick breaths. "I think it's both."

"Are all your workouts this difficult?"

"They vary. But mostly, yes."

"Don't you get tired of pushing yourself that hard?"

"This is Rick's last year before he retires from coaching. I want to make him proud."

I wouldn't have understood the drive to want to please your coach while I was under Clay's wing, but I got it now.

Next, we talked about the upcoming road trip for the race we were working in Waco. It was only a three-hour drive, but Gabe had declared a Buc-ee's stop was non-negotiable. We discussed food options for when we weren't working at the race. I'd been excited before, but now I was nearly giddy about taking a trip with Gabe. Talk of the trip got us through the rest of the workout. We unclipped and dismounted slowly, muscles and joints aching.

Gabe had brought an extra pair of clothes for after the long ride, and I let him use my shower on the condition that he refrain from using all of my raspberry-vanilla sugar scrub. I'd been teasing, but Gabe nodded slowly and said, "That's why you always smell like dessert."

I had to hide my blush because the fact that Gabe recognized my scent unlocked some sort of weird, primal part of my brain. Years of evolutionary coding told me to jump him and continue the bloodline.

When he finished his shower, dressed but hair wet and mussed, the savage side of my brain was still running the show. He cleaned up so nicely, even in his casual marathon T-shirt and basketball shorts. I wanted to get up on my tiptoes to put my face in the crook of his neck and see how my shampoo smelled on him.

"April?" Gabe said, his brows scrunched. "I asked if you wanted me to order pizza while you shower."

"Yes. Pizza is great!" I edged toward the bathroom. "I'll take whatever you want as long as it doesn't have mushrooms on it."

I turned the cold water up and hoped it would be enough to kickstart reason and bring intellectual April to the forefront.

After a cold shower to remind myself that I was more than just my hormones, I was able to enjoy dinner with Gabe. It was almost domestic, seeing him in my kitchen. He lounged in his chair, one arm hooked over the back while the other held onto his slice of pizza. His long legs stretched under the table, which I kept accidentally bumping with my feet.

"I want to hear about your Friday the Thirteenth."

I snorted. "You want to hear me whine for half an hour?" I asked before plucking a second slice of pizza from the box.

"If it means you'll tell me about your day, yes."

Something in my belly swooped at that. I took a large bite of pizza to give my fizzy stomach time to settle before answering.

"Well, one of my favorite parts was when a customer proudly told me he used dish soap to clean his bike, which is fine if you're in a pinch, but when I warned him that using it on the derailleur could eliminate the good grease, he berated me, saying I just wanted to 'push product.'" I used air quotes on the last two words.

"Because a ten-dollar bottle of bike cleaner is really going to help you reach your monthly sales quota."

"Exactly!"

Having someone on my side felt so good that I spilled every miserable part of my day. And as we laughed through all my misfortune, Gabe had somehow cast a different light over the day. How could I think about this Friday the Thirteenth without also remembering Gabe's commentary and how he threw his head back and laughed, only to slap a hand over his mouth and say, "Sorry. That's not funny," though he was still laughing behind his hand?

When the pizza box was mostly just discarded crust, and the conversation had finally found a lull, Gabe stood. "Well, I'd better get going." Then he gave a mischievous smile. "Can I borrow your dish soap? I was going to give my bike a quick wash before I leave."

It took me a moment to realize he was messing with me. Two could play at that game. I passed him, grabbing a wrench from the counter. "Hey, if you want to slow down your bike, I'll just take the wheels off."

"Hey, no!"

I giggled and picked up the pace as Gabe chased after me. He grabbed the wrench from my hand and tossed it back onto the counter.

"Keep your hands off my bike!"

"Just a few modifications," I said, still laughing as he hauled me away from the garage door with an arm hooked around my waist. When I reached for the wrench again, Gabe backed me against the wall and gripped my hands above my head.

At first, we stared at each other, smiling like idiots as our chests rose and fell with heaving breaths. Then Gabe's dark eyes fell to my lips, and the air in the kitchen felt charged. My heart pounded so hard, I thought it was looking for a way out of my chest.

His eyes came back to mine, a question clearly in his widening pupils. I didn't answer. Instead, I closed my eyes and leaned forward. Gabe caught my mouth with his.

That first moment our lips touched was gentle, testing. Then Gabe sighed and pressed in. Just like that, the kiss turned from question to need. He kissed me hungrily, and I wanted to be consumed by him.

His tongue swiped across my lower lip before he sucked on it slowly. My knees buckled. Luckily, Gabe was holding me up—my hands still deliciously pinned above my head. I opened for him, and we tasted each other in between gulps of air that I took like I had no intention of resurfacing.

Heat coursed from my core, molten lava in my veins. He could wreck me. His size, his power, his stamina. All of it should have intimidated me. Instead, I was grinding against him, begging for it with my body.

I needed him—in a way that should have concerned me, but there was something about being with a guy who could destroy you but would never dream of it.

As if testing that theory, I felt his erection push into my stomach. I gasped at the size, and Gabe released me and pulled away. "I'm so sorry," he rasped.

"Why are you sorry?" I took a step toward him, but he put out a hand to stop me.

"That was unprofessional. You're my athlete, and I . . ." He looked at the floor for a moment before meeting my gaze again. His pupils were still huge, but they narrowed by the second. "I'm just sorry."

"I'm sorry too," I said because it felt like the right thing to say even if my body screamed that it was definitely wrong. "We shouldn't have . . . You have A-Team to think about."

He nodded without meeting my gaze.

We worked in silence, unhooking the bike from the trainer and packing it all into his truck. The words neither of us could say hung in the air, making everything seem heavy.

As I watched him drive away from the window, I just kept thinking, of course, I wouldn't get lucky on Friday the Thirteenth.

Chapter 20

APRIL

That morning, I completed a nine-mile run like it was a breeze. My swimming felt less like a struggle with each stroke and more like a glide. Cycling had always been my favorite, but now I felt powerful behind my pedals. Not only was I confident about the upcoming Ironman, I was excited about it.

I used to see the race as a giant in the distance. An impossible, immovable foe. Not anymore. I felt stronger than ever. Gabriel Torres had lived up to the hype. No doubt. He was coach of the year in my mind.

So why was I staring at my phone, expecting more from him?

It had only been three days since our kiss, but he'd been especially quiet. At the very minimum, he'd always text to ask how the workouts felt, but even that stopped after the kiss.

I should have been happy to have a coach who wanted to remain professional. Instead, all I could think about was how his hands gripped my wrists. The heat of his body pressed against mine. The way it felt to be tasted by him.

"Why don't you put the phone down," Billie said, startling me enough that my phone nearly went hurtling toward the floor.

"Could you not sneak up on me?"

"I don't sneak. There was no sneaking. I've been standing here for the past minute, watching you stare at your phone like it's going off to war."

I scoffed and tossed it on the counter.

"Who is it?" she asked, hands on hips.

"What? Nobody?"

She narrowed her eyes at me.

I sighed, then looked over her shoulder to make sure no one would overhear, but Trevor was with the only customers we had in the shop. "It's just . . . I—" There was a finished bike on my stand, ready to go home to its owner, but I spun the tire and pretended to be interested in how the chain looked. "I kissed Gabe," I muttered.

"You kissed Gabe?" Billie said, in a voice that could have warned all of China that the Huns were coming.

"Shhhh!"

"April Baird," she opened her arms for a hug. "The girl finally becomes a woman."

I swatted her arms away, which made her laugh. "You act like I'm a virgin," I said, then my eyes widened—worried a customer had overheard. Luckily, they were too busy jogging around the shop in a prospective pair of shoes. Trevor, on the other hand, made a face and then gagged dramatically.

I rolled my eyes but pulled Billie closer to the counter so we could talk without scarring my cousin for life, a smart move because, in true Bille fashion, she took the conversation to another level of inappropriate.

"Yeah, but I bet with Gabe it will be like the first time all over again. I mean, look at the size of him, and then look at you." My cheeks grew feverishly hot, but she kept going. "Logistically, I'm not even sure how you two would work."

I put a hand on her shoulder to stop the onslaught of her words and the image she'd projected in my mind: lying under Gabe, his weight pressing down on me.

"That's not happening," I said both to her and myself. "Because the kiss was a mistake." *Chocolate chip cookies were a mistake, too, though,* I thought. The baker had wanted the chocolate to melt. Instead, she accidentally invented the world's favorite sweet treat—the *second* most delicious error known to man after kissing my coach.

"Why? Is he a bad kisser?"

A dark chuckle escaped because I only wished he'd been a bad kisser. If he'd used too much tongue, I wouldn't have had such a hard time accepting his wish to keep things professional. "If only."

"Then, is it *you* saying the kiss was a mistake or *him*?"

"Why does it matter? I thought you didn't want me to get with him anyway."

"No, no, no. Do not twist my words. I wanted you to be careful, not abstinent. Big difference." She ducked her head to catch my gaze. "So, what's going on?"

I shrugged. "He said we should keep things professional." Billie rolled her eyes, but I kept going. "And he's right. I finally feel ready for an Ironman. Do I want to make things complicated with my coach? And it's worse for him. This is his livelihood. What if his company finds out?"

"That two consenting adults had sex?" She wore a mock-scandalized face. "Oh, no!"

My lips went to a flat line. "It's more complex than that, and you know it."

"Okay, so again, be careful: have sex, keep your feelings out of it, and don't advertise it to the world. Simple."

"Yes. Simple because we won't be having sex."

She opened her mouth, but Trevor's exclamation stopped her. "Holy shit!" He gaped at his phone for a moment before cutting a glance at the customer. "Sorry." Then he looked right at me. "I got an interview with *Exposure*."

"No way!" My mind reeled. Working for this company was Trevor's version of making the Olympics. "Trevor! That's crazy!"

"It is crazy." He looked like he stood in the center of three concentric circles of excitement, disbelief, and panic. "But it might not mean anything." And there he was, trying to get ahead before his hopes could get up. "It's just an interview."

"No, don't do that," I said. "This is huge! The fact that you even got an interview—" I had to stop, my throat clogged with emotion. When we were kids, he always had an *Exposure* magazine with him. To this day, he kept the latest issue on his coffee table. The photography in it is the reason he asked his mom to buy him a camera for his seventh birthday. "I am so proud of you!" I crossed the shop and pulled him in for a hug, not able to keep from getting his T-shirt damp.

"Are you crying?" he asked, rearing back to look at me.

"No," I lied, sniffling.

He put me at arm's length. "Wait to get your snot on me until after I've gotten the job," he said playfully.

But I knew. I already knew. How could they not hire Trevor? When he took pictures of people or animals, he always managed to capture a part of their soul. The job was his.

"When's the interview?" Billie asked.

"On Monday." Trevor frowned. "And it's in person." He looked at me. "It's going to be tight—with the road trip. I'll have to turn around for a flight to San Francisco early the next morning."

The only reason I hadn't been worried about the trip to Waco was because I knew Trevor would be a buffer between Gabe and myself. Without him, I couldn't imagine how awkward the drive would be, not to mention staying in a hotel room alone with Gabe.

But there was no way I would let anything stand in Trevor's way.

"No. Call one of your photographer friends to take pictures at the Waco race." My tone left no room for argument. "You need to be well rested and at your best Monday. You're getting that job at *Exposure*, Trev."

Chapter 21

GABRIEL

I didn't think it was possible to simultaneously kick yourself for starting something and, at the same time, be so frustrated you hadn't taken things further, but I couldn't think about April without the warring guilt and need. Both were potent, but the need was so strong, it was nearly painful. I tortured myself, letting my thoughts wander to her all the time—to her plump lips, her taste, that fruity scent of hers, how it felt to pin her to the wall.

Every detail tormented me.

According to her training data, April dominated her workouts. I liked to believe that was just my stellar coaching at play, but I couldn't help but wonder if she was using the physical exertion to release some pent-up energy. I know I was.

After my most recent ride, Rick sent me one sentence: **Cool it, Torres.**

Lying on the tile of my living room, sweating and panting, I'd thought it was hopeless. I could chase the thoughts of April away, but they always came back.

There was the temptation to reach out and talk about what happened, but I was afraid even to tell her what a great job she was doing on her workouts because I didn't trust myself to keep it professional, especially knowing she wanted me, too.

She had a real shot at crossing the finish line of an Ironman this year. If I fucked that up, I'd never forgive myself. We only had one month left to keep our eyes on the prize. Maybe after, we could pursue things, but that felt like false hope. I liked April, really liked her. I didn't want to ruin our friendship. Besides, she deserved someone who could offer more than I could. She deserved someone who could afford to be emotionally invested.

So, I kept communication robotic—just workouts through a system, which made things infinitely more awkward when I got this text from her: **Trevor can't join us on the road trip. He has an interview for a competitive position.**

I'd gotten that text between appointments at the clinic, and for a while, I'd just stared at the phone in disbelief.

Without Trevor as a barrier between us . . .

This was either a bountiful reward—a redo of sorts—or the cruelest of punishments.

I sat on the massage table and ran my fingers through my hair. I couldn't go with her. That would be a mistake, right? Undecided, I left my phone on the counter, the message unanswered until after my next client.

By then, she'd texted again: **If you don't want to go with me, I understand. But I wasn't able to find another hotel in the area. Everything is booked for the race.**

Shit. Now I made her feel like I didn't want to go with her. I had to fix this. I didn't want things to be weird between us. I could be professional. We could go back to having a coach-athlete relationship—to being friends.

Me: No. Let's follow the plan.

Chapter 22

GABRIEL

On the late afternoon of our trip, shortly after dropping Chuck off for boarding, April picked me up at my apartment. She wanted to drive, but she'd put me in charge of music and navigation. As I ducked into her baby-blue Subaru, I was encompassed with that scent of hers—raspberry cake, and my mind immediately returned to the kiss.

"You ready?" she asked, looking too good for a road trip. She wore a romper—one with the spaghetti straps—over a tank top. I could easily imagine curling my fingers under those straps and peeling them off her shoulders.

Mierda. Not even a minute in, and I fantasized about getting her naked. I needed one of those electric dog collars so I could zap myself every time I had a dirty thought of her.

"Ready," I lied.

Conversation on the road was polite but sparse. I kept trying to find that usual place of comfort and laughter with her, but it felt like I was trying to climb a steep slide. I'd almost get to the top just to slip back down. It was like that the entire way to our Buc-ee's stop. I worried not even high-quality gas station brisket would lighten the mood. Then, we got back in the car, and my music wouldn't start.

I turned the volume dial as April backed out of our parking spot. Then she glanced at the screen and blanched.

"It's connected to my phone," she said, throwing the car in park and fumbling to pull it out of her pocket.

"You are going to be a good girl," a deep voice blared over the speakers, "and take every inch."

My mouth fell open as a woman's moan filled the car.

April looked like she was having a stroke, trying to get to her phone, until I reached over and turned the volume all the way down. For the longest moment, April just stared at me, the horror apparent in her wide hazel eyes.

I floundered to say something, but instead, a laugh burbled out of me. I tried to get a handle on it, afraid I'd make the situation so much worse, but then April was laughing, too, so hard, she started wheezing.

"Do you always listen to porn when you drive?" I asked, wiping tears from my eyes.

"It's a book," she said but then dissolved into more giggles.

"Wow. I need to read more." I reached to turn the volume back up, but April pulled my arm away.

"No! Definitely not!"

"But it seems like you are missing key plot points."

"Please." She was holding her side now as she laughed. "I'm begging you. Reconnect your phone."

"Our loss," I said with a shrug.

It's not like shared laughter over April's sex book completely healed the crack between us, but after, the gap felt approachable. The rest of the trip seemed less tense, even if just marginally.

As we checked into the hotel, I was sure we would show up to one bed. It wouldn't be the first time I'd have an unexpected bunkmate. The only difference—the last person I'd been forced to share a bed with was Koontz, someone I had zero desire to be intimate with. April, though . .
.

I imagined our legs brushing one another under the sheets, being engulfed in her scent, lying only inches from her body.

I wouldn't survive it. I'd have to sleep on the floor again, like in Costa Rica.

If April seemed nervous about sharing a room with me, she didn't show it. She had her colorful duffle bag slung casually over one shoulder, hands in her pockets. There was this laid-back beauty to her—from her scuffed sneakers to how a few strands fell loose from where she'd tucked the blonde hair behind her ear. She was the embodiment of perfectly imperfect.

However, when I scanned our key card to get into our room, we shared a look, and I saw the tiniest glimpse of nerves in those hazel eyes.

That made two of us.

To my surprise, I swung the door open to two beds. That did nothing to quell my raging hormones, which were very aware that I'd be spending the night alone with a gorgeous woman. At least I wouldn't have to worry about rolling over and pressing a hard-on into April's back.

After three hours of driving, we both fell into an exhausted silence as we settled our things. I brushed my teeth as April put clothes into her nightstand drawers. She swore under her breath.

"What's wrong?"

"I forgot my sleeping shorts, of all things. I packed jeans for tomorrow and overalls for the trip home. So, I'll have to sleep in my romper tonight."

She had the tank top, so I started to suggest she get under the covers and take off the romper, but the idea of her shimmying out of it made my mouth dry.

"Here." I dug through my bag and pulled out an Ironman T-shirt from a few years ago. I tossed it over. "This will probably fit you like a nightgown."

She unrolled the shirt, a smile spreading as her eyes zeroed in on the Ironman symbol. "You don't mind?"

"No. I brought extras. Just make sure to let me borrow one of your shirts if I ever need a crop top."

The corners of her eyes crinkled as she laughed. "You've got a deal, Torres."

I only thought having her undress under the covers would be torment. Then she walked out of the bathroom in my shirt. Her thighs peeked out from the bottom, and my fingers twitched with the urge to touch them again. But this time, I wouldn't be dealing pain—only a little bit of pressure and a lot of pleasure.

"I think I like the way this Ironman symbol looks on me," she said.

"Me too." What I liked was *my* shirt on her. It awakened something possessive in me.

As we settled into our respective beds, my body was painfully alert to how close we were in the dark. How easy it would be to get under the covers with her and pick up where we last left off. I imagined her rolling on top of me. I'd slip my hands under the hem of the shirt she borrowed and . . .

Shit. I was rock hard.

I thought of all the grounding techniques I asked my clients to use when a massage session got too intense.

Breathe.

I forced a five-count inhale through my nose and a slow release out of my mouth. Then, I mentally listed all the sensations that didn't have to do with the straining in my boxers—like the way my head sank into the hotel pillow, the weight of the comforter, and the cool touch of the sheets.

After all that, my blood still hummed with need. So, I started to think about things that definitely did not make me aroused—like bare feet on wet grass, the sound Styrofoam makes when it's rubbed together, and ice baths.

Baths, however, was the wrong word. My mind drew up April in the hotel tub, suds around her breasts.

¡Dios mío!

I wasn't getting any sleep.

Chapter 23

APRIL

I always pictured Gabe as a morning person, that he popped out of bed, ready to tackle his training and any other obstacle that dared to stand in his way. However, judging by the dark circles under his eyes, the ruffled hair, and the way he hunched over, head in his hands for several minutes before finally getting up, Gabe despised the mornings. Or maybe it was just this particular morning. It seemed highly possible the hotel bed didn't adequately fit his monstrous frame.

At any rate, he shuffled around the hotel room as a man of very few words. In fact, he answered all my questions with nods and grunts until we picked up our volunteer shirts at the registration tent.

When I asked for a larger size, commenting about needing a nightshirt, Gabe reached over with that long arm of his to stop the interaction.

"You already have a sleep shirt." Still warming up, his deep voice sounded extra gravelly. "Did it not meet your standards?"

I laughed. "No, your shirt was fine." In all honesty, it wasn't just fine. I loved sleeping in it. The fabric smelled like him, which was probably why it took me forever to fall asleep. The scent had me replaying our kiss over and over. "You don't mind if I borrow it again tonight?"

"No, April. I don't mind." He must have heard how gruff he sounded because he cleared his throat. "You can keep it—looks better on you, anyway." I think that was supposed to be a joke, but there was nothing funny about the intensity in his dark eyes.

"So, are you keeping the small? Or . . ." the volunteer behind the counter asked, looking uncomfortable to be caught in whatever the hell that was.

"Yeah, I'll keep the small."

It was still dark as we approached the technical tent—a delicate crescent moon hung at the horizon's edge. However, the tent was already a blur of mechanics working to assist athletes with last-minute issues.

"How can I help?" Gabe asked as I joined the chaos.

"Don't you need to be at the massage tent?"

"Not until the first athletes cross the finish line." He looked at his watch. "So, I'm yours for a few hours."

I'm yours.

I had to stop taking his words out of context.

I grabbed some handlebar tape and tossed it to him. "She's got some exposure here. Can you rewrap her bars?"

That's how we worked. Gabe assisted with putting bikes on stands or removing wheels, and I handled the more technical side. Lost in the bustle of repairs, we didn't do much talking other than when he asked for clarification or I gave him directions. It was peaceful working elbow to elbow with him—okay, maybe it was more elbow to bicep with his height.

I didn't usually like working with others while doing repairs because I couldn't get lost in the puzzle of the bicycle. But either Gabe sensed that, or he didn't feel like talking. The quiet wasn't uncomfortable. It was cozy.

Most athletes who visited our tent were appreciative. We were fairy godmothers, there to save their race day with a quick fix of a dropped chain or inner tube replacement. Of course, there were exceptions to the rule like when someone wanted me to replace his corroded bolts. They would have to be pried out, and while I agreed the guy needed to have the bolts replaced, we were there for race day emergencies, not freebie repairs.

"Unfortunately, that's something you will have to take to your local bike shop. We're only doing quick fixes today."

"If you start on it now, you could be done with it by the time I get out of the swim."

Doubtful, but more importantly, working on his issue could keep me from fixing a bike that really needed it.

"Sorry, that's not what the technical tent is here for. But good news, you can still ride with it in this condition."

"Sweetheart, thanks for your help," he said condescendingly. "But I want to talk to someone else. Someone more experienced." He shifted his gaze to Gabe, who'd been down on one knee, tying his shoe. "Can you have a look?"

"Out of the three of us," Gabe said, still working on his knot, "I can assure you, she has the most bike experience."

The man looked between us, most likely used to winning *The Customer is Always Right* battle. "Why are you even here if you won't do your damn job?"

I wish I could say the escalation surprised me, but triathletes tended to be on the more entitled side. All that mileage and endurance gave some athletes a God complex. I folded my arms, trying to conjure the politest way to say *scram*, but then Gabe extended to his full height, and, I swear, the guy lost his coloring.

"This isn't our job. We're volunteering," Gabe answered calmly. "And on that note, you can leave this tent voluntarily, or I can let an official know you are berating the technical support." The guy's mouth fell open, but before he could conjure an argument, Gabe continued, "Your choice whether or not you want to start race day with a disqualification."

The guy stood there, beady eyes narrowed. I could see the fight or flight warring in his features. Finally, he grabbed his seat and guided the bike away with a string of expletives.

"That's not fair," I said, peering up at Gabe.

His eyebrows rose. I'd clearly surprised him with my complaint. "What?"

"All you have to do is be tall and people listen to you."

He scoffed.

"No, seriously. You stood up, and I watched the guy's life flash before his eyes."

I meant it as a joke, but Gabe's smile fell. "Do I give the impression that I'd hurt someone?"

"No, Gabe." He was the very definition of a gentle giant. "But self-preservation is loud. And what are they going to do? Argue with someone who blocks out the sun?"

Gabe removed another busted glove. The technical tent only had gloves for regular-sized humans, and they stretched so tight on Gabe's massive hands that the integrity was compromised. He was on his third pair due to tearing. "I don't block out the sun," he said, leaning into my space to toss the ruined glove into the trash behind me. "I provide shade."

"Did you get your height from both parents? Or just one?" I asked, eyeing his frame.

He pulled on another glove, fighting to stretch it over his Jack Skellington fingers. "My father is tall," he said. "My mom is about your size. Maybe a little shorter." He squinted as he scrutinized my height. "How tall are you? Five two?"

"Five three." I straightened my spine so he could behold every inch.

His lips pressed together as he fought a smile. "Yeah, you have her beat by two inches."

I bit back my own smile. "How old were you when you outgrew her? Four?"

He hoisted the next bike onto the stand. "How old were you when you realized you'd never be allowed on all the rides at Disney?"

My mouth fell open in mock offense, but then I had to fight off a laugh, because I wasn't used to Gabe being this sassy. I didn't know if it was from lack of sleep or too much time in my presence or just the real him coming out, but I liked it. "I'll have you know that I'm almost an average height. I'm sure it's hard to tell from your spot in the nosebleeds."

He put his hands on his hips, and that scarred brow of his hiked—a playful warning. The last time things had gotten playful, he'd pinned me to the wall. I felt lightheaded, imagining his body pressed against mine again.

Gabe's eyes flicked to my lips, and the world around us disappeared. I suddenly couldn't even remember what we'd been talking about. The air between us felt magnetized. He must have felt it, too, because he shifted forward slightly. I held my breath in anticipation, but to my dismay, he stopped, shaking his head as if snapping out of it.

"Back to work, Baird."

"Yes—" I had to clear my throat. "Yes, Coach."

· ♥ · ♥ · ♥ · ♥ · ♥ ·

At race start, my shift was over, which left Gabe and me free to spectate for a couple of hours before he had to be at the massage tent.

I loved this race because while it wasn't as big as an Ironman, it still was a sizable party. For athletes and volunteers, they had a tent serving food and drinks, but food trucks were parked and ready for spectators. Vendors of all sorts gathered—most catering to the triathlon community: shirts with sporty phrases, an array of nutrition options, headbands in every color, massage boots, non-alcoholic beer, and on and on.

We were browsing an apparel booth when Gabe held up a shirt that said *If I crash, stop my Garmin.*

I huffed out a laugh. "I need that."

"You do not," he said, hanging it back up. "Because we are done with crashes, Baird." He leveled a look at me. "You hear me?"

"Oh, are we?" I asked, sliding shirts over on the rack. "Good, my bike will be happy to hear that."

"Speaking of your bike. You did a great job with your rides this week." I looked back up at him so I could fully drink in the compliment. His words made me feel like my chest was filled with carbonation—all fizzy and bubbly. "So much so that I wondered if you'd brought your bike computer for a car ride."

I laughed. "Why hadn't I thought of that yet?"

"Seriously, though. You're crushing it."

"Thank you," I said, then my smile faded as I remembered how he'd left me checking my phone all week, waiting for a message from him or a call. I fantasized about him walking into the store about a hundred times. "I wasn't sure, since I didn't hear from you."

He briefly looked away. When his gaze returned, it was hard to hold eye contact for the intensity. "I'm sorry. I just thought we needed space after we . . ."

"Yeah," I said.

"We can't let something like that happen again." I looked down, embarrassed, but he lifted my chin. "I want to." His words teamed up with the sincerity in his eyes, and the gentle press of his fingers on my jaw made my spine feel like it conducted electricity. "But we can't."

I swallowed. "Because you're my coach."

He dropped his hand and sighed. "That's a big chunk of it, yes. But also because I only do casual." So, Billie's information about Gabe had been right. "I won't ever change my mind about that."

My chest felt hot. Why did everyone think I'd be the one to catch feelings? "What makes you think I'm looking for something serious?"

"Nothing," he said quickly. "I just like to make myself clear on that." Then he shook his head. "Not that it matters because I'm here to coach you through your Ironman, and, more importantly, I don't want to complicate things between us because we're friends. Right?"

Friends. What every woman wants to hear out of her crush's mouth. "Right," I said. And even though I felt disappointed, I knew he was making a good call. "Come on," I said, looking for distraction in any form. "We'd better get something to eat before our massage shift."

He folded his arms across his chest. "*Our* massage shift?"

"Yeah, you helped me with mechanical stuff. I'm going to help you with massage stuff."

"And how do you plan on helping with that?"

"Hmm." I chewed on my bottom lip as I considered. "I could check people in or squirt oil into your palm." I ticked off the ideas on my fingers. "Or, oh! I know! I can hold people's hands while you apply 'pressure,'" I said with air quotes.

Gabe rolled his eyes and started walking.

"How many people do you plan to make cry today, Coach?" I called, struggling to keep up with his massive strides. "I can see if the medic tent has any tissues."

Chapter 24

APRIL

As it turns out, there really wasn't much I could do to help Gabe. Athletes who opted for a massage were zonked after miles of endurance, so I would fetch them water bottles. Other than that, I waited by the sitting area and watched Gabe work his magic.

He'd battle the tension by rotating and pulling limbs. Then, he'd use quick circles followed by a hold. It amazed me how he'd use his own body to preserve his strength—folding an athlete's arm over his to help get a deeper stretch, changing his stance to have better weight distribution, or using his forearm to slide across muscles, saving his hands.

I did notice, after a couple of hours of nonstop massaging, he started to look a little stiff himself. Then, when we got back to the hotel, he dropped the room key. He looked at it for a long, loathing moment before I picked it up for him, despite his protests.

"Thanks."

"You okay?" I asked.

"Yeah," he answered, his voice tight. "It's just been a long day." His lips pressed into a flat line. "You'll understand when you hit thirty."

I rolled my eyes as we entered the room. "I'm twenty-nine. I understand enough."

We both wanted to get clean, and he tried to let me shower first, but I would hear none of it. "You have other people's sweat on you," I said, thinking about how athletes had gone straight from the finish line to the massage table. "Go shower."

He conceded, and when it was my turn, I could have skipped to the bathroom. I might have only had my own sweat on me, but it was enough. I felt grimy in every crevice.

Showered and hair combed, I donned Gabe's shirt and inhaled deeply at the collar. It smelled like him—fresh cotton with the slightest bit of spice.

I looked in the mirror and felt like I had the night before—a little self-conscious to be wearing only Gabe's shirt and a fresh pair of panties. Sure, the shirt easily covered my ass, but my nipples tonight were obviously hard under the fabric. I folded my arms across my chest, ready to make a mad dash for my bed.

That is, until I found Gabe leaning against the desk, rubbing his back. He struggled to reach a spot, which was saying something, given the guy's wingspan. My feet stalled on the carpet. He'd spent most of the afternoon taking care of people, but who was taking care of him?

I went back into the bathroom to fetch my lotion and stood right behind him. "Who gives you a massage when you're hurting?"

He let his arm drop. "If it's still bothering me when we get back into town, I've got a friend at the clinic."

"That doesn't help you right now, though."

"I'm fine, April." He tried to walk past me to his own bed, but I put a palm on his chest. He stared at the point of contact for a long moment.

"You're a great coach," I said. "Coach me on giving a massage."

His eyes met mine, and I had to fight to hold my ground because his dark eyes could swallow me whole with their intensity. He wrapped his fingers around my wrist and removed my hand from his chest. My cheeks heated. I waited for Gabe to chastise me for getting too close.

Instead, he surprised me by removing his shirt. The shirt coming off tousled his thick black hair, and his scent filled our space, leaving me feeling like I was floating on a cloud of cotton. And then, of course, there was a chest molded by a strict training schedule, and below were real abs. Not at all similar to the ghost abs I had. With my stomach, you had to treat it like a page from one of those optical illusion books: hold it up to the light and tilt your head this way.

Not Gabe's abs. Gabe's abs left no room for doubt. They were unrelenting trenches that looked to have been built by Spartan battle. It was a struggle to bring my eyes back up to his—to not stare at the stomach that could have been a stunt double for Gerard Butler's in *300*.

Luckily, I didn't have to keep the faith for long. Gabe stepped back and, with stiff movements, pulled the chair from the desk and turned it around before sitting.

Now that I had him there, shirtless, waiting for me to touch him, I couldn't help but keep staring. Cords of muscle rested under bronze skin, a reminder of his strength, his power. I felt a surge of anticipation. My fingers were about to benefit greatly from all the work he'd put into his training. Then, I chided myself. *I'm not here to be creepy. I'm here to help.*

"Where—" I had to clear my throat because the words were too thick. "Where does it hurt?"

He grabbed the hotel notepad and pen and made a rough sketch of a back. Then he pointed as he spoke. "It's my rhomboids—so basically near my shoulder blade. I'm feeling tight, right about there." He pointed to a spot on the chart.

"What's the technique?"

"You don't have to follow a certain technique. It will feel good to have some pressure on it—getting out those knots."

"No, I want to do it right. What would you do if I were sitting in the chair?"

Gabe was quiet, seeming to think that over before he asked, "Can I see your hand?"

I stretched my hand towards him, and one of his swallowed mine. My heart felt like a rabbit in a too-small cage.

"You are going to use your middle and ring finger primarily." He curled my fingers with his free hand. "Make a pad with your fingers. Then, use a circular motion. You can curl them tighter to add more pressure." He looked at my eyes but didn't drop my hand. "The more you use your whole body, the more you'll save your own joints. So, try not to move your wrist. Instead, keep your arm as straight as you can and put your body weight into it." He nodded toward the bottle of lotion in my other hand. "If you use that, you can do dragging motions at the shoulder blade." He dropped my hand to point to the picture again, showing me the direction to move.

"Okay," I said when he was done. "I can do that."

He nodded, but it took him a while to fold his arms on the desk and rest his head, and I wondered if he was as nervous as I was. Thankfully, with his head down, he couldn't see my shaking hand as I put some lotion on my fingers. It wasn't that I was afraid to do something wrong. I knew he'd direct me if I did. But the anticipation of touching him—I felt like someone had removed all my cells and replaced them with Lite-Brite pegs. Every part of me was awake and glowing.

At my first touch, Gabe shivered, and I watched the hair on the back of his neck stand up.

The lotion is just cold, I tried to tell myself, but deep down, I knew it was more. He was physically reacting to my touch. The thought made my mouth dry.

"Is this the right spot?" I asked.

"That's it," he said, a little breathless.

I made circles, trying to keep my arm straight just as instructed.

"Can you add a little more pressure?" he mumbled into his arms.

I did, and sure enough, I could feel the knots. I curled my fingers to get in deeper. Gabe groaned, and I immediately stopped, thinking I had hurt him. "You okay?"

"For the love of God, don't stop," he said without picking up his head.

I smiled and continued massaging. "How long should I work on this area?"

"You should—" His breath hitched as I hit a big knot. "Feel the knots loosen within a few minutes."

I let him relax as I worked, and just as he'd said, the knots started to smooth beneath my fingertips. "How is it feeling?" I asked.

It took a few beats for him to answer, and then he had to almost hum into his response. "Mmmm . . . Like if you ever get bored of bikes and switch to massage, I'll have some real competition."

I laughed, then moved my hand to his other shoulder blade. He only said that one side was bothering him, but I had to even it out, right? Gabe made a sound close to a moan, and I beamed at being able to make Gabe melt the way he made me do so regularly.

When I finished there, I ran my hands up either side of his spinal column until I reached his shoulders, following intuition more than instruction. "This still okay?" I asked.

"Yes, all—" I lost him for a second as I dug into his shoulder. "All of it."

I got to his neck. He was positively pliant as my fingers pressed in. Then, I kept going, scraping my nails along his scalp, and the goosebumps were back. If he had been a cat, I swear he would have started purring. He mumbled something that sounded like Spanish, but it was so quick and quiet I couldn't be sure. I wondered if he was bilingual. I would have asked if I wasn't busy trying to keep a giggle locked in.

I played with his hair, pulling the thick black strands—still damp from the shower— through my fingers, tugging ever so lightly. I didn't want to stop, and I got the impression he didn't want me to either, but if I didn't show some restraint soon, I thought my hands would grow a mind of their own. I imagined rubbing around his back until I reached the plains of his chest. Then I'd follow that ab pathway all the way down . . .

I pulled my hands away with a deep inhale through my nostrils.

"Did I do okay, Coach?"

Gabe lifted his head and turned toward me. He looked barely awake. "I owe you another massage, because that was life-changing."

I laughed. "And have to suffer through one of your pressure fests? I'll pass."

His gaze bore into mine. "Pressure can be pleasurable."

My universe whittled down to Gabe and his deep voice and those four words. Usually, my mind jumped from Gabe's innocent connotation to very dirty images, but right then, it seemed like he knew exactly what double meaning he sketched.

In fact, he was staring at my lips. As he zeroed in on my mouth, I watched his own slacken, his eyes darkening. He didn't look like he wanted to kiss me. He looked like he wanted to devour me, and I wanted him to. I wanted him to kiss me until my lips were swollen, bruised.

I wanted him to taste me as he did at my house when he treated my mouth—my tongue—like it was a dessert to be savored: ice cream on a hot day or whipped cream off the pumpkin pie.

With him sitting, we were somewhat eye-level. I stood too close for friendly conversation, but my feet stayed planted. "Prove it."

His jaw worked. Then, his Adam's apple bobbed. "That's probably not a good idea."

Gabriel was the very picture of a man fighting for the light. I should have put distance between us—backed off so he could think clearly—but I was lost in my own haze, and I wanted him to stay in the dark with me. Fiery need licked across my skin as my mind shuffled through all the possibilities of what Gabe and I could experience together.

"I don't care," I said. Life had stolen so much. So what if we broke the rules? I was claiming this moment with Gabe as mine—as long as he permitted it. "But—" I breathed, trying to calm my pulse, to find a break in the heavy fog, "I don't want to make you do anything you'll regret." I had to fight the urge to tell him how badly I wanted him and how long I'd fantasized about this. I sank my teeth into my bottom lip to keep the words from spewing out.

Gabe's eyes tracked the movement, and I watched his resolve snap in half. In a flash, my world shifted as he pulled me to him. Our mouths met in a frenzy, fumbling before we found a ravenous rhythm. His lips on mine only sent a scorch of desire down my stomach.

We were sealed together. We breathed the same air. It was everything, and yet not enough. Not nearly enough.

Gabriel didn't kiss me as though it might be a mistake. He kissed me like each break between our lips was.

I ran my tongue along his bottom lip. He groaned, and his hands were on the back of my thighs, lifting me into his lap. My ass got caught on the back of the chair, so he scooched just enough to make room for me. I sank into his lap, and his length pressed against my core. The air was stolen from my lungs. Only a few layers of clothes separated him from me.

I had one arm hooked around Gabe, pressing myself to his bare chest. The other hand was tangled in his hair.

Gabe's mouth left mine to kiss along the sensitive underside of my jaw, and I clamped my thighs tight around him. My desire was a blooming flower, and with each press of his lips, another petal unfolded.

He rubbed his nose along my ear, his breath tickling my neck. "Tell me to stop, April." He could have been asking for morphine for the way his voice strained. He wanted me to be the voice of reason, to put him out of his misery.

But I was just as desperate. I ground myself against him. "Sorry, Coach. I can't do that."

When he realized I wasn't going to give him an easy out, he planted his mouth back on mine, then sucked my bottom lip. My head swam as I felt his fingers at my hips, just under the shirt he was letting me borrow, right above my panty line. He traced the area, and I shivered, but he moved upward.

His hand stopped at my ribs, wrapping all the way around. "I can't give you anything more than casual," he reminded me between pants.

I grabbed his jaw to make sure he looked into my eyes and understood I had no problem with that. "Then give me casual, Gabriel."

His pupils were so blown that they almost looked predatory—he was a shark who smelled blood.

A thumb swiped upward, tracing under my breast. "Seeing these in my shirt—" he said, eyes on the hardened nipples beneath the fabric. He caressed my breast, lifting and massaging. "Has been driving me crazy." His thumbs swiped over the buds there, and I drew in a sharp breath.

"I offered to get my own shirt," I said, breathless.

Gabe's soft laugh rumbled between us. "I didn't think I was a masochist, but here we are." He pulled his shirt off me, letting it drop to the floor before he helped to smooth my hair back into place. I found the gesture tender for casual sex, but what did I know?

His eyes roamed over my bare breasts. He cupped them momentarily again before his hands slid down my stomach, fingers devastatingly light. I shivered, and he kept going until he reached my thighs. "Should have been obvious after I offered that massage, really."

"What do you mean?" I asked, struggling to pull together even a basic question when Gabe's fingers raked from thigh to knee.

Gabe watched his fingers work. "Look at you. Do you know how difficult it was to touch you but know I couldn't have you?"

My stomach fluttered. Then I remembered how much I struggled on his table, having his hands all over me. However, he'd seemed unaffected. "You were so professional."

"Do I still seem professional?" he asked in a rough voice. His hand gravitated toward my upper thighs, then to my center.

"Professionalism is overrated," I rasped.

His hand kept traveling upward, and every inch higher left me more and more at his mercy. When he got to the top of my thighs, he moved his hands inward and then spread his legs. Since mine were on top of his, he left me wide open for the taking. The only thing left to stop him was my panties.

I shivered as his finger ran along the seam. Then he stopped. "You're sure about this?" he asked.

"Yes," I whispered, my voice lost.

My stomach flipped as he hooked a finger and pulled the fabric aside.

"Oh, April," he said, teasing my entrance with his finger. "You are so wet."

I didn't even have a response. And any prayer at conjuring one flew out the window when he pressed a finger inside. My breath shuddered.

"You feel so good," he said, removing his finger to add a second one. I whimpered at the fullness of just his fingers. Then, he curled them. I bit my lip, but a moan still escaped.

"I told you pressure could be pleasurable," he rasped. Then he pressed even harder, sliding back in. My nails dug into his back as my body tried to figure out how to react to the all-consuming pleasure.

"Gabriel!" His name left my lips like a prayer—a beg. I leaned my head against his shoulder, watching his wrists pump up and down as he massaged my inner wall.

"Ever since you were on my table," he said hoarsely. "I've been dying to show you these fingers aren't just for pain."

"I'm a believer, now."

He picked up the rhythm, working until I could feel a build. My muscles started tightening, but Gabe slowed down before I could get too close to the edge. "I want to be inside you when you come." And though, technically, he was already, I didn't argue because I knew what he meant, and I wanted that, too.

"I'm clean and on birth control," I offered.

He removed his fingers and hoisted me off his lap. "I'm clean too. Was checked last month." My feet touched the ground just long enough to remove his shorts and boxers. I saw just a flash of his nude body before I was pulled back onto his lap.

But once settled there, I beheld all of Gabe. My mouth fell open. I know it's not always true that height correlates to length. But it certainly did in his case. He watched me drinking him in, his breath heaving until I wrapped my hands around him and stroked. He blew out a long breath, watching the movement like his life depended on the details.

Then I lifted up on his lap to put him at my entrance. He choked back a groan as his head slipped inside. I gasped, feeling myself stretch around him. It was a tight squeeze, but the discomfort didn't really start until I slid further down.

Gabe's head rolled back, the pleasure etched in his tightening features. It encouraged me to keep going, but at about the halfway point, I slowed. There was just too much of him.

I remembered what Billie had said about it being like the first time again. I'd thought it was ridiculous. Now, I wondered if she'd called it.

It had taken so much to convince Gabe. I feared my apprehension would scare him off, so I tried to soldier on, lowering myself another inch. My breath hitched. I didn't know how I was going to take him any deeper.

Gabe grabbed my elbows to stop the movement. "It hurts," he guessed.

"Well." I worked to keep my tone light as I remembered his warning before agreeing to be my coach. "You did say you wouldn't go easy on me."

His mouth fell ajar, but he quickly recovered. "That is not what I meant—"

"I know," I said, stopping his explanation.

"I would never intentionally hurt you."

"I know."

A crease formed between his brows. "Do you want to stop?"

"God, no!"

His chest rose and fell, and I could see his mind reeling when he finally asked, "Do you trust me? Enough to let me take control?"

Let him take control? My skin tingled at the prospect—an entanglement of fear and excitement coursed through my veins.

It was probably a terrible idea, but I did trust him.

I nodded.

In an instant, I was lifted. Gabe brought us to the bed, but instead of laying me on my back, he flipped me over.

As my hands and knees sank into the mattress, I wondered if he used this position to keep the intimacy out of things. Maybe it was harder to catch feelings if we didn't make eye contact.

When he placed himself at my entrance, I braced for pain. He was a big guy, and I could offer very little resistance in this position. Then, his warmth encompassed me. His stomach pressed against my back as he leaned forward to take my jaw in his hand. Gently, he turned my face to the side, kissing me with feather-light touches on the corner of my lips. "This position helps loosen tension—meaning less discomfort." His deep voice reverberated from his chest to my spine. "Try to relax. I'm not going to hurt you, April."

I let out a long breath and willed some of the tension from my muscles.

"That's it." He pushed a strand of hair behind my ear. "*Hermosa*," I thought I heard him whisper. Then he followed it with a, "You're so beautiful."

Just when I thought I could keep a guard around my heart, Gabe had to crack and shake the shell until the whole thing glowed.

Then, his big, warm hand slid down to my core, fingers circling my clit in a way that stole all my attention. That's when he pushed in, just a bit.

Even with him going slow and shallow, it was mind-numbingly good. I relished the movement against my inner wall, the steady rhythm of his fingers.

Tentatively, Gabe picked up the pace, but he didn't push further in. Soon, I found myself not only ready to take all of him but needing to. Feverish for more, I rocked my ass backward, forcing a few more inches in.

Gabe gripped my ribs and made a wounded sound.

His hands slipped to my hips, holding me in place as he went deeper and deeper until—I gasped as my ass finally pressed into his front. We both stilled, taking in the sensation of complete connection.

"Fuuuuuck." The pleasure in Gabe's voice was so thick, it could have been mistaken for pain. Then, after some labored breathing, he asked, "Are you okay?"

I nodded, adjusted, then slid forward so I could push against him again. Gabe didn't need any other encouragement. He rested one hand on the bed next to mine and kept the other at my hip as he thrusted.

Sounds of whimpering and moaning weaved in with our heavy breathing. And as the friction picked up, so did the heat until Gabe's sweat dripped on me. Not even an hour before, I'd let Gabe use the shower first because he had other people's sweat on him. Now, I couldn't think of anything more crude or delicious than feeling his sweat roll down my spine while he drove into me.

I was encompassed in rising ecstasy, but I worried Gabe was holding back for my sake. Only because I knew his athletic ability. I'd seen his power in action. He could go faster, harder. The white-knuckled grip on the duvet suggested more than just pleasure. It was restraint.

My concern snipped free when he ground out a, "You take me so well."

And that, of course, would push me over—praise from my coach. Sparklers lit behind my eyes, and my body seized with an orgasm so intense, I had to blink tears free.

Gabe pumped faster, working to reach his own pleasure. By then, I was so pliant; it wouldn't have mattered how rough he went. I was too far gone.

His free arm hooked under me, and he clamped down, holding me in place as an orgasm ripped through his body. I knew that moment—being secured by Gabe's bicep while he pulsed inside me—would be a savored memory for the foreseeable future.

His forehead rolled against my shoulder as he tried to get a hold of his breathing. I could have spent the night like that, Gabe's breath at my ear, his body leaning against mine. But the moment ended when Gabe lifted his head. "I'll get us a towel," he said between pants. I rolled over, an arm over my eyes as I fought through the post-sex haze to find my bearings back in the real world.

I just had toe-curling, mind-blowing sex.

With.

My.

Coach.

I dropped my arm at Gabe's returning footsteps. His lips pressed into a flat line. Yep, reality had slapped him in the face, too.

He handed me the towel and then sat on the edge of the bed. "We're going to be okay, right?"

"Yeah," I said, my voice a little too high. "We just needed to get that out of our systems."

"Right."

"Right."

He looked at the floor, a line between his brows.

"What's wrong?" I asked. Suddenly, I felt very small. I'd thoroughly enjoyed sex with him, but what if the feeling wasn't mutual? "You didn't like it?"

His head snapped my way. "You know that's not it." The severity of his voice alleviated the self-consciousness building in my chest. "I just—" He straightened my butterfly necklace, resting the charm over my heart. "I like what we have, and now I'm worried I fucked up everything."

"Hey." I grabbed his hand and waited for his eyes to meet mine. "You didn't ruin anything. We're fine." And because I couldn't stand that broken look on his face, I said, "It wasn't a mistake, but it was a one-time thing."

He released a long exhale and nodded before getting under the covers with me. We settled in, his bare chest pressed against my back, his arm strapped across my stomach, fingers absently making figure-eights at my navel.

My own words grew heavier by the minute.

It was a one-time thing.

A one-time thing?

That was the best sex of my life, and I'd never get another taste? I found myself wanting to backtrack—to barter—but I clamped my mouth shut because I knew if I pushed the issue, I'd risk losing him completely.

And no sex, no matter how incredible, was worth that.

Chapter 25

GABRIEL

If April's kiss was nicotine, having sex with her had been cocaine. What had she said, *'We just needed to get that out of our system?'* Bullshit. It was much worse now.

Before, I had only imagined how good it would be with her. Now, I *knew*. And the last thing I wanted was to stop.

After a difficult workout, I'd reward myself with a shower and thoughts of her. But my hand didn't come close. I needed her moans, her gasps, her ass, the way she bit that bottom lip, how she clenched around me when I made her come.

But that couldn't happen again.

The first time I saw her after our trip was in the weight room of the rec. She stood at the squat rack, positioned and ready. I thought about leaving. I could do my swim first, but I stopped myself. If we were planning on being normal with each other—remaining friends—I couldn't run and hide every time I saw her. We could be civil. We had to be. I had an Ironman to coach her through.

Then she did a squat. The fabric stretched over her ass, effectively transporting me back to our hotel room. She'd been so tight and started out so tense. The last thing I'd wanted was to hurt her. It had been a war against instinct to go slow and shallow, but I managed. Up until she'd pushed that ass against me, burying me deeper inside her.

¡Ella me vuelve loco!

At that moment, burning need replaced every logical thought, and standing in the gym, I felt that same animalistic desire snaking its way through my chest.

Remain just friends? Whose dumbass idea was that?

A guy on the pull-up bar hung, openly staring at April's perky ass. A weird, protective wave washed over me, even though I was engaged in the same creepy act as him. I positioned myself right behind April, blocking the view.

Oblivious, she went down for another squat, and I waited until she came back up to say, "Great form, Baird."

She staggered, her eyes wide as they landed on my reflection in the mirror. I threw my hands out to spot her, but she recovered on her own, racking it safely before whipping around to face me.

Something sparkled in her hazel eyes, and her mouth widened to a ridiculously cute smile before she tamped her expression. "Hey, Coach."

It had only been a few days since I last saw her, but it was like coming off a three-day fast and seeing chocolate cake.

She's not dessert.

She's my athlete.

"Where are you in the workout?" I asked.

"I was just finishing up the squats." She wiped her forehead, retrieved her phone from the floor, and gave it to me for inspection. She had hip thrusters next. The idea made me sweat. I would not survive watching her do a set of those.

"And how do you feel?" I asked, my voice gravelly.

She considered that. "Strong." Then she smiled as if surprised by her own answer.

I nodded. "You looked strong." I handed her back the phone. "Which is why you're going to add more weight."

Her face fell. "I walked right into your trap."

I took the liberty to add ten pounds to each side. "When I said I wasn't going to go easy on you, *this* is what I meant." I leveled a look at her.

A blush deepened on her already pink cheeks as she tried to wrestle a smile back into submission. It was no use, and she finally positioned herself in front of the bar, smile and all.

"Go for five," I said, standing close, ready to spot her. She went down with it, nice and steady, but grunted on the way back up.

"You've got it," I said, and she did. She breezed through the next three, then slowed on what she thought was the last squat.

"You're doing one more," I said.

She made a choking sound. "You said five."

"And now I'm saying six." I met her eyes in the mirror. "You can take it."

A small voice in my head tried to warn me that I sounded more like a narrator for one of April's audiobooks than her coach. However, that voice was muffled by the sound of my own thrumming pulse.

Her delicious, plump lips parted, making any and all internal chastising worth it. It dawned on me that April liked dirty talk. I thought back to her audiobook; it was my turn to fight a smile.

She brought the bar up, legs quaking. "You can do it. Come on," I encouraged. When she got it to the top, I helped guide the bar back into position. She was flushed and panting, but she'd done it. I stayed in her space until her eyes met mine in the mirror. "That's my good girl."

She gasped, and I forced my feet to walk away before I could cause any more irrevocable damage.

Chapter 26

GABRIEL

We had a big group swim scheduled in the neighboring town over—at Gemini Lake. Open water swimming was vastly different from the chlorinated lanes of a pool. Many practiced swimmers got to the murky lake on race day, panicked when they couldn't see the bottom, and kept veering off course because they hadn't practiced sighting, or were forced under when other swimmers passed over them.

Even on race day, when you had people out on kayaks serving as unofficial lifeguards, you got the distinct feeling that your survival depended on your athletic ability, and that magnitude could break anyone.

Which is why Beck joined our group swim. It was our last chance before the relay. He'd agreed he needed the practice, but now, surveying the still lake, he looked less than pleased. "You'll be fine," I said, giving his back a slap.

Beck had to step forward to catch himself. He turned back and glared at me. "And we're sure there aren't crocodiles in there?"

"No, Beck. There aren't crocodiles." I walked away before he could see my widening smile. "Alligators, maybe."

"You're fucking with me!"

I once had a client who worked at a reptile rescue. She told me alligators were so prevalent in our area that there was likely an alligator in every body of water larger than a ditch. I hadn't had a restful open water swim since, but Beck was already on edge, so I let him believe it was a joke.

As we tugged on our wetsuits—an effort that always made me feel a tad claustrophobic—April joined us under the pavilion.

"Coach," she said, plopping her duffle onto the picnic table. She wore an unreadable expression. We'd been having normal conversations over text, but I hadn't seen or spoken to her since that day at the gym.

"That's my good girl."

I'd crossed a line. My own line that I drew with a permanent marker, and I couldn't tell whether or not she was pissed with me, but she had every right to be.

I could do better. I would do better. I just had to hold my ground.

"April," I tested and was pleasantly surprised when she didn't give me an earful for teasing her at the gym. "This is Beck—our swimmer for the relay."

Beck stood to shake her hand. "You must be the cyclist. Nice to meet you."

"Beck?" April exclaimed. "As in Beck and Emily, *Beck*?"

Beck laughed, then gave me a look. "Depends on what this guy told you."

April's smile was huge. I could almost see the Costa Rica story playing behind her eyes. "Oh, all good things," she finally landed on, then changed the subject. "Do you do a lot of racing?"

"Not since high school," he admitted.

"But he's a strong swimmer," I cut in, then regretted it because Beck smiled wickedly at my compliment. "We just have to get this city boy used to real water," I said, slapping him between the shoulders again.

His glare was back, just as I preferred.

"Well, today should be some good practice," April offered.

"You look familiar," Beck said, head tilting.

"She's the swimmer who got kicked in the face when we were volunteering."

April's lips pressed into a hard line while Beck's eyes widened with recognition. "Oh, yeah." He gave a sympathetic wince. "Guess that's something to look forward to during the swim."

"Only if you have my kind of luck," she said bitterly before removing her T-shirt.

My gaze dropped to her breasts, and I started salivating. April had on a swimsuit, but it was sporty, which meant aerodynamic, which meant skin-tight. This one had no padding, and her nipples looked like they were fighting to be freed. I realized I'd made a grave mistake that night I'd had sex with her. I hadn't tasted them.

Less than three minutes, and I was already losing my footing, ready to pole-vault over those boundaries I'd set.

April hiked an eyebrow. She didn't look angry to catch me staring. She looked pleased with herself, which was much worse. I averted my gaze as she removed her shorts, not willing to subject myself to further suffering. Instead, I kept my eyes on the group gathering at the dock.

"Better get that wetsuit on quickly, Baird." *¡Dios mío! Cover that body.*

"What's the temperature?"

"Seventy-five."

"Pssh. That's barely wetsuit legal. I'll pass."

I snapped my attention to April, forcing my eyes to stay glued to her face. "You're going to be cold," I tried. "And you'll want the extra buoyancy the wetsuit offers."

"If I practice without the extra buoyancy, it will be that much better if I do use it on race day," she countered, not completely wrong.

"Are you sure?" I asked.

She reached up to put her hair in a short ponytail, and her breasts were back to taunting me. "Absolutely." She tugged on the ends of her hair to secure the ponytail further up, then strode down to the dock. "See you in the water."

I told myself to look away, but then there was her perfect ass.

Goading her at the gym had been a fatal error. I'd played with fire, and now I was being burned alive.

I looked over and found Beck reading my face, a question in that crease between his brows.

"Come on," I said before he could ask. "Gotta keep up with the group if you don't want an alligator to pick you off."

Chapter 27

APRIL

M ost of our group chose to shower at home, but the idea of sitting in lake water for the drive made my feet shuffle toward the outdoor shower stalls. I wondered if Gabe had already left. He'd been conversing with Beck when I'd gotten out of the lake, but I lost him when Jessica asked me to unzip and peel off her wetsuit. Then we started talking about some modifications she wanted for her bike. By the time our conversation died down, the group had dispersed.

The slap of my flip-flops on concrete echoed between the stalls, accompanying the spray of the one running shower. I opted for the open door across from it, figuring the person in there was most likely someone from our group.

There is safety in numbers. That's the thought I had before a hand tightened around my wrist.

I yelped as that hand yanked me backward into a stall. Before I could thoroughly panic or imagine becoming the topic of a crime podcast, Gabe's dark eyes came into view. I only saw a flash of them before he cupped my face, lips on mine—hungry, greedy.

His condition was contagious. My mouth became embarrassingly frantic, like I was kissing him for the last time—not an illogical thought, considering the last time was supposed to be the last time. Without breaking our kiss, his hand hooked under my duffle bag's strap, relieving me of it. I suspected he put it on the nearby bench, but I didn't open my eyes to look. Honestly, he could have thrown it under the shower spray for all I cared, as long as he didn't stop kissing me.

Luckily, Gabe's appetite seemed as insatiable as my own. He tilted my face, plunging his tongue deeper. Meanwhile, I snaked a hand under his arm and around his back, fingers digging into his shoulder blade as if I could keep him from retreating—from snapping out of it and telling me this was a bad idea. As I sealed myself to him, Gabe's length strained against his swim shorts, pressing against my stomach. He was hard—so hard it had to hurt.

I could relate. An unbearable heaviness grew between my thighs. I had to have him completely on the hook or I would face a very disappointing evening.

Fighting every instinct, I broke the kiss, gulping in air I hadn't realized I'd gone without. "I thought we agreed not to do this again," I whispered, then sucked his bottom lip, relishing in the way it made his cock twitch.

A groan rumbled from his ribs to my chest. "That was before I knew you were going to torture me today, April." He went back to kissing me with commanding lips, but this time, he backed me into a wall. His hand left my jaw, and I heard the door's lock slide into place. There was no escape now. I was going to pay thoroughly for teasing him. The promise hummed down my spine.

"Tortured you?" I tried to feign innocence, but it sounded nothing short of salacious.

He put just enough space between us so his hands could roam over my breasts. With a whisper of a touch, he brushed the back of his fingers over nipples that pebbled beneath my swimsuit fabric. I shivered.

"You know exactly what you were doing," he accused, eyes glued to my breasts like he was afraid they'd vanish if he didn't watch carefully enough.

I considered letting him win the argument, only so he'd keep touching me, but I forced the words out. "Like you didn't know what you were doing." I gasped as he lightly pinched. My back arched off the wall, but I closed my eyes, focusing on the words I needed to say. "The other day. At the gym."

He'd gotten me all hot and bothered during my squat set. Then he'd just walked away, leaving me confused and aroused and frustrated.

"You're right," he said, his voice as deep as a cavern. Sure fingers edged my swimsuit straps down, peeling until fresh air hit my breasts. "Let me make it up to you."

He licked his lips and moved in, but that's when my eyes fell on the edge of the shower stall. I put a hand on his chest. "Wait. We can't." He stopped instantly, searching my face like he'd find some hint of some-thing he'd done wrong—a cue he'd misread. "I want to," I hurried to say, "so unbelievably bad. But—" I pointed at the open area between where the concrete stopped and the shower stall started. "What if someone sees our feet?"

I was pretty sure we were the only swimmers left, but I wasn't certain. The idea of him losing out on A-Team because I'd seduced him made me feel like a siren dragging him under dark waves.

His gaze could have burned a hole in my irises. "Is that all you're worried about?" He tilted his head. "Someone seeing our feet?"

I nodded, eyes fluttering. "It's a little suspicious."

He peeled off his suit and the rest of mine before hoisting me up. My bare core resting on his pelvis was enough to make me feel sparks. Then he said, "Guess I'll just have to fuck you against the door, Baird." And in a snap, the sparks ignited into a full-on forest fire, engulfing every thought except Gabe and what he planned to do with me.

He started by lifting me further to taste my breasts, taking turns sucking and nipping them. My head rocked against the shower stall, and I bit down on my lip to keep the moan inside.

Gabe sucked on my nipples until they were nearly to the point of being raw. When a cry did escape, he let my body slide down his and kissed me. My core was still achingly empty of him. I reached down to rectify that but released the reins to Gabe when he put himself at my entrance.

One push inside, and I was seeing stars. Gabe adored my lips with his own for a moment. Then he asked, "You okay?"

The tenderness in the question made my heart swell. "Better than okay," I whispered into his mouth.

He caught my lips with his again and then continued rocking into me. I'd gotten the feeling that he'd been holding back on our first night together. I didn't want him to do that here. "You know," I said between pants, "you're not going to break me."

He pulled back to read me as if trying to ensure he hadn't misunderstood.

"You'd tell me if it hurts, right?"

I nodded.

"Promise me, April."

"I promise."

Even with my promise, he worked us up to it slowly, but it was like clicking up a roller coaster. Eventually, he got to the point where he let go of restraint and drove me into the shower stall.

The rhythm and the pressure were perfect, so I wasn't going to say anything about being cold. The only part of my body touching the shower spray was my legs. Gabe's body blocked out the rest. I shivered, and Gabe stopped.

"Are you cold?"

"You're kind of hogging all the water," I said, nipping at his bottom lip.

"Not being a very considerate lover, am I?" he rasped.

Before I could contradict him, he spun us so both our bodies were under the gush of water. Then, he pinned me with his hips against a different wall so he could reach over and point the shower head at both of us.

The water made my legs slip down his backside, but it didn't matter because Gabe's grip kept me secure. I kind of hoped his fingers would leave imprints on my ass—a little souvenir of this time with him.

Satisfied with his hold on me, Gabe went back to rolling his hips into mine, and I had to work to keep quiet at the build of pressure.

"You drive me crazy, April," he said before kissing me. His lips were slippery from the water, and the glide made me that much hungrier for purchase. Water dripped from his face to mine, rolling down my jaw in streams. I couldn't get enough. He swept his tongue across my bottom lip, and my stomach swirled. I hooked an arm around his shoulder to pull myself closer to him. He held me up with one hand and braced the other against the wall. I could tell he was in the same boat, in need of release—so bad it hurt. He whispered something that, again, sounded like a Spanish prayer, but I could have imagined it for how clearly he next asked, "May I come inside you again?"

"Yes," is all I managed. I slapped a hand over my mouth to keep from crying out as he picked up the pace. Gabe watched my features like he would find the solution to world hunger in my eyes. It was too much, the way he looked at me. Too intimate. Eye contact was not for casual sex. I broke my gaze, squeezing my eyes shut and dropping my head to his shoulder. It wasn't long until an orgasm tore a hole through my reality, pulling me away from everything that wasn't Gabe and the sensation he'd created.

Gabe's pleasure followed directly after. He shuddered forward, leaning into that arm he had propped on the wall. When the climax loosened its grip on him, his entire body relaxed like a puppet whose master snipped the strings. "April Baird," he panted. "You are going to be the death of me."

I quietly laughed. "There are worse ways to die, though, right?"

"I can't think of a better way." He adjusted me in his grip.

"Speaking of dying. Your arms must be killing you."

"You weigh nothing." He backed us up until our faces were under the water.

I laughed, and Gabe said, "We have to shower all that lake water off if we want to get dinner."

Butterflies. I had butterflies. "Dinner?"

"Yeah," he said, pulling us from the spray to get his bottle of soap.

"Here," I offered. If he was going to hold me up, I could at least do the lathering. Besides, I needed something to look at other than his eyes, afraid I'd melt. I squirted some in my hands and made small circles over his shoulders, up his neck, across his chest.

"I don't want to be done seeing you today."

I did look back at his eyes at that. The words were such simple colors, but they painted a complicated idea.

It's more than sex, then.

I countered that thought with a normal one. *Dinner can still be casual.*

"Tell me you can come," he said.

I went back to lathering. "That depends. Do you know of any good places to eat, Torres?"

I learned that Gabe is a bit of a foodie which, if I had to spend a considerable amount of time fueling that tank his soul drove, I'd probably be more of one, too.

He took me to Freedom Park because the food trucks rolled in on the last Saturday of every month. So many cultures were represented, and different mixes of spices melded in the air. I didn't know where to start. I wanted it all.

"How will we ever choose?"

"This is one of my favorites," Gabe said, pointing to a truck that smelled like a taqueria. My stomach growled. "Do you like TexMex?"

I walked toward it as an answer. The line was long, which I figured was a good sign. I squinted at the menu while we waited. An item caught my eye: a corn tortilla stuffed with beef, cheese, cilantro, and onion.

"Do you know how to pronounce that?" I asked Gabe while pointing.

His eyes narrowed at me as if trying to see if I was serious. "Yes?"

"Do you speak Spanish?" I finally asked.

"I hope so since that's what my mom speaks."

Add bilingual to the long list of things that made Gabriel Torres hot.

"You never told me that."

He shrugged. *"Nunca preguntaste."*

I stared at him blankly. "Should I get out Google Translate, or . . ."

"You never asked."

"So, how do I say it?" I asked, looking back at the menu.

He gave a mischievous smile. "How do you *think* it's pronounced?"

The line moved forward, and I had the distinct fear that this was going to be the equivalent of someone ordering fajitas as *fah-jigh-tahs*.

"I don't know. That's why I'm asking."

"I want to hear you give it a try."

"You know what? I'm just going to go get that Thai I saw," I said, turning away from the truck. "They have little numbers next to the menu items."

Gabe grabbed my arm, laughing, and the warmth of his touch made me feel like I harbored a star in my chest—becoming brighter by the second.

"What if I promise not to make fun of you?"

"You're already laughing," I accused.

"I'll stop," he said, clearly struggling to keep his features neutral.

I sighed and squinted back at the menu. Okay, I knew the first part, *quesa*—only the best ingredient of all time. It was the second half that felt like a calculus problem. I blew out a breath, then guessed, "Burr-ia?"

As promised, he didn't laugh, but there was no mistaking the twinkle in his eye. "So close. It's pronounced bee-rryah."

"Bee-rryah?" I tested.

"That's it. You've never had it before?"

"It's just like a taco, right?"

"No, Baird. Not *just* like a taco."

It was our turn at the window, and Gabe ordered for us. He started with a friendly, "*Hola*," and then ordered in Spanish that rolled effortlessly off his tongue. I did catch, "*quesabirria y sopapillas*" and a "*por favor*." The rest was lost upon me. But I didn't need to know exactly what he was saying to realize this was the first time I'd ever thought someone ordering food sounded sexy.

Gabe turned back toward me, and I'm sure the wonder must have been plain on my features. I felt like a sunflower turned toward the sun.

"What?" he asked as we stepped to the side, waiting for our food.

"Nothing." Then I laughed at myself. "Just ashamed that I took two years of Spanish in high school and couldn't keep up with a food order."

"You don't remember any of it?"

"I know the basics. Colors, greetings, how to ask for the bathroom." I thought for a moment. "Oh, I know like half of *Despacito*. Does that count for anything?"

"I don't know." He pretended to mull that over. "You'd have to sing it for me."

"Yeah. That's not happening." I laughed, and so did Gabe. "Was Spanish your first language?"

He bobbed his head from side to side. "My dad wanted me to know English. So I grew up learning both."

"Wow." I wondered how hard that must have been for him as a child. Learning two names for everything. Then again, kids are pretty resilient. "Did your dad grow up bilingual, too?"

Gabe paused so long that I thought maybe he hadn't heard the question, but then he said, "No. He didn't learn Spanish until he was an adult."

"Don't tell me he learned it to communicate with your mom, or I will melt."

Gabe watched the people passing by on the sidewalk. "He did."

I got it. Gabe was a guy. It was normal for him to be unimpressed with his parents' love story, but I couldn't take how cute that was. "That's so romantic."

Gabe didn't just look unimpressed. He looked disgusted. I tried to figure out what I'd said wrong but was saved when they called his name for our order.

The awkward moment between us was forgotten as Gabe unbagged our food on a picnic table. Cheese oozed out of my taco, causing my mouth to water. I picked it up, ready to take a chunk out of it, but Gabe stopped me.

"Woah, hold up, Baird."

"Oh." I lowered the taco. "Sorry. Were you going to say grace or something?"

He chuckled. "No." Then he opened a lid on what looked like a container of soup. "It's traditional to dip the tacos in the stew."

"Seriously?" I asked.

"Seriously." He took his own and dunked it before taking a bite that deleted half his taco.

I followed suit, still skeptical, until I took a bite of savory heaven.

"My God," I said.

"Beats cold spaghetti or whatever the hell you planned on eating tonight," he said, grinning into his bite.

"Hey," I said, wiping my mouth. "I don't *always* eat my spaghetti cold."

"I'm sure you don't." He sounded unconvinced.

I would have argued further, but honestly, the taco was taking all my attention—that is until Gabe opened a bag of sopapillas dusted in cinnamon and sugar. We ate and commiserated about swimming in lake water while watching a group of teens trying skateboard tricks.

I'd just finished comparing the grass at the bottom of Gemini Lake to the *poor unfortunate souls* in "The Little Mermaid" when Gabe's eyes dipped to my lips.

"Here. You have a little—" He reached out, and his own mouth went slack as he watched the movement of his thumb drag down my bottom lip. I felt particles of sugar fall from my lip, but his thumb stayed there. He was entranced by my lips, and I was entranced by him.

Someone hollered, snapping us from our hold on each other. We both turned to find a teenager on his back, skateboard rolling down the pavement, but he laughed, letting everyone know he was okay.

Gabe gathered our trash. "We better get you home. You have an early run."

I hated to part ways. I wanted to spend the night spellbound by him, let him lick sugar off my lips until the sun came up. But that was the problem. I wanted it too badly, and that was a recipe for heartache.

"You would know," I said, helping him pile containers in the paper bag.

"You're damn right I would."

This was easier. Flirting was fine, but I would not catch feelings for Gabriel Torres.

Chapter 28

GABRIEL

If that kid hadn't hit the pavement at the park, I would have started kissing April again, and I knew what her lips did to me. I would have asked her to come home, and I would have spent the night devouring them—among other things.

And damn it, I'd just fucked her not even a few hours before. Sleeping with her was supposed to scratch an itch. Usually, when I kept things casual with a woman, I could go days—even weeks—between seeing her.

Not April.

On the drive home, I pictured April in her car, listening to another romance novel. The image had me smiling. If I'd driven her home, I wondered what we'd talk about—a customer who was shitty to her or maybe the bike she was restoring. I suddenly found myself hungry for all the little details of her life. It was new for me to want more than sex, but I did.

What would it be like if I allowed myself to see where casual went naturally—if I didn't torch a relationship at the first sign of life?

Maybe I could try with April. I *wanted* to try.

I approached my apartment with phone in hand, a message typed out, asking her to send progress pictures of the Schwinn she'd been fixing up. I'd been about to hit send, but Chuck didn't run to me like usual when I opened the door. Instead, he cowered on the couch.

"Hey, bud," I said, crossing the room. He wagged his tail but wouldn't look at me. "You okay?"

Then I saw them. On the floor, next to the couch, were my race shoes—the Nikes I'd just gotten from Trevor. I hadn't even put thirty miles on them yet and they were chewed beyond recognition. Two hundred dollars down the drain.

"Oh, shit."

I put my hands on my head, and the movement made Chuck flinch. He hunched against the couch, head low enough that his jaw touched the cushion. The fear was so human, so sad, so familiar.

It took me a beat to realize he was cowering because of me.

"Oh, Chuck, no."

I pulled my hands from my head, staring at them. I knew why Chuck's position looked familiar.

The memory of slammed cabinets and shattering glass assaulted my mind. I could feel my hands over my ears again. My eyes squeezed shut. The tears streaming down my cheeks. The way I hid between the couch and the shelf with my mom's porcelain knick-knacks, my knees curled to my chest.

He's mad again.

I covered my mouth, fighting the onslaught of images flashing behind my eyes before dragging my attention back to Chuck. My vision swam as I slowly approached, my hand outstretched so he could sniff me. *"Está bien."* From the waver in my voice, I wasn't sure if I was talking to him or me.

To my relief, he licked my hand and then inched closer, head still low but tail wagging. I sat on the couch and let him put his paws on my lap. He tried to lick my face, and I rubbed behind his head the way he liked. "I would never hurt you, bud."

But my chest ached as I realized how hollow that promise was. I'm sure my dad never pictured hurting my mom when he wanted to communicate with her so badly he learned a whole new language.

But he had.

That wouldn't happen to me. I wouldn't be so blindsided by love that I let my emotions override my mind. I'd completely control the situation. Break the cycle.

Which is why I couldn't keep Chuck.

It's why I had to keep my head clear with April. I could be in her life for as long as my feelings stayed small.

I deleted the unsent message and tossed my phone to the other side of the couch.

Chapter 29

GABRIEL

The thing about being nervous when you're a coach—you can't let it show on game day. Both Beck and April had a quiet, anxious energy as we took turns laying out our things in the shared transition area on the morning of our 70.3 Ironman relay. I had to be the calm in the chaos.

So, I slowly reviewed the game plan, which was a simple one. Beck: stay to the left, don't drown, and don't get picked off by a shark (because this swim was in the bay, after all). April: keep the pace steady and comfortable. No wrecks.

Then I checked they had all their gear, that April had her bottled nutrition, and Beck had the tracker on his ankle—it served as the baton for our relay.

The longer we talked through the plan and checked off the gear, the easier the two seemed to breathe. All the while, the knot in my stomach pulled tighter and tighter.

I'd been so focused on how much I thought this plan could help April, I hadn't considered the damage it would cause if it backfired. If, for whatever godforsaken reason, she had to DNF today, she'd claim this as evidence of her Ironman curse. I could see her adding a string to her mental *Crimes Committed by the Universe* board. How could I ask her to complete a full—on her own—after that?

While Beck pulled on his wetsuit, I turned to April. She absently rubbed the tiny wings on her butterfly charm.

"You doing okay?"

"Yeah." But her voice was a little too high-pitched. She was overselling it.

I put my hands on her shoulders. "You've put in the work. Now it's time to show off."

She nodded, but my words didn't seem to permeate.

"I have something for you."

That got her attention. "You do?"

I handed her a square of packing tape with the sticky sides pressed inward, making a protective case for the four-leaf clover.

By the look in April's eyes, you would have thought I'd given her a diamond, not a weed. "Did you find this?"

I rubbed the back of my neck. "Yeah. Chuck probably thought I was a nutcase, kneeling in the grass to look for one."

"That must have taken you forever."

It had been forty-five minutes, minimum, and for the entirety of that time, I kept reminding myself that what I was doing did not strike as casual, but she didn't need to know that. "No. It wasn't too bad."

She threw her arms around me, so hard that I rocked back from the impact. "Thank you."

I returned the hug, relishing the whiff of raspberry and the surge of warmth that spread across my chest at being close to her. So much for keeping my feelings under control. What was it about her that had my resolve in pieces within minutes? "It's no problem," I said, voice rough.

When I released her, I realized Beck was looking between us, an eyebrow hiked. He didn't say anything, but I knew he would when we were alone. He loved to give me hell. Mercifully, he rarely shamed me publicly.

"Go, Team Trouble!" We turned to find Emily. She leaned over the transition gate with a poster board. Our team name had been swooped and swirled onto the sign in the elegant penmanship that attested to Emily's craft. Emily had been the one to come up with the Team Trouble name after realizing Beck and I would be on the same relay.

Beck laughed, clearly surprised and delighted to see her. We followed him over.

"I thought you had to be at the live lettering event," he said.

Strands from Emily's bun came loose, red hair whipping in the wind as she shrugged. "I told Hailey I'd join her in a bit. I didn't want to miss your swim."

Before Beck could jump the fence and make out with her, which is exactly what he looked like he wanted to do, I reached over the gate and hugged her. "Hey, Emily."

"You ready to crush this race?" she asked, face muffled by my chest.

"No crushing," I said, releasing her. "We are just taking an easy day."

I looked between Beck and April, and because I knew teasing them would take their minds off the race, I put a hand on each of their shoulders. "We're a little nervous," I said with exaggerated sympathy.

As predicted, my hands were instantly shoved away. I chuckled at the look April gave me, then neutralized the situation by introducing her to Emily. Unfortunately, they didn't have long to talk. An announcer came over a creaky speaker, giving directions to athletes. That's when Emily looked at the other spectators, claiming their positions along the course.

"Well, I guess I should go find a spot before they fill up."

"My cousin, Trevor, probably found the best place." April pointed to where Trevor crouched, giving Johnson a scratch. "He's the guy with the camera and the wiener dog."

"Thanks!" Emily replied, then to Beck, "Good luck with open water." He gave her a playful scowl, then kissed her on the nose.

"Your girlfriend is adorable," April said as we walked back to our spot in transition.

"She is," Beck agreed, wearing that same smile he always wore when someone mentioned Emily. Then his head jerked up. "So, is your cousin a photographer?"

"Yes," April answered proudly.

"And is he any good?"

"I'm biased, but he's been doing it forever. He's actually waiting to hear back about a job at *Exposure*, the nature magazine."

"Do you think he'd be willing to take pictures of a potential engagement?"

I stopped and stretched my arm out to make him stop, too. "Are you finally going to ask her?"

"Yeah." He gave one of his normal cocky smiles, but I could read the nerves beneath. "In two weeks. I'm going to ask her where we first met."

"That's so sweet," April said. "I'll talk to Trevor for you."

"Thank you. And you are both invited." He looked at me. "I made the mistake of telling Victoria and Emily's sister, Hailey, my plan," he said grumpily. "Now, they are making a whole event of it."

"What day?" I asked.

"The twenty-ninth. It's a Sunday."

"Shit."

"What's wrong? You have plans?"

"No. That's the problem." I looked at April who was trying to suppress a smile. "That's the day after our local triathlon club is throwing a party. I was hoping to have an excuse to miss it."

Beck cocked his head. "Why? You love parties."

I thought of all the parties Beck and I had attended in college. I never drank—afraid I'd turn out like my dad. Beck, however, was a fun drunk. All unbridled laughter and quick-witted remarks.

"It's not the party," April said, giving me a knowing smile. "It's the host." Because, of course, it had to be at Clay's house this year. "We don't have to go," she supplied.

"No," I said. "It's fine. I should make an appearance if only to socialize with my athletes for a bit. It will be the last time I see most of them before race day."

April nodded. "Probably a good idea."

"Anyway, I'll be there," I said, returning to the main topic—Beck getting engaged. "I'm so happy for you, man."

"Well, don't celebrate early. Emily hasn't said yes yet."

My lips pressed into a flat line. In high school, Beck could just smile at a girl and have her number. Now, he had a woman who openly loved him, and he was an anxious wreck.

"She's going to say yes." I reached down to pinch one of his cheeks. "You are so cute when you're nervous, Beckett."

He dodged my hand. "I'm not nervous. It's just presumptuous to assume she'll say yes."

I chose to ignore his ridiculous fear of Emily saying no. Some humility would do him good, anyway.

I noticed one of my athletes sorting through his gear and decided to check on him and some of the others, telling Beck and April I'd catch up with them later. Everyone on my roster, except April, had a full Ironman under their belts, so the seventy miles were no big deal. Still, I reminded them about the choppy water of Galveston and told them to be braced for strong winds on the bike.

"I didn't realize you were racing today, Torres." I recognized the voice as belonging to one of my least favorite people. I took a long inhale before turning to face Clay. He wore his little matching sweat kit over his tri-suit, no surprise there.

"Yep. We're relaying it."

He scrunched his nose. "With who?"

"An old friend." I couldn't keep the smile off my face. "And April."

Clay's eyes narrowed. "What's your goal here?"

I didn't understand the question. "To have a good race?"

"No." He laughed bitterly. "I mean with April. Are you hoping the board will give you extra points for taking on a charity case?"

"Okay," I said, turning. The guy was a parasite. He loved getting under other people's skin. I wasn't going to give him the satisfaction. "Have a good race," I said woodenly.

I left him to go back to my team. It was childish, but I had a new reason for wanting April to kick ass today.

I wanted Clay to pay for dropping her.

I watched another wave of swimmers come out of the water. As predicted, the bay was choppy. Knowing Beck did ninety-nine percent of his training in a pool as flat as glass kept my nerves bubbling under the surface. So, when one of the swimmers ripped off his swim cap to reveal a head of curls, I felt both a surge of relief and a little shock. Beck had been among some of the first to reach land. He swam daily, but I hadn't expected him to do that well in his first open-water race.

He got to transition, dripping and breathless. Going straight from swimming to running was incredibly disorienting, so he wavered when he reached to remove the tracker from his ankle. April stopped him and crouched to pull it off instead. I would have helped, but only two relay members could be in transition at a time during the race, so I watched from the gate.

"You had a great time," she said, freeing the Velcro.

Beck hunched forward, hands on his knees as he caught his breath. "I felt something touch my leg as soon as I got in the water," he panted. "It was quite motivating."

"Take your time!" I called. "It's not a race or anything."

"Why are we friends with him?" Beck asked, stepping out of the tracker.

April pulled the band tight against her own ankle. "He gives good massages."

Beck scowled. "We don't do that."

April laughed while yanking her bike off the rack.

"You've got this, Baird!" I yelled. "Break the curse!"

She saluted me, then jogged with her bike to the exit. I didn't take my eyes off her as I took her place in transition. When she was out of view, I realized Beck was staring at me.

"What?"

"You tell me," he said, pushing his wet curls off his forehead. "What's going on between you two?"

"Nothing. How about you get in some dry clothes? You're off duty now."

"Stop changing the subject," he said as he reached around to pull the string on his wetsuit zipper.

"When have you ever known me to kiss and tell?"

"I'm not asking for details, Gabe. Jesus. I just don't think I've ever seen you look at a woman with love eyes before."

"I do not have love eyes."

"You do," he said, peeling the wetsuit down. "And it's okay, you know? You can let yourself be happy."

"I am happy," I said flatly.

"You know what I mean."

"What I know is that you smell like cheap seafood."

He frowned but dropped the conversation. Beck was my closest friend, and there was no denying life had dealt him plenty of shit. I just had a hard time believing he understood the gravity of my situation when he had grown up in a healthy home. He'd had issues with his own dad, but they were vastly different than my experiences.

I stared at the bike entrance archway. We had about three hours before April returned, and I didn't know how I would do anything else besides watch for her.

My mind played all the scenarios that could keep that from happening. She didn't lack power. She'd been so solid in her training. The wind was formidable but nothing she couldn't handle. If she got a flat tire, she could change it, no problem.

The only real concern was another wreck. What were the odds of that happening again? They had to be low. That didn't stop me from thinking of how I'd found her last year, lying on the asphalt.

Quieta como la muerte.

Still as death.

No one else stopped to help her.

How long would it take for someone to help if she wrecked again? The idea made my stomach feel as choppy as the bay.

Chapter 30

APRIL

The wind on the Galveston course was absolute bullshit. Every pedal cycle felt like an uphill battle. But I just kept pumping my legs, moving forward.

I thought of my mom. She'd always been such a fighter. When diagnosed with cancer, she'd stood tall and faced it head-on. I tried to channel her strength, her resilience.

And at the last half of the race, when my spirit was just as tired as my body, I pictured Gabe in a patch of clovers, looking for one with four leaves. It gave me this burst of energy, this lighthearted floating feeling like my tires would take off the ground—a total E.T. and Elliott moment.

I stopped worrying about my curse. I didn't need the universe on my side—Gabe was enough. When I saw the arch, tears blurred my vision. I wiped them with the back of my hand. This was it. I was going to break my Ironman curse.

I dismounted, running for our spot. Gabe, who'd been leaning against the gate talking to Beck, straightened. Then he started jumping and yelling, and my hand had no hope of keeping up with the steady roll of tears. I tried to focus. We were in the middle of a race. I could have my emotional moment after I'd passed off the tracker.

I racked my bike and went to undo the tracker, but Gabe was already on it, bending down to transfer it to his leg.

He straightened, looking race-ready with his bib and running belt. I backed up to let him speed away, but he surprised me by pulling me close. His lips collided with mine, and I dissolved into him. The moment felt like a fireworks show. All bursts of color and light—feelings loud and celebratory.

Gabe pulled away but grabbed my face so I'd look at him when he said, "I'm so proud of you, April."

My insides switched to zero gravity at that point. All my organs floated on Gabe's words.

Proud? Of me?

It wasn't until he was out of transition that I realized my fingers were still on my lips. I lowered them, turning to talk to Beck about the race, but my attention caught on a pair of eyes watching me. Clay's brows furrowed, and all those organs that had been floating around came crashing down.

He'd seen Gabe kiss me.

Clay clipped his race belt, holding my gaze until he finally turned and took off after Gabe. The thought of Gabe getting in trouble and losing out on A-Team was too much to stomach. My legs felt wobbly as I walked over to Beck, but that could have also been the fifty-six-mile ride.

"You okay?" Beck asked.

"Yeah," I said because there was too much to unpack with Beck, even if he was Gabe's buddy. "Let's go get a good spot to watch Gabe finish."

The gates along the red carpet were congested—naturally. And I didn't think we'd find room, but then a family of four packed up just as we arrived, leaving a gap large enough for us to camp out comfortably. I leaned against the railing, ready to people watch for the next hour and a half, when I noticed Trevor. He stood under a tree with Johnson in one hand and his phone in another. The crease between his brows grew deeper and deeper.

"Can you watch my spot?" I asked Beck. Too worried about Trevor, I didn't hear his response as I made my way over to my cousin. By the time I made it through the crowd, Trevor was off the phone, his face in his hand.

"Trevor?"

When his head popped out of his hand, his eyes were red-rimmed.

"What's wrong?" I asked.

"Can you . . . ?" He handed Johnson to me, then lifted his glasses, pressing his fingers to his eyelids.

"That was *Exposure.*"

"And?" I was afraid to hear the answer. I'd pushed him to apply, but only because I couldn't see rejection as a possibility.

"And I got the position," he said, like he couldn't believe the words.

"Trevor!" With Johnson still in my grasp, I wrangled my cousin in for a bear hug. "That's amazing!"

I released him and Trevor nodded, still looking shocked. "I just—How do I leave everything I know? And what about the shop?"

"What about it?" There was no way in hell I was letting him back out of this opportunity. "Billie and I will handle things. You have worked so hard toward this. It's time to cash in."

Trevor nodded, but I could tell he was processing too much to really hear anything. I convinced him to watch the race with us, and I felt lighter than I had in a long time. Sure, I'd miss him, and we would have to find a replacement for the shop asap, but things were finally working out.

One hour and fifteen minutes later, Gabe came barreling down the red carpet. I wouldn't be surprised if beneath his skin were gears, pistons, and jet fuel. That's how powerful—how solid—he looked as he made it across the finish line.

Then he slowed, and I could see the toll the run had taken in how his chest shuddered for fresh breath, the way he leaned his hands on his knees and gulped air. He'd hit it hard, and I wasn't sure why until Beck showed me his phone. "We just got second place for the relays."

"No," I said, grabbing the phone from him. "There's no way." Sure enough, Gabe's time had pushed us over.

"I've never made podium before," I said, laughing.

Beck smiled. "Gabe said as much." We weaved through the crowd to make our way over to the end of the corral where he'd come out. "When he was tracking your bike, he realized we might have a shot if he pushed himself."

I felt pressure behind my eyes.

He just likes to win, I told myself. *He's competitive.* But it felt like more. It felt like he'd done it for me.

Luckily, with Gabe being a giant among men, we spotted him easily in the crowd.

"We did it!" Beck said. "Second place."

Gabe wearily pumped his arms, seemingly too winded for vocal celebration.

"You okay?" I asked, putting a hand on his sweat-soaked back.

"Yeah." But he was still breathing heavily. "I'm fine."

"You didn't have to hit it so hard."

"You inspired me," he said between breaths. The words illuminated me.

Trevor took our picture on the podium. The guys had me stand in the middle—on first place. Beaming on that number one, I realized we hadn't just broken the curse. We'd decimated it.

Gabe wanted to go out and celebrate, but Beck left to bring Emily lunch since she'd had to hurry straight to work after watching him swim. Likewise, Trevor had to return to the shop to help Billie, leaving Gabe and me to meander Ironman Village on our own.

I pointed to the massage tent as we approached. "Should we go in?"

"I think I'm offended," he said.

"What?" I laughed. "Why?"

"*I'm* your massage therapist."

"You're a busy man."

"What are you doing later?"

His deep voice, that spark in his eyes, made me hungrier than the free pizza they were giving athletes. Then logic seeped in. Gabe offering to give me a massage would be work for him, and he'd already pushed himself to the brink. "You're tired after racing, too. The last thing you need is more work."

"I'm fine, April. Look, why don't we both go home, take a shower, maybe a nap. Then you come over to my apartment tonight. I'll take care of you."

I'll take care of you. Were there any words as sweet and seductive as those? "That sounds really nice," I said. "Are you sure?"

"Of course, I'm sure." His dimples were out. "I can't think of anything more important than post-race care." As that smile turned delightfully wicked, my heart skipped a beat.

I don't know when trouble had become so appealing, but at that moment, doing all the wrong things with Gabriel sounded like the perfect way to celebrate a podium finish.

Chapter 31

GABRIEL

I'd tried to rest while waiting for April to come over, I really did. Freshly showered, I lay on my couch. Chuck picked a spot next to me, and I rubbed his back, which usually put me to sleep. At least it sent one of us over. He snored while I stared at the ceiling and thought about April.

How incredible she was: her determination, her strength, her resilience.

Her curves. Her lips.

I pressed the heels of my hands to my eyes. She was going to be the death of me. Luckily, Coach Rick messaged, knocking me loose from April's hold.

Rick: Congratulations on such a quick run.

Coach Rick wasn't quick to praise, so I stared at my phone warily until, sure enough, the second message came through.

Rick: You must really like ice baths, Torres. See you tomorrow.

"Fuck," I said to the ceiling.

That did it. I wasn't going to sleep. Careful not to wake Chuck, I pushed up from the couch. My calves and abs were the most tender. They weren't too bad yet, but tomorrow they would be. Slowly, I moved around the kitchen, marinating chicken and cutting up vegetables.

Anything to keep my hands and mind busy.

When the doorbell rang, I was just finishing the training plans for the next week. Chuck beat me to the door, but he'd have to get in line. My blood hummed as I swung it open for April.

We took a long moment to drink each other in. She had on this black romper that cinched at her waist and stopped mid-thigh. She looked great in it. But I was already imagining peeling it off her.

Similarly, I watched her eyes roam from my legs up to my chest—a savoring perusal. I was just wearing basketball shorts and the finisher shirt from the Sugarland Triathlon, but judging by the blush on her cheeks, she liked what she saw.

Then her hazel eyes slipped past me, and she shook her head laughing. I followed her gaze to the massage table, which was taking up half of my living room.

"I didn't realize how serious you were about the massage thing."

I stepped aside to let her in. "I never joke about post-race care."

"Nice place," April said, eyes roaming over my cozy apartment. There honestly wasn't much to look at. Besides the massage table, I had basic, nondescript furniture. The second bedroom—that I used as an office—had a little more personality, but only because that's where I kept my racing memorabilia. However, I was aware that displaying racing medals and plaques rode a fine line between being impressive and douchey. On the plus side, Chuck and I did manage to keep the place clean. At least we had that going for us.

"Thanks."

I guess Chuck figured he'd been patient long enough because he jumped up on April, paws on her knees, tail going a mile a minute. I started to scold him, but there was no point when she crouched down and cooed, "You are by far the cutest Chuck I've ever laid eyes on." Chuck managed a lick under her chin, eliciting an adorable giggle from April.

I can't keep them, reason warned. I knew the sooner I came to terms with that, the better. But I wasn't ready.

"You okay?" April asked. She stood, but her movements were slow, and she winced ever so slightly.

"I'm fine," I lied. "But I can tell *you* are sore from the race."

"I'm a little stiff," she admitted.

I nodded toward the massage table. "Let's fix that."

"Right now?" she asked, eyeing it warily.

"You'll feel better after," I said, removing her overnight duffle from her arm and placing it on the couch. She scowled, so I said, "No deep tissue. I'll keep it light."

She put her hands on her hips, obviously unconvinced.

I ducked my head to be closer to her level. "No waterboarding or bamboo under the fingernails today. Promise."

The corner of her lip twitched. She tried to subdue it, but then a full smile cracked. "Fine," she said. The smile turned wicked. "Last time I kept my clothes on during the massage. Do you mind if I make myself more comfortable?"

And that's how I knew I was going to be the one tortured today. Right in my own home.

"Be my guest," I said, barely managing to keep my voice even.

Her eyes bounced between mine for a moment before she reached to the back of her neck and pulled a string. The top of her romper fell loose around her collarbone. She held my gaze as her shoulders rolled out of the fabric. The material fell to the cinched part of her waist, stopped by another tie.

Her breasts strained against a lacy black bra. Just above one of the cups, that little silver butterfly charm she wore stuck to one of her voluptuous curves. A piece of jewelry had never looked so good.

Fuck.

I'm not going to survive having my hands on her.

How was I supposed to behave myself when she looked like *that*? I imagined throwing her over my shoulder and taking her to my bedroom—fucking the tension out of us before it ate me whole.

Then I chided myself. She'd feel so much better—enjoy sex so much more if she weren't stiff. I didn't want her to leave my apartment tomorrow in worse shape than she'd come. I invited her over to take care of her, and that's exactly what I would do.

I forced my eyes back to hers and closed the distance between us. I slowly pulled the string at her waist, and her lashes fluttered. The rest of the fabric fell to the floor.

My hands slid down to her hips, and a small moan escaped April. My fingers found a strappy thong, and my dick strained in my shorts, desperate for me to rip the lace off her body and bury myself inside her again.

"These can stay on," I said, my voice sandpaper.

My palms rode her hourglass figure up. "But this—" I traced around her bra straps until I reached the clasps. "Has to go." April shivered as I undid them. Her breasts bounced free, and I salivated at the sight of perfect nipples.

Both previous times with April, we'd been frantic, like two people getting one last lay before the end of the world. Tonight, I'd take my time savoring her—worshipping her.

I backed away from her to lift a corner of the sheet on the massage table. "On the table, Baird. Face down."

She blinked, looking lost in her own lustful haze. Then she gave a slight shake of her head as if to clear it. "Yes, Coach."

At this rate, I'd have to ban the other athletes from calling me Coach. She'd turned it into something so sweetly salacious for me.

With her comfortable under the sheet and my hands oiled, I started on her back. I knew she'd have a lot of tension there, the same with her shoulders and neck. Hours hunched in aero position, holding up a head—made heavier by a helmet—will do that. I'd stretch, smooth, press, and pull until she was all better.

The goosebumps sprouted instantly. Then came the first moan as I swept my hands from shoulders to hips. I eased up.

"That little sound you just made," I said, beginning at her neck again. "It was from pleasure, right? I'm not hurting you?"

"No hurting," she murmured. "I can't believe I'm saying this, but can you add more pressure? Just a little?"

I grinned and pressed deeper with my next pass.

She responded with an, "Oh, Gaaaabriel."

My dick twitched. She wasn't done moaning my name tonight. That much I knew.

I worked her until she was boneless. After I'd eased all the stress from her back, legs, and ass—massaging those curves had taken every ounce of restraint—I moved up to her neck again. I remembered how, back at the hotel, she'd played with my hair. I'd practically had an out-of-body experience. I wanted the same for April.

"April?" I asked quietly, sitting on the table next to her.

"Hmmm?" she murmured in a way that made me wonder if she'd fallen asleep.

I draped her arm over my leg and rubbed circles around her shoulder. My other hand snaked into her hair. My forearm rested along her spine as I rubbed her scalp. "Are you tender-headed?"

"No. Why?" I grabbed a handful of hair and held, giving a gentle tug right at the roots. "Oh!" April froze for half a moment before melting with another moan. I felt all the blood in my body flow to one eager appendage.

When I released her hair, she let out a shuddering sigh.

"That okay?" I asked hoarsely, fingers running along her scalp again.

It sounded like she mumbled, "New kink unlocked," but it was so quiet I couldn't be sure.

"What?" My question released with a huff of a laugh.

"Feels so good."

I chuckled. That's definitely not what I'd heard the first time, but I decided to let it slide, reaching to grab another fistful of hair.

She gasped.

My other hand squeezed and pulled on her bicep. "I love making you feel good," I admitted before releasing my grip.

"Part of the job? Right?"

"No, this is." I blew out a breath, then placed both my thumbs on her neck, applying pressure and sliding them upward into her hairline. She hummed her approval. Her pleasure was my pleasure. I wanted to be her chauffeur to ecstasy every single time. "So different."

I had her flip over, and it was almost too much being able to see the pleasure on her face when I hit just the right spot—her hips, her deltoids, when I gripped her hand while I rubbed down her forearm.

Towards the end, I washed the oil off my hands and pulled a chair so her head was practically in my lap. She melted as I erased the tension from her forehead, cheeks, and jaw.

I placed a hand on her chest and leaned her head against my forearm so I could give her neck another stretch while I massaged the scalp just beyond her temple. The way she relaxed into my arm made my chest pinch.

Hermosa.

She was so beautiful it hurt.

Then her full lips parted, and I couldn't help myself. I raked a hand down her face, watching my thumb catch on that bottom lip.

She opened her eyes slowly.

"I'm obsessed with your lips," I confessed.

"Just my lips?" she asked with a breathless smile.

"No. I'm obsessed with all of you, April." I swiped my thumb down her jaw. "I can't get you out of my head." I brushed my knuckles ever so lightly across her throat. "I think you know this already." I elicited a shiver from April as my fingers skated over her collarbone. "But you torture me in all the best ways."

She blinked up at me, and I wondered if I'd gone too far when she grabbed my face and pulled me down to her. Kissing her upside-down gave me a whole new perspective of her mouth. I let myself enjoy just the press of her lush lips before I slid my tongue from corner to center. She opened, and we were tasting each other. I stood, wanting to have more control, more reach.

That's when she found the waistband to my shorts. She propped up on her elbow, yanking me closer, then stopped, laughing. "Your kid is watching."

"My what?" I whirled to find Chuck sitting up on the couch, tongue lolling out of that smiling mouth, tail wagging.

"Pervert," I tossed over my shoulder to him as I whipped the sheets off April and hiked her up. It was becoming a favorite pastime of mine, feeling her legs around my torso, my fingers pressing into her ass cheeks. Her core against me, right where it belonged.

"Bye, Chuck!" April said, still laughing. She relieved me of my shirt and tossed it right before I shut my bedroom door with my foot.

Moving with purpose, I carried us toward the bed.

"Wait!" April said. Reluctantly, I paused. If I had to wait any longer to be inside her, I thought I'd lose a year off my life.

What would be a legitimate reason not to continue?

Tornado?

There weren't any windows in my closet. We could do it in there.

She felt like she was coming down with something?

I made killer tortilla soup. We could be sick together.

Nuclear war?

All the more reason to get one last fuck in.

The only reason I'd stop was if she wanted me to, which was why I was so relieved when she said, "I'm covered in oil. Couldn't that stain your bedding?"

I laughed. "Fuck the bedding." I tossed her onto my comforter, and she landed with a delighted giggle.

I felt predatory, shucking off the rest of my clothes and heading for the space between April's thighs, but she stopped me with a hand on my chest.

"I don't think so," she said. "On your back."

My jaw worked. That massage had depleted my self-control. I was ready to let desire engulf me, not hand over the reins. But it was April. Her wish was my command.

"Yes, April," I said, using the same tone she did with her, *Yes, Coach.*

Her eyes sparkled as my back sank into the mattress. April knelt next to me and set a hand over my sternum. My heart banged against her palm, and she gave a slight smile. She knew exactly what she did to me.

Her hands slid over my ribs, across my abdomen. I shivered as she went lower and lower. The reward for handing over control came quickly.

"What do you think about when you look at my lips, Coach?"

She wrapped a hand around me, and I short-circuited. I was already hard, of course. I'd pretty much spent the entire fucking massage hard.

"Do you want to know what they'd feel like? Here?" Her mouth hovered over my head.

My brain scrambled for purchase, but every thought was a slippery surface, feeling her breath on me. "April—" Her tongue swirled over the head, and it tore a sound I didn't recognize from me. April's hazel eyes were bright as she lowered her mouth, lips stretching over me.

I threw my head back against the pillow. As she moved up and down, taking me deeper, I forgot how to breathe. That was fine. I didn't need oxygen.

She kissed up the side. When she got back to the top, she paused to say, "Keep breathing for me, Torres." I wanted to retort, but my mind went blank when she put me in her mouth again. I was proficient in two languages, but when April's plump lips were sliding down my dick, my vocabulary dropped to zero.

I could die now. This was the peak of my existence.

She picked up the pace, and I knew an orgasm was on the horizon. April didn't seem like she had any intention of stopping. And, shit, I didn't want her to either. The idea of her sucking me to completion almost sent me over the edge, but I got a hold of it. She felt too far.

"April," I tried, but she kept going. My head rolled against the pillow as I fought for control. I asked her to stop, or at least, I meant to.

She was so mind-numbingly good that I didn't realize I'd spoken Spanish until April paused to say, "¿Qué?" with a playful spark in her hazel eyes.

I placed my fingers under her chin, knowing if she put her mouth back on me, I was a goner. "Get up here," I said, sounding guttural.

She obeyed, crawling on top, but I flipped us over. She let out a surprised little squeal at the sudden shift. Her eyes danced with laughter until I discarded her thong and dropped to my forearms between her thighs.

"Gabriel," she gasped, a hand pushing up her forehead as if just the idea of my mouth on her drove her wild. I knew the feeling, and it was time to return the favor.

I lowered my mouth and devoured her.

Her body immediately tensed—like paper curling in a flame. Her thighs clamped my head, her fingers in my hair.

I didn't let up.

She was delicious.

So incredibly delicious. I thought back to the first time I'd caught a whiff of her scent. How she smelled like some sort of dessert. If only I'd known.

I was intoxicated by not only her taste but those little whimpers she made. How she gasped and squirmed when I sucked just the right spot.

"Gah—" she panted, her legs clamping tighter against my head. "I'm gonna—I'm close."

"I'm aware," I said, kissing the bud before grabbing those legs and spreading her wide. I latched back on and, within a minute, had her arching off the bed, screaming my name.

I absently wondered if the neighbors could hear. I didn't mind. Let the entire world know the intimate, vile things we did together. I couldn't promise her a future, but I selfishly claimed her as wholly mine in the present.

As her body relaxed, I crawled my way up to her, kissing her stomach as I went. With a flushed chest, mussed hair, and rosy cheeks, she was devastatingly—beautifully—spent. I loved that I'd done that to her.

"It's not fair," she panted. "You didn't let me finish you."

I ran my nose along her jaw as I positioned myself at her entrance. "Let's fix that."

Her swollen lips parted, and her eyes rolled as I slowly moved into her. Meanwhile, I palmed different parts of her greedily: her shoulders, her hips, her breasts. She registered every subtle shift, gasping and moaning at the different spots I hit as I pushed into her.

I wasn't sure if I'd be able to make April come again, but I took it slow, trying to give her enough time to recover. It was so hard to keep the pace controlled, but my resolve paid off when April tensed beneath me.

I slid a hand into her hair. What had she said about a new kink? I lightly pulled a handful. She cried out in pleasure and gripped my back, nails digging in. We were both close. I wanted to look her in the eye as she came, but her lids were already closed.

"April." Her name sounded like a beg out of my lips. "Look at me."

Slowly, her lids parted, and her eyes reminded me of the sun cresting a hill—the gold spilling onto green earth. That's when I came undone, and so did she. We clutched each other as we orgasmed. I was pretty sure April was leaving scratch marks on my back, and I was okay with that. More than okay. The pleasure was so intense, so bright, it was like watching a star being born. A nova, right here in my vast, empty galaxy.

After ecstasy released its hold, I collapsed on the bed next to April, listening to our lungs try to find some sense of normalcy. When I felt stable, I looked over at her. She had an arm thrown across her forehead, features completely relaxed.

"That was—" I started.

"Ruinous," she rasped.

I propped myself on an elbow, not sure I loved that description.

She peaked open one eye, still shaded by her elbow. "You've ruined all other sex for me. How am I supposed to ever enjoy myself with another man after that?" Her tone was playful, but the words were serrated.

April with another man?

Pressure swelled in my chest, and it took me a second to clock it as jealousy. I was jealous of simply the idea of another man taking her like I just had—of being able to enter her, grip her hips, listen to her gasp his name, watch her come undone.

But that's what would inevitably happen. We weren't anything close to permanent. Our time together was sand in the wind, and that was my fault. I'd prescribed casual for our relationship, just like all the other relationships I'd had, except none of the other times had felt like this. Just the idea of letting her go barbed.

It was getting harder and harder to ignore the fact that having sex with April was different. I didn't just feel a release or the normal appreciative companionship that came with friends with benefits. I felt connected to her, and that scared me.

"You sure you're okay?" she asked, removing her arm from her eyes.

The question made me realize I was clenching my jaw. I forced myself to relax. I didn't have to worry about saying goodbye tonight. "Yeah. Sorry, I'm always a little out of it after races."

She nodded, and her necklace caught my attention again. The tiny silver butterfly rose and fell with her shallow breaths.

"*Mariposa,*" I said, tracing a finger around the wings. "You wear this a lot."

"My mom used to look for meaning in everything, and butterflies were always a sign of magic to her." April gave a sheepish smile. "And I know it sounds silly to think of an insect as magical, but I like the idea that there's more out there."

I picked up the butterfly, and the silver winked in my palm. I had April Baird naked in my bed. How could I not believe in magic? "That doesn't sound silly at all." I thought of my own mom's culture and beliefs. "Did you know that when the Day of the Dead is celebrated, Monarch butterflies migrate through Mexico? They're often viewed as souls of loved ones stopping by."

"That's—" Her eyes shined. The emotion there was so raw, I almost regretted telling her. That is until she smiled that gorgeous smile of hers. "That's beautiful," she finally managed. "I had no idea."

Her fingers curled around mine over the necklace, and I could have spent the rest of the night there, just like that, enjoying April's warmth. Unfortunately, it was bittersweet, knowing every moment we drew closer to our impending end. For all I knew, this could be the last time I had her in my bed, the last time we held hands. That kiss could have been the final time my lips touched hers.

Just in case, I leaned in, catching her mouth with mine. She sighed into me, and I was frantic, trying to memorize her delectable lips, but I already knew I'd never accurately capture April. Breaking things off with her was going to rip me to shreds.

Chapter 32

GABRIEL

While April showered, I got started on dinner. I had this inexplicable need to take care of her after *taking care of her*. Starting with dinner—it was all cut up. I just had to cook it.

I'd just added the broccoli steamer to the pot when fingers ran up my back. I shivered.

"Sorry," April said, tracing my shoulder blades. "I left a mark."

The girl could fucking brand me for all I cared. That's how crazy I was about her.

But that sentiment didn't quite jive with the casual tone we'd agreed upon. So, instead, I said, "A souvenir to remember a great night."

April laughed and folded herself around my body. I traced her forearm, and she rested her head against my back.

I could get used to this.

The problem was that I couldn't allow myself to.

"Is there anything I can do to help?" she asked, releasing the hug.

"Yeah, actually." I grabbed a glass from the cabinet and filled it with water. "Sit on that stool and drink this." I handed her the cup.

"You know, I have ridden fifty-six miles before," she answered but sat at the bar as instructed.

"As fast as you did today?"

"Okay, you got me there." She drank deeply.

"I've already updated your training plan. A light walk tomorrow, a swim the next day. We'll play it by ear from there. We have the century ride in two weeks and want to be completely healed for that."

"What about you?" she asked. "You hit it hard, too."

"Don't worry," I said with a strained smile. "Coach Rick already has an ice bath with my name on it."

April's eyes widened. "That sounds awful."

I shrugged even though I dreaded the next day. "It's not my idea of a good time, but it works."

"Your coach seems like a hard ass."

"He is. But, I mean, something he's doing is working." I gave a smug smile.

April gestured toward my bare torso. "Clearly."

I winked at her before flipping the chicken. The spices swirled in the air, making my stomach growl. "Were you able to get some rest after the race?"

"I tried, but my mind was busy."

"That's normal," I said. After a particularly hard race, athletes often report playing it over and over again, even after falling asleep.

"I think—" She rubbed her arms absently. "I think we might have a problem."

I put my tongs down, alarmed by the sudden shift in the air. "What's wrong?"

"Clay saw us kissing today."

I released my breath in a relieved laugh. "And . . . ?"

"And . . . aren't you worried he might tell someone? I don't think he's very happy with our team-up."

"You think I give a shit if he tattles on us?"

"I just don't want you to lose A-Team because of me."

"If it makes you feel better, I'll tell the board myself."

"You will?"

"Sure," I said. "I'll email them Monday morning." I mimed typing. "I'm getting some one-on-one cardio with one of my athletes. Is that cool?"

"Gabe—" April said, trying to sound stern, but she fought a smile so I kept going.

"Endurance training has never been so *hard*," I said, trying my best to match the seductive tone of the narrator in her audiobook.

"Gabriel Torres!" April shouted, but then she had to slap a hand over her mouth because she'd laughed so loud. She fanned her rosy cheeks and then downed her water. I reached for the glass to fill it back up, but she waved me away. "Focus on cooking. I can refill my own water."

I smiled to myself as I checked the chicken. However, when it flopped back into the pan, searing grease splashed on my stomach.

I hissed out a breath and backed right into April, knocking the water glass from her hand. It collided against the tile in a deafening shatter.

I braced myself.

Dad's mad again.

"Gabe?" Hands shook my arms, and I found April staring at me, her head cocked. "Gabriel?"

She took a half-step toward the stove, reaching to turn it off, but she was barefoot—we both were—and glass littered the floor.

"Sorry, I—" With one hand, I grabbed April's shoulder, stopping her before she could get a shard in her foot. With the other, I reached to turn off the stove. Then, I lifted her to sit on the counter and tiptoed around the glass to get to my shoes and the broom.

I felt April's eyes as I swept. "Are you okay?" she asked.

"Fine," I said. "It's just a light burn."

She sat quietly for a moment before saying, "You don't like loud noises."

The tips of my ears warmed. I hated that loud noises bothered me so much. It made me feel like the kid crying over thunder or fireworks. "Does anyone like being startled?" I asked defensively.

"Well, no." She paused again. "But it seems like we lose you for a second whenever there's a loud sound."

I let the clinking of glass shards fill the silence as I plotted where I wanted this conversation to go. The easier path was to deflect—come up with an excuse. We could spend the evening weightless, in laughter. Then, I thought of all the times April had been vulnerable with me about her mom, about her fear. It couldn't have been easy, but she'd trusted me with her hurt.

I emptied the dustpan into the trash and leaned against the counter across from April. "When I was a kid, if my dad came home quietly, we'd have a good night. Laughter at the dinner table, Mario Kart on bean bag chairs, bedtime stories, and hugs before sleep. But when he didn't come home quiet—"

It was like a tornado siren. I'd hunker down, cradling myself—hoping just to make it to the other side of the storm.

Already, the conversation felt too raw. The topic was a scraped knee. I didn't want anyone poking or prodding. The urge to slip out before I could further expose the wound was strong, but April watched me with bated breath. She deserved to know why I could never give her a real relationship, to know she was keeping company with a cracked man.

"Sometimes, my dad would announce his homecoming with a door slam. Right away, I knew we were in for a bad night." The memories were a lot, even after so many years. I blew out a long breath through my nose. "It usually started in the kitchen. He'd drink beer after beer, and if he didn't go into a drunken slumber, we could expect shattered plates and glass—maybe a hole in the drywall." I shook my head. "We had so many picture frames, most without any family photos, because my mom just wanted to cover the evidence. Cover for him."

"Gabriel," April whispered. She ducked her head to get me to look at her, but I couldn't. "Did he hurt you?"

"Sometimes." I tipped my head towards the ceiling, wishing I could say the words without summoning the memories. "It was mostly my mom. He'd push her or slam her into the wall. Sometimes, he'd grab her face so tightly, he'd leave finger marks." My stomach roiled. "And for years, I just let it happen. Because I was too scared."

"Gabe." April's voice cracked on my name. I opened my eyes at her touch. She'd reached across the distance. I let her pull me to her.

I rested my forehead against hers, relishing the coolness of her skin. "I should have done something sooner. We both made excuses for him. 'He had a *really* bad day at work,' or 'He's just tired. He does a lot for our family. We should be grateful.' That sort of thing." I lifted my head off hers. As hard as it was to say, I needed her to hear me—needed her to understand.

"One night, though, he had his hands around my mom's throat," I said, voice hoarse. "It finally got me out of the corner." I remembered running on shaking legs for the phone. How the receiver slipped in my sweaty hands. "I tried to call 9-1-1, but my dad pushed me into the coffee table, and I blacked out."

April's eyes, now filling with tears, shot to my scar. "You said you fell," she accused.

"I mean, technically—"

"Gabe," April covered her mouth with her hand as a sob racked her body.

"Please don't cry." I wiped her steadily falling tears with my thumbs. Then I pointed at my scar. "This is one of the best things that ever happened to me."

April's eyes searched mine, her brow scrunched.

"I'm serious. My mom saw me lying there, so still."

Quieta como la muerte.

Still as death.

"She thought I was dead. And all of a sudden, the excuses dried up. My mom pressed charges, and we never went back home after the hospital. We moved cities and started a new life, just the two of us. I don't know what ever happened to my dad, and I don't care. When I turned eighteen, I legally changed my last name to my mom's. It felt like finally cleansing myself of him."

April pulled me to her, burying her face in my chest. Her arms wrapped around my ribs, constricting so tight it was almost hard to breathe. "I can't even imagine the hell you went through," she mumbled. "How old were you when you left?" She lifted her gaze for my answer, and I pushed her hair behind her ears.

"Ten."

"You were just a kid," she said, closing her eyes tight, only for them to pop open in horror. "I called him romantic."

"That's the problem, though, April. He was. And there were times when he'd put me on his shoulders, and I thought I was flying. He'd bring me fishing or to the park to ride our bikes, and I felt like the luckiest kid in the world, but my mom said it best, '*El siente demasiado.*' He feels too much."

I watched my words click into place. "He's the reason you don't do relationships."

I held her gaze. "If I keep my distance, I can manage my emotions."

"Gabriel—" The tears were back. Instead of wiping them away, she grabbed my face. "You deserve love—to be happy."

Just like with Beck, I felt the need to defend myself. I grabbed her wrists. "I am happy."

"It's not your fault your dad was abusive, Gabe. You are a victim." She sniffed. "You are the gentlest person I've ever met. You would never hurt someone."

This is where her argument and everyone else's fell apart.

"Do you think when my dad learned a whole new language for my mom, he imagined slamming her face into the frame of their wedding picture?" April's mouth opened, but I wasn't finished. "Do you think when he held me in his arms for the first time, he pictured shoving me off the porch and breaking my wrist?"

"God, Gabriel." April sobbed.

I wiped away her tears. Then, with a lowered voice, said, "No one dreams of becoming a monster, April."

"People break the cycle all the time."

"I know. I broke the cycle the minute I decided not to have a serious relationship."

"Have you ever hit anyone?" I just looked at her. I knew where this was going, but my answers didn't matter. "Ever pushed someone?" She was satisfied with my silence. "I haven't even heard you raise your voice unless it was to encourage someone."

"You're right. I'm a pretty calm person. But that's easy to do when emotions aren't running high."

"You've been angry before. Have you beat the shit out of anyone because of it?"

"My grandma—my dad's mom—said he'd never had a violent streak before my mom. Love will make you crazy, April. It's just not worth the risk. I can't imagine reaching my breaking point and hurting you because of it."

"Listen to yourself. You can't imagine hurting me because you would never do something like that."

She was probably right, but that little bit of doubt made me hold my ground. It was for the same reason we replace the batteries in our fire alarms when they chirp instead of ripping them out of the ceiling like we all want to. It's not that any of us expect a fire, but it's a precaution. Better safe than sorry.

It had been so easy with women in the past—to call it quits when things started getting heavy. I knew the right thing to do was to stop seeing April. If I'd been a good man, I would have done it long before. If I was a decent man, I'd have done it right there in the kitchen.

I apparently wasn't either of those because I hugged April and rested my head on hers.

Eventually, I'd find the strength to do the right thing, but it wouldn't be that night.

Chapter 33

APRIL

A group of about thirty riders waited outside Just Tri. Bicycles were nearby and loaded with water, electrolytes, and nutrition for a hundred-mile ride. It had been quite the turnout, which was great. There was better visibility for cars in numbers, but my eyes roamed over the crowd, looking for my coach.

We'd spent the last couple of weeks nearly inseparable since our relay. For the most part, it was lighthearted and fun. We trained together and took Chuck on walks. Gabriel taught me a little Spanish here and there and came over on a few of his days off to help replace my half-broken baseboards.

I got a new part in for his bike, and we hung out in my garage while I put it on. Gabe had convinced me to play my current audiobook over the Bluetooth speaker in my garage. My cheeks flamed for about half an hour straight until Gabe turned it off and carried me over his shoulder to the bedroom.

He took me to his favorite food trucks, was bossy about my water intake, and gave me mind-numbingly good massages that were only slightly painful. I was sure I'd never had as much fun with anyone else, but there was this nagging warning in the back of my mind—quiet but repetitive: *This isn't casual anymore.*

I didn't even know when we'd crossed the line of something more, but we had. Or I had, at least. It was like when you back up from your parking space at work after the longest day. Then suddenly, you are pulling into your driveway. You can't remember a single stoplight or detail from the drive. All you know is you're home.

I didn't dare broach the subject with Gabe. After learning his apprehension for relationships was less about personal life preferences and more about protecting others, I felt this urge to help him realize there wasn't anything wrong with him, but it would take baby steps. We'd have to ease into it bit by bit. Still, I was hopeful.

By the time I spotted Gabe in the crowd, he was already weaving his way toward me. The congestion outside the shop delayed our rendezvous. Then Dan, one of his athletes, intercepted him.

About an arm's length from me, I could hear Dan say. "I saw Jamal. I'm going to ride like hell today, Coach."

"Thanks," Gabe said. "Just don't overdo it. The last thing we need is an injury two weeks out from Ironman."

Dan gave a little salute before guiding his bike away.

"Who's Jamal?" I asked, looking in the crowd for a new face.

"He—" Gabe tried to get to me, but as he went to step forward, Ned pulled his bike between us and stopped to chat with another group of riders. "He's on the board for Triple Threat. He lives in North Houston, so we rarely see him here."

"What does him being here mean for you?"

Gabe shrugged. "Officially, nothing. But I'd be lying if I said I don't feel a little bit of pressure to perform today."

I nodded. "Like having a supervisor looking over your shoulder."

Gabe laughed. "Exactly."

"Okay, so what I'm hearing is that Team Torres is burning this century ride to the ground."

"It's okay, April. We can stick to the plan. A hundred miles is a long distance to go all out."

"Okay, so we don't go all out. We just push ourselves a little."

His gaze pulled away from me, landing on Clay, who was guffawing with a man I didn't recognize. "Is that him?" I asked.

Gabe nodded.

"Oh, yeah." I walked around Ned's bike, trying once again to make it to Gabe. "It's happening." I stopped short. The path was blocked by a ladder that had been left out—Trevor was trying to wrap up as much maintenance work as possible before he left. He still hadn't found a replacement to run the shoe section, and he was paying for his guilt by running himself ragged at the shop. Honestly, I was starting to worry about what we'd do after Trevor left, but I'd never tell him that.

Undeterred by the obstruction, Gabe ducked right under the ladder to get to me.

I blanched.

His smile dropped when he looked at my face. "What?"

"You just walked under a ladder."

His eyebrows furrowed before it clicked. "Oh! Shit." He ran a hand through his hair. "Superstitious, right. I forgot that ladders are a thing."

"Work with me, here, Gabe!" My fingers flew to the butterfly on my chest. I needed all the magic I could get. Unfortunately, the curves against my thumb did little to soothe the dread. "How are we supposed to do well when you are collecting bad luck?"

"I'm sorry," he said. "If it makes you feel better, I won't ride with you today."

"You're damn right you won't ride with me." He frowned, but I continued. "You are going to go fast. Stop worrying about being a coach for a second and show off as an athlete."

His frown was still in place. "I was looking forward to riding with you today."

"Me too, but keep your eyes on the prize, Torres. You are so close to A-Team."

He narrowed his eyes, considering. "Fine." He reached over to fix my necklace. As his hand slid the clasp to my back, his deep voice rumbled by my ear. "But you are coming over tonight."

Heat blossomed in my lower belly. "Deal," I answered, breathless before the ride had even begun.

He smirked. "That is, if we make it back after the whole ladder thing." I glared at him, but he kept going. "Who knows? A tsunami could engulf Texas."

I laughed at the ridiculousness of it.

"Or a swarm of locusts could get us," he continued.

"A rogue dust storm could roll in," I added, and somehow, blowing my superstitions out of proportion made them seem silly, small.

Gabe laughed. "Exactly. Anything could happen."

After hours of riding, I was over it. My ass hurt. My head felt like a bowling ball on my shoulders, and my legs were ready for me to pick a new hobby—I wondered if I'd be any good at cross-stitching or maybe knitting.

But I kept going, and I kept fighting the urge to slow down. I thought of all the times and ways Gabe had shown up for me. The least I could do was showcase his coaching abilities by holding my own.

"Rider up!" someone in our group called. I veered to the right to see. Of course, it was Gabe, kneeling in the grass as he checked out a wheel. The universe was cashing in on that bad luck. I thought of Clay somewhere ahead, trading jokes with Jamal, and sighed.

"I'll help him!" I called.

I unclipped from my pedals and pulled over. "What happened?"

Gabe's eyebrows popped up in surprise. "You've been hauling ass. I only just stopped a few minutes ago."

My legs felt like they belonged to a wooden puppet as I knelt. It didn't take long for me to locate the problem. A busted spoke waggled in the wind.

"See! I knew that fucking ladder would get us," I grumbled as I went back to my saddle bag for supplies.

Gabe laughed. "It was a pothole, actually."

I leveled him a look. "Hold the bike still for me," I said before wrapping the loose spoke around a neighbor.

"Anything else you need?" Gabe asked. "I could hold your water bottle over your head so you can drink out of it like a gerbil."

I barked out a laugh. "All I ask is that you avoid any other potholes or *ladders* on the way home." I secured the spoke with a tie-wrap. "We can replace this as soon as we get back to the shop."

"No more holes or bad luck. Got it."

I watched a gust of wind roll through the field, then looked behind us in the direction it had come from. A dark wall of clouds loomed on the horizon. I straightened and dusted my hands on my sweaty tri-suit. "Did you happen to catch the weather today?"

"Fifteen percent chance of rain."

I nodded toward the sky behind him. "That doesn't look like fifteen percent."

Gabe turned. "We'd better get going. We've got what? Twenty more miles to beat that storm?" We both mounted our bikes. Gabe looked over at me. "Well, a busted spoke and a thunderstorm are still better than locusts, right?"

"It's too early to count out locusts," I grumbled.

For forty minutes, we booked it. But at mile ninety, we started feeling drops.

"This is going to get bad," Gabe said. "Let's stop there." He nodded toward a barn that looked to have survived the Great Depression with its waist-high grass and leaning frame. The structure belonged in a horror film.

"Let me get this straight," I panted, wiping my face on my shoulder, trying to get the raindrops off my lashes. "You wouldn't let me ride my bike through a short stretch of woods after Billie's party, but you're okay with chilling in the Texas Chainsaw barn?"

Gabe laughed loud and deep. "I'm surprised you remember anything about that night."

"Just bits and pieces," I admitted.

"You're right. I wouldn't let you wander the woods *alone*. But there are two of us—safety in numbers."

"I think the serial unaliver would just see us as a two-for-one deal."

"Seeing as I walked under a ladder earlier, being hung on a meat hook seems like the next plausible event for us," he deadpanned.

"I pick storm over meat hook."

"Okay, come on. There's a donut shop probably a mile or two down the road. But we're going to have to move fast, okay?"

I nodded and pushed my already-worn legs.

Gabe wasn't the only one to have thought of using the donut shop for shelter. A row of bicycles leaned against the front of the building and wrapped around the side. We picked an open spot toward the back and ran in—even though we were already thoroughly soaked.

The shop owner came from behind the counter with a pair of mismatched towels. "My wife brought a stack of these when I told her we had some wet cyclists in for donuts."

"Thanks, Aaron." Gabe handed one to me as Aaron talked about how much better his lats were feeling after Gabe's massage. I laughed as I toweled off. The guy massaged the whole flippin' town.

Semi-dry, Gabe and I sat in a booth together. I kept having to remind myself that Gabe was my coach here and not my fuck buddy, but when I shivered violently, he put a long arm over my shoulders. "Do you want me to call Trevor to pick you up?" he asked.

"No," I said, teeth chattering. "We have less than ten miles."

"I'd just hate for you to get pneumonia." He cocked his head. "You know, since I stepped under that ladder."

I opened my mouth to say something when Jamal stopped at our booth. I tried to slide out from under Gabe's arm, but he held tight. I thought of our conversation at his apartment about emailing the board. Though I know he didn't actually tell the board we were fucking, this felt like an equivalent. Or, at least, proof that he wasn't worried about Clay telling on us.

"I don't think I've introduced myself," Jamal said, putting out a hand for me to shake. "I'm Jamal Hudson. I work for Triple Threat."

I shook his hand, surprised he wanted to speak to me of all people. "April Baird," I said, but I got the impression he already knew my name.

"Congratulations on your recent Ironman. I heard you made podium."

"Oh." I blushed. "Gabe and Beck are the ones who really carried the team."

Jamal shook his head. "Now, don't go underselling yourself. The bike is the longest stretch, and you held your own." He smiled. "And when one of our athletes does good, it makes the whole team look good. So, thank you."

Gabe's dimples were out. The sight made my heart catch. "Well, I do have a pretty great coach."

Jamal looked delighted. "There's no denying that." He eyed where Gabe's arm draped across my shoulder. "You two stay warm and take it easy on the ride back. Only two weeks before race day."

After Jamal was out of earshot, I turned to Gabe. It felt like the excitement would leap out of my chest, like one of those spring-loaded snakes in a can. "A-Team is totally yours!"

The power could have gone out, and Gabe's smile would have kept the room illuminated. "I told you, April, you are doing an amazing job."

"That's it!" I squirmed out of his arm.

"Where are you going?"

"I have some money in my saddle bag. We're celebrating with donuts."

It was down to a sprinkle when I made it outside. I rounded the corner and nearly ran smack into Clay's chest.

We both backed up. His eyes widened as he looked at me, then they darted away. "Excuse me," he mumbled, stepping around me with red cheeks.

The reaction seemed weird, but I realized I'd probably just narrowly missed him peeing on the side of the building. They had bathrooms inside, but after eighty-odd miles, there'd been a constant line at the door.

Oh, to be a man and not have to wait in a restroom line. I rolled my eyes as I dug out a crumpled five from my saddle bag.

Two donuts later, the rain had stopped entirely. I was stiff but ready to close the distance between me, a hot shower, and Gabe's bed. Just as the group started to take off, an athlete of Gabe's asked him about that week's training plan. Gabe waved me on.

It wasn't like Gabe would have any trouble catching up to me, so I followed the group. We fell into line on the bike lane like a flock of birds. My right shoe snapped easily into my pedal. I shifted my weight to clip into the left side, but my foot found empty space. The world went sideways.

Wind whooshed past my ears, and my stomach flipped with a falling sensation. Colors blurred together until I hit the pavement rolling. Then, it was washed out by white-hot pain.

My back might as well have been tarred to the road. I couldn't move, couldn't even inflate my lungs after the hit. I gasped, trying to gulp for air like a fish on land.

When tires screeched across wet road, all I could do was squeeze my eyes shut and wonder if those were the last sounds my mom heard too.

Chapter 34

GABRIEL

From my spot in the parking lot, not even ten feet away, I had a front-row seat as April went down. I watched her body slam into the asphalt. Watched her bike bounce violently off the ground. Watched her roll into the middle of the road.

I threw my own bike down, already running. The harshness of her fall would have been enough to steal my breath, but then came the scream of rubber as April lay there.

Quieta como la muerte.

Still as death.

I wasn't going to make it to her in time. I'd watch April, the woman I loved, die in front of me.

I love her.

What should have been a beautiful realization hit like a knife to the chest. Her death a twist to the handle.

The car jumped to a halt, and I stopped, too, waiting for the world to fall on top of me.

Then, my brain processed the scene. April's helmet lay three feet away from the car's tire. My eyes kept tracing between her and the car. I'd never appreciated empty space as much as I did at that moment. She hadn't been hit.

I still couldn't move. Couldn't breathe.

Her head rolled, and she bent her knees with a groan.

She's okay.

She's alive.

I gasped for air, stumbling as I ran toward her again.

"April!"

The other cyclists were starting to dismount, but I wove around them, desperate to see her up close, to make sure my eyes weren't playing tricks on me and that she was actually okay.

She unclipped her helmet with another groan, her eyes squeezed shut.

"*¿En dónde te duele?*" I asked, helping to ease her helmet off.

"What?" She blinked through squinted eyes. I worried she'd really hit her head hard until I realized I'd asked "Where does it hurt?" in Spanish.

"Is she okay?" It was the driver, rounding the car to get to us.

A surge of anger rose at the sight of him. He could have killed her. The rage burned. Keeping my knees on the pavement took tremendous effort. I felt this animalistic need to defend April.

But then I exhaled. It hadn't been the driver's fault. It was a freak accident. She was alive *because* he had been paying attention to the road. And most importantly, April wasn't in danger anymore. My anger lessened, but my adrenaline still ran on rabbit legs.

"I'm fine," April leaned onto her side to ease herself into a sitting position. "I went to put my foot on the pedal, but it didn't catch."

I grabbed her elbows to support her. "Take it easy."

Our crowd of cyclists gathered and cars on both sides of the road were stopped now, hazards on.

"Her pedal is missing," someone called. "The screws must have come loose."

"We need to move her to a safer spot," someone else said.

I nodded. Of course. We were still in the middle of the road. My brain felt like it was trying to catch up with my heart, hand on its knees, breathing heavily.

My eyes roamed her body. I didn't want to make any injuries worse. I scanned for any obviously broken bones, any gushing blood, then wondered if she had some sort of internal bleeding we couldn't see.

"April, sweetheart, where are you hurting?" I asked again—this time in English.

"I'm okay, Gabe, really. It was just a bad fall."

I scooped her in my arms, slowly in case the movement woke up pain, but as I carried her to safety, she soundlessly laid her head on my chest.

I tried to convince April to let me call an ambulance, but she declined. And everyone else agreed with her. She'd fallen off her bike, but it had been at a low speed. I reluctantly set her down in the parking lot, making her test out all four limbs. It was decided she had some scrapes, but nothing was broken.

If my brain had been in a logical state, I would have agreed with the group. But my adrenaline was still running the show. She could have died, and my pulse was having the hardest time accepting that she was no longer in danger. Bringing her in and having her checked out seemed like a good way to calm my nerves.

Instead, it was a call to Trevor who came to bring us to the shop. I took it from there, driving April straight to my apartment. We would get some of her things the next day. Right then, I just wanted to bring her home to clean her up, get her in bed, and care for her.

On the drive, I kept her hand in mine, wanting her to know I was there but also needing the reassurance of her touch. The silence in the car was so thick, it was almost loud, and I wondered if she was doing what I was, playing the scene over and over again, thinking of all the fucking things we could have done differently to have avoided it.

We could have stopped at the barn instead of the donut shop.

I should have been at her side when we took off for that final stretch. If I hadn't been talking to my other athlete, maybe she would have fallen into me instead of the street.

I should have walked anywhere else other than under that fucking ladder.

And I'd teased her for being nervous about it. What would that do for her fear of bad luck now? Because hell, I was starting to believe in it.

In my bathroom, I helped her strip down for the shower. When I unzipped her tri-suit, I found a scrape the size of my palm on her ribs. The top layer of skin was gone, leaving an angry, raw wound.

My breath caught, and April tried to smile, but her eyes were shining. "I'm sorry. I know we agreed I was done with wrecks."

"April—" But that's all I could manage. I thought my chest would crack open.

My fingers rose, wanting to do anything to make it better. Then they dropped because there wasn't a goddamn thing I could do.

"I'm okay, Gabe," she said, but her tears threatened to spill over. "It could have been so much worse."

"You don't have to do that," I said, looking over the wound. "Make less of your pain. It's okay to say this sucks."

"Okay," she said with a humorless laugh. "This sucks."

"Does it hurt to breathe?" I asked, gingerly feeling around the ribs that still had skin.

"No, I—" Her breath caught. "That doesn't feel great, though."

"Sorry," I said, easing up. "I just want to make sure you didn't crack a rib."

"This doesn't feel anything like when I broke my collarbone. It's just tender."

That would have to be enough. I couldn't feel the spots that were missing skin, and I wasn't a doctor anyway. I nodded and kissed the top of her head before unbraiding her hair and turning on the shower. She could have taken care of herself, I knew that. But I wanted to. So, I peeled off my own tri-suit and got in with her.

When the spray hit her left side, her breath hissed, and she moved away from the water. I wrapped her in my arms and rubbed her back before murmuring, "We need to clean it."

She didn't resist when I guided her back under the water, but she held her breath, and her body trembled. I winced. Training for long races, it was commonplace to find spots where garments rubbed you the wrong way—left your skin raw. Those burned like hell in the shower, and they were normally just dime-sized wounds. This was a massive patch of missing skin.

"Breathe through it," I softly encouraged.

When she exhaled, a whimper released with it. She bit it down and pressed her forehead into my chest, her fingers clutching my back.

"That's it, almost done," I whispered, laying my head on hers.

"Eres muy fuerte." You are so strong.

When we were both clean, I dried her off, then sat her on the bathroom counter. With just a towel around my waist, I gathered supplies to dress her wounds. It felt like a car battery charged my body, but April looked exhausted on the counter. Her shoulders drooped, and her lids looked heavy. I thought she'd fall asleep right there if I didn't hurry.

I started at the edge of the scrape, barely touching the wound to spread a layer of antibiotic cream.

"Gabe," she said quietly.

"I know," I said, ever-so-gently dabbing some more around the circumference.

"Gabriel," she said, grabbing my wrist.

Her eyes were red-rimmed. I opened my mouth to apologize for hurting her, but what she said next knocked me off guard.

"This doesn't feel casual to me anymore." My hands dropped to her legs. The first aid I was supposed to provide completely forgotten. "And I'm sorry. We agreed to keep our feelings out of it, and I was going to wait to say something . . . but after what just happened—" Her lip trembled. "I don't want to waste time lying to you or myself." She kept her chin high, eyes never leaving mine. "You said you can't give me more, but I can't give you less."

I leaned my forehead against hers, trying to find my bearings in the swirl of emotions in my chest. From that angle, I noticed her tiny silver butterfly was caught on her collarbone instead of hanging on her chest. I straightened it before answering. "Things haven't felt casual to me for weeks now," I said.

She must have read the pain in my voice because she sniffled. "Does that mean we have to stop seeing each other?"

"I can't think of anything I want less." My voice cracked, and I bought time to recover by pushing a strand of wet hair behind her ear. "But I'm feeling a lot, and it scares me."

"Please," she said, and the tears did fall. "Please, can we just try?" The panic was so thick in her voice that it made me want to cry with her. "I'm not ready to stop seeing you."

I wiped her tears with my thumbs. "I'm not going anywhere tonight. Okay?"

And as she laid her head on my chest, I held her tight, wishing I would never have to let her go.

That night, I had a hard time falling asleep. My brain was running the accident into the ground. Over and over, it played. I couldn't make it stop.

Screeching rubber.

April's body hitting the pavement.

Her head so close to the car's tire.

April woke up and must have realized I still hadn't fallen asleep because she ran her fingers over my arm, a light scrape of her nails making circles and patterns until my muscles relaxed.

Eventually, I fell asleep, but when I got up, I couldn't find April.

I padded into the living room. Only it wasn't my apartment, but the living room from my childhood. I surveyed the yellow wallpaper and corduroy couch warily. Then whimpering came from Mom's shelf of angels. I edged forward, confused by the crying, until I rounded the couch and found April there, head on her knees, sobbing.

"April!" I reached for her, but she yanked back from my touch, and that's when I saw the black and blue bruise ringing around her eye. The image made my blood gallop. "What happened?"

I reached for her again, but she backed up into the wall so hard the frames rattled. "Please don't hurt me, Gabe."

"I would never—" I put out a hand to show her I meant no harm, but my knuckles were bloody.

I woke up gasping for air.

"It was just a dream," April murmured, a hand on my back.

I nodded. That's all I could manage after my sprint through hell. I let my head fall into my hands while I focused on the facts.

April is okay.

I'd never hurt her.

She is safe with me.

But is that what Dad had thought? I didn't know. The question kept me up for the rest of the night.

Chapter 35

APRIL

As far as recovery went, Gabe was the best possible nurse. Sure, he was a little fussy about my water intake and changing my bandages often enough, but he made us tortilla soup and always had cut-up fruit and veggies nearby.

He tried to get me to stay home from work, but I didn't have to explain to him that small-business owners rarely got the privilege to call in. After hours at the shop, I came home to him, and we watched a movie marathon with my head in his lap. He lightly stroked my hair while Chuck snored at my feet. It felt awfully domestic for a relationship that was supposed to be casual, and it gave me hope—a window into what could be.

The next day, I risked a look at my bike. It wasn't as banged up as I feared. The frame had some scratches. Other than that, I just needed to replace the lost pedal.

I could have been hit by a car because a few miserable screws had come loose. I wondered how long I'd been riding with the pedal barely hanging on, and it made me feel like a shitty mechanic that I hadn't felt a difference in the ride.

More than anything, the wreck had felt like a warning shot—one last chance to back out of Ironman. The idea made me nauseous, but it also gave me a sort of mad determination to finish what I'd started. I had come so far. This wasn't going to be what stopped me. I was going to complete an Ironman or die trying.

I wasn't the only one affected by the wreck. The dark circles under Gabe's eyes told me that despite going to bed with me at a reasonable hour every night, he wasn't doing much sleeping. Then there was the staring out into space over long periods of time, and the delayed responses—always a beat too late with his reactions.

I knew the feelings were a lot for him. So, I tried my best to create a safe space while he processed. I could be the calm while his mind and heart went to war.

Which is why I tried to talk him out of Clay's party. The last thing he needed was to be bombarded with conversation and questions. However, he had his other athletes to think about. Ironman was only a week out. This would be the last time he'd see most of them before the big day. It's not like he would impart some game-changing wisdom at the party, but it was about morale. That, I understood. So, when we got to the party, I led him to the kitchen, which had Trevor, queso, and fewer people. The only drawback to the location—it's also where the elite crowd was hanging, meaning we were in for a debate about shoes or the aerodynamics of helmets or some other shit that would maybe add or shave off a whopping three minutes from your thirteen hours of racing.

"Why are you here?" I whispered to Trevor as Clay argued very animatedly with Ned. The excess from Clay's sweatshirt flapped as he waved his arms.

"I came for the queso," Trevor answered, dipping his chip into the bowl.

I dipped my own and took a bite of liquid gold. "Mmmm. Mkay. That might be worth this conversation."

"Time will tell," Trevor said, eyeing Clay. "Do you think they would notice if we walked off with the bowl?"

I nearly choked on my chip, and Gabe unscrewed a water bottle cap for me.

"Hey," Trevor said, looking at Gabe. "I'm glad you're here." He dusted his hands on his shirt and stood up straight. "The no-kill shelter has room for Chuck now. So, let me know a day that works for you, and I'll pick him up."

Gabe's chip stopped on the way to his mouth.

Chuck: my big-headed buddy. The one who snored and gave too many slobbery kisses and looked like he was smiling when he panted. No. There was no way he was going to a shelter, no-kill or not. I started to say I'd take him, but Gabe beat me to it.

"I'm sorry. I should have said something sooner, but I'm keeping Chuck."

That moment when the sun breaks through the clouds after a storm—that's how my heart felt.

Trevor smiled. "No need to apologize. I'm glad he found a home with a good guy."

Those words might have seemed simple enough to someone else, but I watched the impact on Gabe. Maybe if enough people told him, he'd start to believe it.

Trevor's attention flicked between Clay and Ned, who had moved onto the topic of shoes. "They really will argue to the death over any topic."

"Trevor, don't—"

But he was already joining the debate about the latest model of Hokas. I wasn't going to survive the conversation without a buzz. "I need a beer."

Gabe obliged, pulling options from the ice chest for me. Corona won. "It's not a twist off."

"Clay, where is a bottle opener?" I asked, not caring that I interrupted their argument.

His eyes roamed over the counter. "Someone must have grabbed the one I had out." He pointed to a drawer across the kitchen. "There should be one in there," he said before diving back into the argument.

I crossed the kitchen and checked the drawer Clay had pointed to. It was full of silverware, but no bottle opener was in sight. The next was Clay's junk drawer. I started to close it, but something caught my eye—a random bike pedal.

I lifted it for inspection. Clay didn't use that brand on his bike, but I did. I had the pedal's twin at home. The hammering of my pulse drowned out the rest of the party.

A hand on my shoulder made me look up. Gabe's eyes locked onto the pedal. He plucked it from my hand, eyebrows furrowed. I could see the gears already spinning—dots connecting.

"I—" I covered my mouth with my hand as I recounted what happened right before my wreck. "At the donut shop. Clay had been by my bike. While we were inside." Suddenly, the embarrassment on Clay's face made perfect sense. He *had* almost been caught—but not peeing on the building. He'd tampered with my bike.

I watched the information click in Gabe, but instead of a lightbulb turning on, it was like one shutting off.

"Gabriel?" I asked, my chest heaving.

I watched his jaw work, watched him struggle to keep his emotions in check. Finally, he pivoted.

"Gabe, wait!"

"It's fine," he said. "We're just going to talk." His voice was a forced calm. The anger thrashed beneath though, like a jungle cat restrained by ropes.

The guys were still arguing over shoes when Gabe tossed the pedal on the island. It slid across the granite until it stopped in front of Clay.

"Why do you have that?" The question hadn't been asked in an accusatory manner, but I noticed the way Gabe stood ramrod straight, how his eyes lasered into Clay.

Clay's eyes fell on the pedal and widened. "I—That—" His face grew redder by the second.

"Why do you have April's pedal?" Gabe repeated, his voice deadly quiet.

"I found it at the donut shop," he said, trying to sound casual but missing the target by a mile.

"Then why didn't you try to return it? Everyone on that ride knew she was missing a pedal."

"I was going to. I just hadn't had the chance—"

"I don't believe you," Gabe said, his voice louder.

"Everything has just been so busy with Ironman coming—"

"Bullshit!" Gabe yelled.

The room stopped moving. I swear the entire party held a collective breath. Clay swallowed before murmuring, "I never expected her to get hurt."

Gabe's throat made a choking noise. I put a hand on his arm, but honestly, I was having a hard time staying grounded myself.

"Wait," Trevor said, giving a humorless laugh like he was pretty sure he knew exactly what was going on, but that couldn't be right. He *had* to have missed something. "Are you saying you messed with her bike?"

"She's a mechanic. I thought it would be a silly little inconvenience," Clay said, his voice climbing higher and higher.

"What was your end goal?" Trevor asked. "Delay a ride? Or wreck her bike?"

"No! That's not what—"

"Because if you fucked up her bike enough, she couldn't race with it, right? So, A-Team would be yours."

"No!" Clay tried to laugh, but it was strained. "You are reading too much into things. It was supposed to be funny."

"She could have died," Gabe said, his tone venomous.

"I didn't think she was going to roll out in front of traffic!"

Gabe growled something quiet in Spanish before switching back to English. "It's obvious you weren't thinking!"

There was a charge in the air, so I tried to intervene—to snuff it out before it grew into something that couldn't be controlled.

"Hey, hey! Okay." I stood in front of Gabe, wishing for once he wasn't so tall, so I could block his view of Clay. But I wasn't, so I opted for a hand on his chest. Gabe's jaw was set, and he looked ready to lay hands on Clay. There would be no coming back from that. Gabe would become the monster he'd always feared. I would lose him.

"Gabe, look at me." It took a moment for him to process my request, and when he finally did, his eyes were still wide. "I want to go home. Can you please take me home?" A muscle in his jaw ticked, but his features softened, if only by a little.

He looked back at Clay, but he was at least calmer when he said, "You don't deserve to be a coach."

He took my hand, and relief washed over me with each step we took from Clay.

Chapter 36

GABRIEL

It would have been hard to walk away from Clay if April hadn't taken my hand. My adrenaline was still running the show, and it said Clay was a threat. I decided to listen to April instead.

Then Clay had to open his big fucking mouth.

"At least I don't sleep with my athletes."

I stopped. The blood in my veins ran cold.

If it was just disrespect towards me, I probably could have stomached it but openly discussing something we (April included) privately indulged in—it felt like a bell tower had rung in my ear. More than that, his voice dripped with malice.

He'd messed with her bike, knowing she could get hurt, because he couldn't stand the idea of her doing well without him.

Flashes of the wreck were back.

Screeching tires.

April on the ground.

Her helmet three feet from the car's front tire.

Quieta como la muerte.

Still as death.

The sight of her wounds.

The sound of her whimpering in the shower as the water licked raw skin.

He'd caused it all because he was petty. She could have died over his hubris.

"Although, if I'd known that was all she needed, I would have fucked the inspiration into her a long time ago."

The last bit of my resolve cracked in half.

I let go of April's hand and pivoted, throwing my weight forward. Clay's nose crunched under my knuckles as my fist connected with the middle of his face.

He stumbled backward, one hand scrambling for something to keep him upright, the other trying to staunch blood flow. It didn't work, rivulets trickled between his fingers and rolled down the back of his hand—dripping onto the front of that fucking sweatshirt he was always wearing.

"Fuck, man!" Clay's fingers ran up the ridge. "You broke my nose!" His eyes were huge from shock and fear.

He had every right to be afraid. I was just getting started. My hand ached from the blow, but I shook it out, ready to deliver another. Then, arms wrapped around my middle. The strength in the hold didn't stop me, but the voice did.

"Stop!" April pleaded. She tugged, but I didn't immediately give in, too locked onto Clay. "Gabe, please." Her voice shook, and that was enough to pull me through the fog.

She was scared. I was scaring her.

The realization was like a splash of water on my face. It woke me up, and I relented. I let her guide me to the front door. On the way, I noticed the same apprehensive look on everyone's face. I was no longer the person who gave nutrition advice or stretch routines but a wild animal.

Once we stepped into the cool night air, I slid my hand from hers. Afraid the beast would be back any second. She reached for me, but I backed up. "Don't," I said. She looked hurt, so I added, "Please, I just need a minute. I—" What? I didn't even know.

April kept her hands to her sides, but it looked like a battle. "Are you okay?" she asked, voice still shaking.

"Yeah," I said, but my voice shook, too. "I'm not the one who has a broken nose, though." I ran both hands through my hair, then raked them down to my jaw. My adrenaline was wearing off, and my brain prickled to awareness. "I didn't even think about it. I just hit him."

"Come on, let's get you home. We should ice your hand."

I inspected it. Sure enough, the skin had broken over my knuckles. "I hit him," I said again, still trying to make sense of what happened.

"It's okay. Everyone gets angry, Gabe."

"No. Not this angry. I don't get this angry. I don't even know who that was back there." My chest ached. I knew where this was headed. I'd known the entire time that we wouldn't have a happy ending. "This is why I don't let things get serious. I feel too much, April. I feel too much with you."

"You've been under a lot of stress." She was already making excuses for my behavior. Just like my mom used to do for Dad. This is how things started. I hadn't ended the cycle like I'd hoped; I only delayed it.

How long would it take before April was on the other side of my fist? The thought made me sick. April's hand landed on my arm, and I flinched, stepping away so quickly that I nearly tripped over my own feet.

"Come on. Let's get home." She sounded panicked. "You'll feel better after some rest."

"I told you I couldn't do more than casual," I said because I warned her this would happen. I tried to prevent this. I really did. "I should have ended things a long time ago."

April swayed on the sidewalk but let me walk alone to my truck. She didn't say anything until I opened the door. "Don't do this," she begged. Seeing those tears—you'd think someone used my chest to snuff out a cigarette.

"I don't want to hurt you," I said, choking on the words.

I closed the door, but I still heard her plea, "Then don't leave." As I started the ignition, I knew that picture would haunt me for years to come—just like her wreck would. I'd close my eyes at night and see her standing alone, an orange glow from the streetlamp illuminating the path of tears rolling down her cheeks.

You deserve better, April. You'll find better. I put the truck in drive, and as her silhouette grew smaller in my rearview mirror, the promise of a better future for her was the only thing that kept my foot on the gas.

Chapter 37

APRIL

I tried calling Gabe and talking sense into him, but it went straight to voicemail. I sent twelve texts, but he left them all unread. He'd made up his mind, decided he was dangerous—Gabe who took in strays and spent his career mending and encouraging. All because he'd hurt the man who'd hurt me.

A part of me thought he needed space—that he'd be fine if I allowed him time to process. So, I was patient . . . for maybe eighteen hours. By lunch, I made myself try to eat some leftover pasta. I had the first bite of cold ravioli halfway to my mouth when I remembered Gabe's comment at the food truck park about me eating cold spaghetti.

And suddenly, I wasn't in my living room but standing outside on a breezy evening while Gabe brushed sugar off my lips.

The fork clattered back onto the container, my lip trembling as I worked to hold back the emotion. I didn't want the crying to start—afraid grief would swallow me whole like it had when Mom died.

"Screw this!" I said, tossing the container on the counter. I wouldn't grieve him. He wasn't dead. I hadn't lost him indefinitely. He was hurt—stuck in his past, afraid it would dictate his future, but he didn't have to navigate it alone. Once the decision was made, it was a fight to walk to my Subaru instead of run.

Then I was at his apartment. Knocking and knocking and knocking. Chuck's muffled barks sounded on the other side of the door, but they quieted down to whining when I started talking.

"Come on, Gabe!" I pounded. "I know you're in there! I saw your truck in the parking lot. I need to talk to you!"

Desperation made my heart feel like it was in the claws of a hawk. "Please! You don't have to do this!" Frantic tears made hot paths down my cheeks. "You just made a mistake! You'd never hurt me. Do you hear me?" I yelled. "You'd never hurt me!" I rested my forehead against the door. "You deserve love." Big sobs shook my body, so heavy they made my knees weak. I didn't stop until a door down the hall opened. I might not have cared if the elderly woman didn't look so frightened by me.

"Sorry," I said and worked to wipe my face clean from the tears because I realized I was the very picture of a hysterical ex-girlfriend.

Then I sobered completely.

I wasn't just the picture of one. That's what I was.

He told me from the beginning he didn't do casual. I fell for him anyway. Now he'd ghosted me, and I was banging on his apartment door. Who knew if he was even there? He could have been out on a ride or a run. I could have been yelling at an apartment with only Chuck inside.

I wiped my eyes once more, sniffling loudly as I tried to fix my face. "Sorry," I mumbled again to the lady down the hall before walking away.

Despite everyone's warnings, I'd fallen in love. Now, I had to live with the consequences.

Chapter 38

GABRIEL

My skin stretched painfully over busted knuckles as I buttoned my dress shirt for Beck and Emily's engagement party, but that was the least of my concerns.

My phone had spent the morning vibrating with texts and calls from April before I finally shut it off. I could stay away from her if it meant keeping her safe. Eventually, she'd get the hint, and she'd moved on.

But as my fingers fumbled with a button at my chest, the knocking started. Chuck jumped up from his bed in the corner of my room, barking ferociously. That is until April spoke. Then, his tail started going, and he whimpered at the door—eager for me to open it wide so he could see his favorite girl.

I wanted to so badly—to throw open the door and pull her through. To put my face in the crook of her neck and breathe her in as I held on for dear life, but I couldn't do that. Not when my anger had taken over the night before. I couldn't guarantee her safety with me, so I couldn't have her.

"Come on, Gabe!" she yelled. "I know you're in there! I saw your truck in the parking lot."

I'm a coward, I thought, leaning against the wall. A better man would have opened the door—told her to leave, but I knew I'd take one look into her hazel eyes, and it would be over for me. So, I just leaned my head against the wall, gritting my teeth to keep from saying something.

"I need to talk to you!" The stress in her voice broke my heart. "Please! You don't have to do this!" I squeezed my eyes tight, willing her to leave before I caved. "You just made a mistake! You'd never hurt me. Do you hear me? You'd never hurt me!"

She started crying, and I rolled over, resting my forehead against the door while she sobbed.

Letting her cry, knowing she was hurting, I almost couldn't stand it. But then I thought of my mom's tears when my dad pushed her into our kitchen table—her scream when he grabbed her face while he yelled at her. That would never be April. I'd make sure of it.

I held my ground, and when she finally left, I seeped to the floor, feeling like my bones had been replaced with rubber.

I tried to tell myself that things would feel better. I just needed to give it time. The breakup was still fresh. We'd both move on. We'd both find peace.

Despite my internal encouragement, I had this sick feeling in the pit of my stomach. This didn't feel like a clean break but a cataclysmic shift. Neither of us would be the same after.

I put my head in my hands. Emotionally wrecked and exhausted, I just wanted to go back to bed, pull the covers over my face, and let my heart corrode in my chest. That wasn't an option, though, because I had an engagement to witness. The punishment seemed cruel—watching two people who were madly in love promise to be married—but it was Beck and Emily, my favorite couple.

So, I left my heart on my doormat, fixed my face, and headed for The Atteridge.

From my spot on a hotel balcony, I watched Trevor crouch into position behind a sparse bush. I'd forgotten all about him agreeing to take pictures of the engagement. The site of him brought a fresh wave of what could have been.

I imagined pressing April in close, wrapping her in my arms when the October breeze picked up. We would have plucked Hors D'oeuvres off passing silver platters and laughed about the ridiculousness of an engagement party being more extravagant than most weddings. Instead, I stood beside Beck and Emily's sisters—Victoria and Hailey—who linked arms in eager anticipation.

"Here they come!" Hailey squealed. Then she quieted down, probably remembering Beck's threat to withhold wedding invitations to anyone who Emily spotted before she'd made a decision. He didn't want her to feel peer-pressured into saying yes. "I see Beck's curls!" she whisper-shouted.

Sure enough, there they were, walking hand-in-hand down the waterway. Emily chatted away, clueless to the audience that took up an entire side of the Atteridge. Friends and family occupied several balconies, giving us all a bird's eye view of the proposal.

"I hope our nieces and nephews have Beck's hair," Hailey said.

"No way," Victoria said, reaching out to touch the red hair Hailey had, identical to Emily's. "We're getting redhead babies."

I think on a normal day, I would have rolled my eyes. Emily and Beck weren't even engaged, and these two were already talking about becoming aunts.

Unfortunately, this wasn't a normal day for me. I was happy for Beck and Emily—truly—but I was also insanely jealous. I'd known for years that becoming a dad would never be an option, but suddenly, that fact felt like a terminal diagnosis. April had started opening doors, showing me new paths, and I'd wanted to go down every single one with her—journey the miles together.

Then I'd ruined everything. So instead, I'd have to settle with watching Beck and Emily and the thousands of possibilities their future held. It was like staring directly into the sun—so bright it hurt.

When they got closer to our spot on the waterway, they stopped to look at each other, and Beck pushed Emily's hair behind her ears. They were too far below to hear, but he was saying something to her. She threw her head back and laughed, giving him a light shove before he pulled her back toward him. Then his expression turned serious. Her features softened as he spoke. The look they shared felt almost too intimate. I wondered what Beck was thinking about as his eyes searched hers. Was he remembering a secret moment between the two, admiring her beauty, thinking about how much he adored her? Those had been frequent thoughts when I'd looked at April.

I was able to pull out of my funk for just a second and appreciate the gravity of the moment. I'd given Beck a lot of shit about being nervous, but just waiting for the question to land felt huge.

Beck's hand shook as he reached for the box in his back pocket. When his knee hit the ground, Emily was already crying, a hand over her mouth.

It was easy to read the question on his lips.

"Will you marry me?"

Emily didn't keep him in suspense for long. She nodded vigorously. The balconies erupted in thunderous applause and cheering. Emily gasped, then laughed as her eyes roamed over the hotel.

My best friend, ever calm and cool, had tears in his eyes as he bellowed, "She said yes!" Then he dipped his bride-to-be and kissed her like the future was theirs for the taking.

The engagement party, which immediately followed, was every bit as extravagant as you'd expect from people who owned a hotel chain. The average participant might think they'd save some fanfare for the vows, but I'd been to an Atteridge wedding before and knew it was a whole other level of class.

I got the feeling Victoria had planned the party—or her people had—her elegant taste apparent in the low lighting and jazz, the option for guests to hang out in the ballroom or the rooftop, champagne flutes stacked in a pyramid. I wished I drank. Maybe that would have made the evening a little more manageable.

Beck, who'd been socializing in that charming way of his, stopped by my spot overlooking the waterway. He handed me a water bottle. "Thanks," I said. "Where is your fiancée?" He smiled wide at the new title and nodded back towards a huddle by the bar.

My bunk buddy from Costa Rica—Koontz—told a very animated story to Victoria, Emily, and Hailey. They all laughed at whatever Koontz was saying, even Victoria, who promptly pressed her lips back into a flat line as though remembering she was above Koontz's antics.

"Congratulations, man. I'm really happy for you," I said, and I meant every word, even with my miserable circumstances.

"It's hard to believe we're old enough for things like marriage," Beck said with a laugh.

"Yeah." I gave a short laugh in return. The years since high school graduation had been swallowed whole.

I eyed the waterway. In one week, that's where the swim for the Ironman would take place, and part of the run would trace along it. I'd been excited to see what April could do, but now I couldn't be there for her. If I hadn't gotten tangled up in her—physically and emotionally—I could have taken part in her big day and made sure she had everything she needed. Instead, I could only hope my guidance over the past three months would hold. Luckily, this close to race day, there weren't even any training plans left to give. It was time to taper: eat carbs, drink water, and rest.

"You okay?" Beck asked.

Shit.

As the night wore on, the fake smile had slipped. "Yeah. Sorry—just tired. I don't mean to be a downer on your big day."

Beck rolled his beer in his hand before finally asking, "Did something happen between you and April?" If it had been anyone but Beck, I might have been surprised at how quickly he'd come to that conclusion.

"Just—" I sighed. "Things were getting serious, and I don't do that." I shrugged as if it didn't feel like my heart had been run over by a semi.

"I'm sorry," Beck said. I kept my eyes on the lights reflected in the waterway, but I could feel his eyes on my face, downloading all the information he needed. "I thought April might be . . . different for you."

I could have ended the conversation there. Shut it down with a, *No, man. We were just messing around*, clapped him on the back and let him enjoy the rest of his party. That's what he deserved, but fuck, I needed someone to talk to. So I surprised myself by being honest.

"She was."

Beck was quiet for a long moment before asking, "What happened?"

Where to even start? The events of the past couple of weeks ran through my mind. I steadied my breath, realizing I hadn't yet had to say the words out loud.

"We were going on a ride, and April lost control of her bike. She fell into oncoming traffic." Beck froze. Whatever he'd expected from my story, this wasn't it. "The car stopped in time, but—" I closed my eyes. The picture of her helmet, an arm's length from the tire, was still so vivid. "I haven't felt the same since."

When I opened my eyes, Beck was just watching, waiting for me to say more, so I did. "Come to find out, her accident wasn't truly an accident. Her former coach is my rival for A-Team, and he's not exactly happy with the progress she's made this season." I tipped my head back, looking at the few stars visible this close to Houston. "He admitted to messing with her bike." Just talking about it made my pulse pick up. "Then he—"

"At least I don't sleep with my athletes."

"Although, if I'd known that was all she needed, I would have fucked the inspiration into her a long time ago."

I couldn't repeat Clay's words with an even voice, so I landed on, "He disrespected her in a room full of people." I pulled my hand out of my pocket. I'd had it hidden there all evening, but now I turned my wrist to allow Beck a good look. The suggestion of bloodied knuckles sat beneath the wrapping. "So, I broke his fucking nose."

Beck's eyebrows hiked. He opened his mouth and then closed it. Normally, I'd revel in the ability to stun Beckett to silence, but now it just highlighted how messed up the situation was.

"You can say it." I scoffed. "I lost my shit."

"You made a mistake," he corrected. "Depending on who you ask. If someone did that to Emily—" He shook his head and took a long pull of his beer. He swallowed, then straightened as realization dawned. "That's why you broke up with April? Because you hit him?" He sounded almost disappointed.

"I can't put her in danger." Why couldn't he see that? I realized I'd hoped for a little chastisement over punching Clay. It would have validated my decision to break up with April. When Beck didn't offer it, I reminded him why I was so hellbent on this issue. "I won't turn into my dad."

"Gabe, cut yourself some slack." He leaned against the railing, staring out at the waterway. "Trauma literally alters your brain chemistry. You said you haven't felt the same since April's wreck. In a messed-up sort of way, that's normal." He may have been an entitled rich kid, but he could write a textbook on grief and trauma, so he had my attention. "You think you're fucked up? Well, you're right, but it's not because of your genetics or your past. It's because you're human. We're all broken."

I didn't say anything as I chewed on those words. They were bitter at first, but there was something in the center of them. The camaraderie of human existence—of us all being in the thick of it—held hope. We were all damaged, but we weren't alone.

"I'm emailing you my therapist's details." He tipped his beer bottle toward me. "Not because I think you have some sort of anger problem or because I think you're a danger to society, but because I know you have unresolved shit to work through."

"Thanks," I said. I might not trust myself enough to be with April, but maybe I could work on myself for me.

"Beck!" Koontz bellowed, snapping our attention over to the bar. "She's lying, right? You didn't steal her promotion."

I'd nearly forgotten about the party, but Emily smiled smugly, hands on her hips. She looked like she was daring Beck to argue. Beck gave me a playfully miserable look. "She always makes me out to be the villain in our story."

"By telling the events exactly as they occurred?" I asked, thankful for the distraction from our dismal conversation.

"Hey! I thought you were on my side," Beck said before sipping his beer.

"I don't know what gave you that impression, but you should go tell your version anyway."

He gave me a long look. "You sure?" He was worried about me, but tonight, he had a future bride to celebrate.

"Yep. I'm going to call it a night, but congratulations again." I stuck out my uninjured hand, and we shook.

"Thanks, man."

"And Emily!" I yelled. "Don't forget the part where he got upset over a wet shirt!" Emily dissolved into giggles, and I ruffled Beck's curls before heading for the elevator. "That's my favorite part."

As the elevator closed behind me, I saw Beck heading towards the group, trying to put out the flames. "Don't listen to them. That is *not* what happened!"

And I had this pang, once again, wishing April had been there—that the night before had gone differently so all our future nights could have gone differently.

Chapter 39

APRIL

The waiting game was my least favorite on the planet. I remembered it all too well when my mom first got her cancer diagnosis. We held our breaths between doctor's visits and test results. This felt eerily similar, but if my mom's journey had taught me anything, being idle equaled misery. The trick was to keep moving.

When my hands were busy adjusting gears, checking tire pressure, or lubricating chains, my heart didn't seem to hurt as much. If I could just keep going, I'd be okay.

At home, I did the same. Working myself to complete exhaustion. My fingers were covered with nicks and shallow scratches because I rushed through projects, trying to stay one step in front of my bleeding heart. I didn't allow my mind to stop and check on the weeping organ in my chest. I kept an audiobook blasting in my eardrums at all waking hours—though I'd had to switch genres, mid-book, dropping romance for a graphic murder mystery. I needed something disturbing enough to hold my attention away from the train wreck that was my life.

It worked.

Sort of.

It worked until, finally, I'd climb into bed, loose-limbed and depleted. I'd lie there, willing sleep to have mercy and drag me under, but it never let me off that easily. Inevitably, I'd think of Gabe. The breakup, yes. The look in his eyes when he backed away from me, of course. Then there were all the painfully beautiful moments we had together—those stung.

But mostly, I cried because Gabe was afraid of love, and how could he not be when the man who was supposed to care for him had made him bleed—broken his bones in acts of rage? I ached to think of him as that scared little boy. I hated that we lived in such a cruel world, where children were broken, and cancer diagnoses existed, and moms died in car accidents.

I'd been wrong. The universe wasn't out to get me. It was out to get everyone. We were all hanging on by a fucking thread, weren't we?

Somewhere along the way, my pain turned to anger. I knew he was hurting, but so was I, and it didn't have to be this way. He'd made me feel like I was different for him, but he didn't trust me enough to let me in. It felt like rejection. It felt like I hadn't been enough for him.

I was angry—not because we'd slept together—but because he'd held me after, made me warm meals, told me stories of butterflies. I was angry because he'd looked into my eyes like he was seeing a window into my soul. I was angry because he let me believe we were something more.

Maybe I clung to the anger because it seemed better than the hurt.

Even still, I cried every night. Then I'd wake up hollow with my aching ribs and swollen eyelids, wishing I lived in a cave halfway up a treacherous mountain so I could grieve in peace, but that's not how life works. The world keeps spinning, no matter how off-kilter everything seems.

So, I did what everyone who is going through a mental breakdown but still needs an income to live does: I lined up the seams of my cracked heart the best I could and wrapped that shit in masking tape. It wasn't pretty, but it would have to do.

With nearly our town's entire triathlon community at Clay's party, our relationship and breakup had become a glass house. Having everyone tiptoe around me should have been awkward, but I was too grateful for the space to care.

Trevor and Billie worried over me in their own way, heating up my lunches, cleaning the bicycles before they reached my workbench, and taking calls so I wouldn't have to. Both had tried to broach the breakup, but I wasn't ready for that conversation and always found a way to slip out of it.

All things considered, I kept my composure at the shop. I mean, everyone knew I was sad, but I could have joined Johnson under my workbench and cried myself into a tighter and tighter fetal position until I just ceased to exist. But I didn't, and that deserved a gold star, in my opinion.

As the days passed, I stayed a little later each night at the shop, dreading those evening crying marathons. Trevor, I noticed, had been staying longer as well. He still hadn't found a replacement to man the running portion of the shop. The stress was eating at him. It probably would have gotten to me too if the breakup had left any crumbs.

By the middle of the week, Billie was sick of it.

"Come on," she said as I lifted the next bike onto my stand. "You are not working on another one. I allowed this staying-late bullshit earlier this week because you had all those tune-ups before Ironman, but those have been completed and picked up. The big race is in a few days. You need to focus on you. Go home."

I looked at the time. I'd finished working on the Schwinn the night before, which meant I'd have hours of open time. The evening stretched before me like a desert—far as the eye could see.

"Just one more," I said, tightening the clamp.

"No. Not one more. You need rest."

"I'll get plenty of rest," I said, "after this one." I plucked an Allen wrench from the wall.

"Give me the thing," she said, hand outstretched.

I looked down at the Allen wrench. "The thing?"

"Yes." She sniffed. "The tool."

"Tell me what it's called, and I'll stop."

"April Eloise, give me that fucking screwdriver right now!"

"Oof, the middle name is correct, but this isn't a screwdriver," I said, sidestepping her to get to the bike, but she caught my arm. She tried to yank it from me, I twisted, and she wrestled me into some sort of bear hug pretzel. She was surprisingly strong for someone who considered laughing at reels as her cardio. "Get off." I huffed.

"You are being so immature," she panted. I felt the wrench wriggle in my grasp as she got hold of it. "Let go!"

It slipped from my palm, but I'd held so tightly that Billie knocked into the wall, rattling it. A crash behind the counter made us both freeze with an *oops* face.

"What the hell is going on out here?" Trevor asked, emerging from the back.

"Nothing," I said, then looked at Billie. "You okay?"

She waved off my concern, and we joined Trevor to see what had fallen off the wall. I didn't have to round the counter to know. I looked at the place where the framed picture of my mom and me used to hang and felt a wash of guilt and loss.

Trevor went to get a broom, but I couldn't wait. I dodged the larger shards of glass and made my way to the frame. Small bits of glass crunched under my sneakers. Careful not to cut my fingers, I turned over the frame and undid the latch to remove the picture. When I did, a folded piece of notebook paper popped free.

I blinked at it for several moments before my curiosity took over. I placed the broken frame on the counter to unfold it. The slant of the letters made my stomach swirl before I even saw the signature.

"What is it?" Billie asked.

"A note." I swallowed. "From my mom."

And not just any note, but a letter—to me.

My dearest April,

The number one rule to completing an Ironman is to remember your "why?" If you can't remember why you started, you'll never finish. You are my why for everything. Why I get out of bed in the morning, why I work so hard at the shop, why I can't find my favorite sweater . . .

So, naturally, you are all I thought about during the Ironman, and it's also why you are all I can think about today after my cancer diagnosis.

I never knew the number three could be so scary, but put it between stage and cancer, and it's, well, it has me thinking about a lot.

I know I'm going to need all the strength to pull through this, so I'm remembering my why: you—my baby girl, grown into a beautiful young woman who is funny and caring and falls asleep every night with a book on her chest. I don't know how we got here. It's my fault for blinking, I suppose. But when I think about you and this time I've had being a part of your life, I don't feel

anything but lucky. Even with the cancer, April, I'm the luckiest woman in the world because I get to be your mom.

I don't know if you'll ever see this. Who knows, maybe I'll make it to the other side of cancer, and you'll find this sorting through the shop after I've died at a ripe old age.

Either way, I just want you to know that having you as a daughter has been my greatest joy. I'll always love you. In this life and the next.

Look for me in the butterflies, sweet girl.

Love,

Mom

I don't remember how I got to the couch in the shoe section. But I was thankful for Billie and Trevor guiding me there and smooshing me between them while I cried.

"Lucky." I sobbed. "She felt lucky." My mom—who feared curses and bad fortune—counted herself lucky when facing down cancer.

I bawled so hard my ribs felt cracked, but that was okay. Billie and Trevor held me together. They passed the letter between them, and though they didn't weep quite as thoroughly as me, neither had a dry eye.

When my body finally turned off the leaky faucet, I felt a sudden wave of clarity for the first time in weeks. Everything seemed to be falling apart but maybe, just maybe, some things could fall into place on the way down.

"I want you to stop worrying about finding a replacement, Trevor."

He scooted back, trying to read my expression—probably thinking I'd lost my mind. He pushed his glasses up, wiping at his eyes. "I have to find someone. You need me."

"What I need is for you to be happy. And I get the feeling you are considering not going to San Francisco over this."

Trevor looked away. Nail meet head.

"You better not," Billie growled. "I'll kick your ass if you throw away this opportunity so you can sell shoes for the rest of your life."

"You guys are family," he argued. "How can I just leave when you need me?"

I shrugged. "We'll find a way, even if that means doing things differently." If my mom could look on the bright side in light of a cancer diagnosis, then I could find a way out of this dark tunnel. One step at a time.

As Trevor considered this, Johnson waddled over to the couch. I'm sure we were quite the sight, the three of us huddled there, red-eyed and sniffling. He sat back on his haunches and eyed us with a *Get it to-fucking-gether* look.

"Do you think Johnson was a mean girl in his past life?" Billie asked.

And her tone had been so serious that I barked out a laugh, which surprised me. I didn't know I was capable of that noise anymore. Billie and Trevor laughed, too, and it felt good to have that moment of levity with them—a little sunshine amidst the rain.

Chapter 40

GABRIEL

When my mom told me she'd be back from Mexico in time for my race, I let her know she didn't have to be there—this was my ninth Ironman, after all. As expected, she shut that down right away. She'd always been my biggest supporter, and she loved the Ironman experience: the race, the spectators, and the village.

On the day of packet pickup, I invited her along for the ride. Mostly because I missed her company, but also because I needed someone to distract me from thoughts of April. When my mom climbed into my truck, she reached over the console to give me a hug, and I swear, it felt like she was getting smaller.

"How was Mexico?" I asked her in Spanish.

"You leave for a few years, and everything changes," she replied, also in Spanish. It had been a while since I'd held a conversation in my mother tongue, but it came naturally talking to Mom. She patted some of her graying hair back into place. "The family misses you. I told them you'd come next time."

I surprised myself by laughing, something I hadn't done in days . . . maybe weeks. Leave it to Mom to sign me up for family functions in another country.

I grabbed the shifter to put it in reverse, but she pulled my hand off it to inspect my knuckles.

"What happened?"

My hand looked better by the day, but scabs still marred my skin. The evidence was incriminating.

I gently pulled my hand away to put us in reverse. If we were going to have this conversation, I needed somewhere to look other than at the disappointment on her face. "I hit someone."

She laughed. "Tell me what really happened."

I flashed her a look, and the laughter died as soon as she realized I was serious.

"What happened?" she asked again, alarm rising with the question.

I tried to map out the easiest explanation. She didn't need to know about April and the complexities she'd brought. So, I left her out as if she was a minor detail and not the reason for my rusting heart, with its pieces flaking off by the day.

"Another coach put one of my athletes in harm's way, and I snapped."

I kept my eyes on the road, but I could feel her eyes scanning my face. I wondered what she saw when she looked at me—another version of my father? I couldn't bear the thought.

"That doesn't sound like you," she finally said.

"I'm not proud of it."

"What do you mean he put your athlete in harm's way? Explain."

I knew she wouldn't let the story rest at that. I sighed. "He deliberately messed with her bike, and because of that, she almost got hit by a car."

My mom didn't answer at first. When she did, it was quiet. "That must have been scary."

I nodded, but my head felt heavy; most of my body felt that way. Everything felt heavier without April. "It was."

I could usually read my mom pretty easily, but at that moment, I had no idea what she was thinking. Was she embarrassed? Disappointed? Scared of me? The silence in the car stretched until it thickened and soured.

I couldn't take it any longer.

"It was a one-time mistake. I'm not dangerous." And I believed myself. I would never get so caught up in my feelings again.

Her head snapped my way. "Of course you aren't, Gabriel."

"I just don't want you to be scared of me." I hated how small I sounded, like I was a little boy again, huddled in the corner, but that's the place I went back to when I pictured my mom being afraid.

"Pull over," she said calmly.

"Mom, I—"

"Right now, Gabriel!"

Surprised by my mom's outburst, I yanked us into the closest parking lot. As soon as the truck rocked to a stop, she reached over the console and grabbed my face. "Why do you think I'd be afraid of you?" Her soft brown eyes danced with tears.

"I just don't want you to think I'm going to be like Dad."

She shook her head. "Son, the only thing you got from that man is your height. To me, it sounds like you were defending someone you care about."

I grabbed her hands to free my face but didn't let go. "I still shouldn't have hit him. I never wanted to hurt anyone."

"Could you have handled things differently? Sure. But that doesn't mean you are dangerous. Okay?"

I looked at her. We had the same nose, same eyes, same dark hair—in the places where she wasn't graying. We couldn't deny kinship if our lives depended on it. Then there was the Ironman T-shirt she wore. She had to gather the loose ends of the shirt in a rubber band so it didn't swallow her. She'd had it for years. It was from my first race. I'd crossed the finish line, picked up my medal and finisher shirt, and handed both right over the corral to her—my biggest fan.

Of course, she would see the best in me. She always had.

But I didn't see the point in upsetting her further, so I put on my best attempt at a smile and kissed the back of her hand.

"Okay."

Bike and gear checked in, the two of us meandered Iron Village. We walked in and out of tents, looking at products and people-watching excited athletes. I tried to let the pre-race high permeate. Tried to allow myself to feel something other than the loss of April, but it was all still too fresh. I tried to tell myself I'd eventually feel better, but I was having difficulty believing it. As if to give my theory of everlasting misery more weight, who should step out of a tent but April?

The sunlight hit her, turning strands of her blonde hair golden. With it being a mild October day, she wore her overalls with a flannel tied around her waist. She was effortlessly beautiful, as always.

I tried to read her expression, but it didn't offer much. Her eyes looked puffy, as though she'd either been crying a lot or missing sleep. Those lips that I loved so much were in a neutral line. She looked okay, not happy, but like she would be with enough time and space.

She hadn't seen me yet, but there would be no going back if I didn't move. I pulled my mom into the Ironman store—where we'd just come from.

"What are you doing?" she asked.

"I changed my mind," I said, feigning interest in the ungodly-priced outerwear. "I think I do want a finisher jacket."

"Are you hiding?" my mom asked, stepping on her tiptoes, unabashedly searching out the culprit.

I gently pulled her to face me. "Can you just—" I blew out a breath and settled my hands on her shoulders. "I just need a second." I risked a glance outside the tent where Billie pulled April toward a stand with drinks. April gave a half-hearted laugh and relented.

It's a good thing she's here, I tried to tell myself. It meant she still planned on racing in a couple of days.

My mom looked over her shoulder, scanning. Then her eyes narrowed on Billie and April before snapping back to me. "Which of those girls are you hiding from?"

I got the distinct feeling that if I didn't give my mom answers, she'd launch her own investigation.

"The blonde." My voice automatically sounded thicker, just talking about her hair color. "Her name is April." I sighed, letting myself have an unguarded moment. "I really like her—love her," I amended. "I love her."

"You say that like it's a prison sentence."

"I had to let her go." I reached over and refolded a shirt that had been thrown over the neat piles. I hated having this conversation with yet another person, but if anyone could understand, it would be Mom.

"Why?" she asked, eyes swinging back to April. Then her mouth fell open as it dawned on her. "She's the athlete who almost got hurt."

"She did get hurt," I said miserably. "But it could have been so much worse."

"So, you were defending someone you love. Can you explain why that's so horrible?"

"Because I exploded. I don't even know who I was when Clay—the guy I hit—told us what he'd done." I let out an exasperated breath. "I feel too much with her."

"Then let yourself feel too much, Gabriel."

"I can't do that. What if she is on the other side of my fist one day?"

My mom's eyebrows drew in. "We both know you would never do that."

"No, I don't know. That's the problem."

"Do you not love me?"

"What?" I asked, confused by the question. "Of course I do."

"You've never been violent with me. Never even raised your voice, and I know there were more than a couple of times in your teen years when you wanted to."

"Grandma said Dad wasn't always abusive—that he wasn't that way until you two got married." I shook my head, thinking about how off the rails I'd gone since April's wreck. "Love makes people crazy."

"You think love made him talk with his fists?" She shook her head. "I thought we decided, a long time ago, that we weren't going to make excuses for him anymore."

My mouth fell open. I wasn't making excuses for him. Was I?

Her expression softened. "When you act like he had no choice, you let him off the hook. He chose to yell. He chose to break our home—to use his hands for harm." She grabbed my hands. Hers were so small compared to mine, and yet she had a fierce grip. "You've chosen to use yours for healing. To defend those you love." She looked close to crying. "Where he used his strength to tear others down, you've used it to help."

"You have to see the best in me," I finally voiced. "You're my mom."

"Because I'm your mom—because I experienced firsthand how dangerous your father was, I know better than anyone. Do you think I would ever let you be with a woman if I thought you'd bring her harm?"

I looked at her for a long time. You'd never know that she'd carried bruises across her cheeks, worn them around her eyes. You'd never be able to guess the sounds of her crying when my dad shook her or slammed her into a nearby wall.

The memories were haunting, but she'd moved on. She'd healed. Even still, she was the one person in my life who understood what it was like to be broken apart by someone who was supposed to build you up. So I believed that she'd protect others from that, even if it meant protecting them from her own son.

"But ultimately," she continued, "the choice will always be up to you. You can choose fear—as your father did. Or you can choose love." She turned her head, and I followed her gaze back to April.

What did choosing love look like right now?

I imagined running to April, begging for her forgiveness, professing my feelings. There was a possibility I could still guide her through Ironman. I could be a part of her big day. More than that, I could have her in my arms tonight. I wanted that so bad it hurt.

But I kept my feet cemented to the ground because there was a chance she wouldn't welcome my apology. I'd hurt her—enough that she might want nothing to do with me. As she'd once said, self-preservation is loud. What if she built up a wall to protect herself? Or worse, what if she'd gotten wise after I'd hit Clay and realized I was dangerous after all? I really didn't know how she felt, and how could I, after running and hiding?

I watched April push Billie away as she tried to take a sip of the drink she'd just purchased. The two laughed, and even though I could see the residual effects of hurt, April was okay. She was doing fine without me.

The day after tomorrow was a huge day, and I knew within my bones what loving her meant at that moment—it meant watching her walk away.

So that's what I did.

Chapter 41

GABRIEL

It was torture, keeping my distance from April on race day. I wanted to go through her supply list with her, see how her nerves were doing, let her know that I'd slipped another four-leaf clover in her bike pouch, but I wouldn't risk ruining her big day. I'd talk to her after the race.

At least I knew April had shown up. I'd watched her from a few aisles over in transition. She wore her short hair in two braids, and she was already in her wetsuit. She looked athletic, competitive, steady. She'd overcome every obstacle this season—had worked her ass off. I had no doubt she would defeat this race.

This was her year.

I forced myself to turn away before she could notice me and nearly ran right into Clay. I almost didn't recognize him with the greenish bruise blooming under his eyes. I was saved from a conversation or altercation when he side-stepped me to get to his own transition area.

May the best man win, I thought sourly, knowing that between us, it would just have to be the lesser of two evils.

·♥·♥·♥·♥·♥·

By the ten-hour mark, I was worn to the bone, had an aggressive side stitch, and was about eighty percent sure I'd find a detached toenail when I took my shoe off.

I was so miserable that I almost missed Coach Rick off to the side on the waterway. He'd stopped racing full Ironmans a few years ago, so he had the luxury of focusing solely on his athletes. We'd decided at each stop, he would give me a quick rundown on my athletes' progress.

He didn't like that plan at first, but I told him he either took the minute to update me or I'd take five minutes going through the Ironman tracker myself. He'd grumbled something about me being stubborn but hadn't argued any further.

The last time I'd seen him was at mile fifteen of the run when he'd told me April had made it off the bike. I'd been saturated in relief.

She's got this.

She's going to be okay.

Then, I reached mile twenty of the run. Coach handed me a cold water bottle and jogged with me along the waterway. Although, at this point, it was less of a jog and more like a shuffle forward. I was so tired, but it was only six miles until I finished. In the grand scheme of things, it was nothing, and at the same time, it felt like flying to the moon on sparrow wings.

"You're on track to PR, kid. All you have to do is keep the pace."

I nodded, too drained to acknowledge more than I had to. "How are they doing?"

Rick started giving me the rundown of my team, and I was proud. All that hard work was paying off.

My attention prickled when he finished the update and skipped over a specific athlete.

"What about Baird?" I managed.

"You are six miles from the red carpet. Finish, and you can check on her yourself."

I planted my feet, and Coach had to skid to stop when I did. "To hell with that. Where is she?"

"Mile three."

"*What?*" She'd been at mile two when I'd last checked five miles ago.

That's when I spotted my mom up ahead. She usually stayed close to Rick and his wife during races. She must have read the stress on my expression because the poster board in her hands drooped.

My mind had replayed her words hundreds of times in the past couple of days, like a melody on repeat. *"The choice will always be up to you. You can choose fear. Or you can choose love."*

I turned around.

"Torres," Rick growled, grabbing my tri-suit. "She's not going to finish, but you might. You are so close to A-Team," he said, exasperated, letting me go and taking a step back. "I don't want to see you throw it away for one person. One of Clay's athletes—Ned—quit at the bike, so you two would be neck-and-neck for the position if you finish this thing."

"Right now, I'm not worried about making A-Team. I'm worried about her." He looked wounded, so I broke it down for him. "Rick, you want me to do well because I'm your athlete. I want her to do well because she's mine."

"You're not just an athlete to me, Torres."

I blinked, touched by the emotion in Coach Rick's voice. I'd always thought of him as a father figure, but we'd never said those words out loud, and he had his own kids—a family that wasn't broken. So, I just figured my sentiment was one-way.

"Coach—"

"Watching you grow from this gangly, scared kid to who you are today—" He stopped, and I felt a pang in my chest as I realized Coach Rick was fighting tears. I'd known the man for my entire adult life, and I'd never seen him cry—except when the Astros won their first World Series, of course. "You were dealt some shitty cards in life, and it's been my pleasure to watch you overcome. I want you to keep going, Gabe. I want all the best for you."

I wet my lips. *How to explain April?*

"Do you remember after I broke up with Ashley, you accused me of having a fear of commitment?"

His bushy brows pushed together, and I really didn't know if my explanation was going to help or piss him off to no end. "Yes?" he said, and I could read the question underneath: *What's that got to do with anything?*

"You called it. I never planned on being in a serious relationship. But then I got to know April—" I blew out a breath, trying to organize my thoughts as athletes went around us, racing towards the finish line. "It's like I didn't have a choice. I fell fast, and I fell hard." I shrugged even though the conversation felt like it was turning me inside out and exposing myself to the world. "She's more than just an athlete to me. Just like I'm more than just an athlete to you. So, I'm sorry. The last thing I want is to disappoint you, but I have to go."

For an agonizingly long moment, Coach just squinted at me. He really didn't give a shit about making other people squirm. Finally, he relented, swearing under his breath. He hiked a thumb over his shoulder at an old mountain bike leaning against a tree. "There's my bike. Take my backpack, too. See if you can revive her."

Chapter 42

APRIL

I'm going to finish.

For Mom.

. . . For me.

My thigh just had to stop feeling like it was being electrocuted. Luckily, I had Billie and Trevor. They'd started walking with me when the cramps began at mile two.

My leg locked up for what felt like the hundredth time, and I grabbed hold of them to keep upright.

"It's bad again?" Billie asked.

I nodded, groaning and digging my fingers into their shoulders. Every step, I fought the voice that told me to sit down. To give up. To go home.

"What's going on?" My eyes shot open, but then I didn't believe what I saw. It had to be a mirage because there was Gabe gliding to a stop on an ancient mountain bike, concern etched between his brows.

I think my heart stopped. After weeks of wishing he'd pick up the phone or stop by the shop or let me in, there he was. Rushing in to save me, to fix the hurt. It was so good to see him.

Then I slammed into reality. The reason it was so good to see him was because he'd shut me out.

"She's having some intense quad cramps," Trevor supplied.

"I'm fine," I said through my teeth, forcing myself to move forward because, though the pain in my leg was intense, it was nothing compared to what Gabriel had done to my heart.

Gabe got just ahead of me, walking backward so he could get a look at the damage. He winced. "I can see the spasming." He looked at Trevor. "There's a first-aid tent not even a mile down. Can you see if they have any ice left? I need a cup's worth."

"Be right back," Trevor said, seeming glad to have a task.

"Take the bike," Gabe said, then he looked at me. "If you lie down, I can help you stretch it out."

"I can't do that," I said, adjusting my grip on Billie and picking up the pace as the cramp relaxed. "I'm in the middle of a race."

"Ten minutes out of seventeen hours probably won't kill your race," Gabe said. "However, taking an hour to finish each mile definitely will."

Billie bent her head close to whisper, "You don't have to forgive him, but maybe you should let him take a look."

I tried to soldier forward, but then another cramp tore through my thigh. I squeezed my eyes shut and bit down so hard I thought I'd crack a molar. I crumpled against Billie until a strong hand wrapped around my arm, holding up my other side.

"Please," Gabe begged. "Please let me help you."

I opened my eyes to his dark ones. They were endless pits of misery. Still, I wanted to deny him because all I'd wanted since the incident at

Clay's house was for him to let me in, to let me help, but he'd locked me out. If I hadn't been desperate for relief, I would have made him leave, but as it stood, the pain had worn me thin. Defeated, I nodded and let Gabe lead me just off the course to a grassy area.

"Lie down," he said. "We're going to stretch it out, then we're going to hit the sodium and hydration hard."

My head in the grass, I looked at the sun's placement in the sky. Gabe was fast, but it seemed early for even him to be done. A glance at my watch confirmed it was. Despite my anger, I had to know. "What was your finishing time?" I asked.

Gabe wrapped a large hand around my ankle and worked my leg in small circles.

"Gabriel," I said, alarmed by his lack of an answer. "What was your time?"

He sighed, then stopped the circular movement to look at me. "I didn't finish."

Three words. They were just three words, but they towered in front of me. I thought of the way Gabe's breath sawed out of him when he did his bike ride in my garage, the pool of sweat on the floor, the ice baths. He'd worked so hard for this.

"Tell me there was a reason you stopped other than me." I thought of how he'd lost A-Team because of my wreck last year. It couldn't be my fault again. "Tell me that you couldn't hold down your nutrition, or you had a bike malfunction, or you have really bad blisters, or you just weren't fucking feeling it today!"

He held my gaze.

"Dammit, Gabriel!" I pulled my leg away from him, shooting to a sitting position.

Billie cleared her throat. "I'm gonna . . . go see if Trevor needs help getting that ice."

Neither of us acknowledged Billie's exit, too wrapped up in our standoff.

"You do *not* get to do that."

"Do what?" He tried to grab my leg again, but I yanked it away.

He gave me an exasperated look. Well, that made two of us. "You don't get to sacrifice your race after ghosting me. That's not fair!"

"I know."

I didn't want him to agree with me. I wanted a fight. "And I get that you were hurting, but so was I," I said, surprised when my angry outburst converted to a dry sob—because I was too dehydrated for tears.

"April—"

He tried to get closer, but I stopped him, just like he'd stopped me at Clay's house. "Don't."

Annoyed that we'd forgotten them, my muscles tightened again. I clutched my leg, fingernails digging into my skin as if I could squeeze the pain back into submission that way. My arms shook with the effort, and I had to press my mouth into my shoulder to keep silent through the pain. It felt like my muscles were trying to escape through my skin—Alien style.

Gabe gripped my shoulders, and despite my anger, the counterpressure kept me grounded. "Breathe," he whispered, forehead pressed to mine. "Let me get you through this, and you never have to see me again, okay?"

I let out a sigh of relief as the cramp finally relaxed. Gabe gave me a reassuring squeeze before kneeling. I lay back, the grass tickling my ears as he worked my leg in circles again.

No longer consumed by pain, Gabe's words finally settled. The idea of never seeing him again made it feel like the spasming had moved to my heart. "I don't want that," I said, sounding broken.

Gabe looked down at me.

"I don't want to never see you again," I clarified.

His exhale shuddered. "I don't want that either."

"Then why haven't you answered your door or my calls? Why are you avoiding me?"

"Because I thought I was doing the right thing. I thought I was protecting you." The hurt was so plain on his face. "It scares me—how much I feel with you."

"But that's the thing. If you want any kind of future for us, then you will have to trust me with all your feelings—the good and the bad. Knowing my luck, it will be a lot of bad."

"I want that." He swallowed. "If that's how I keep you, then give me the anger, the fear, the pain. I want it all if it's with you."

My stomach flipped, but my leg had to steal the show again. Gabe's eyes shot to my thigh. In a flash, he tilted my toes so they pointed at my body, and then he leaned his weight onto my foot. I gasped, my leg protesting at first, but after a few seconds, relief, sweet relief, flooded my leg. It was as if my muscles had been in a game of tug-of-war, and the position forced the rope to drop. The cramp miraculously relaxed.

I let out a shaky exhale, shocked at the magic he'd worked.

"That a little better?" he asked.

"Yes." If I'd had any tears left, I would have cried from relief. "So much better."

He smiled slightly, then released my foot, moving my leg in circles again before pressing deeper. He worked silently for a long while, but the quiet was like a raincloud, gathering droplets by the second. It was only a matter of time until the downpour, and I didn't know if this rain would soothe the drought or flood the lands.

"I want you to know that I started therapy," he finally said. "And if you want to wait to be together until I've started going a while, I understand."

"Gabe, stop." He paused his circular motions to look at me. "It's great that you are going to therapy. I think it will help you work through a lot of your pain." I sat up, taking his hands in mine. His knuckles were still scabbed from the night he defended me. I brushed a thumb carefully around the wounds. "But I was never once scared of you." I swallowed. "Only scared of losing you."

His features softened. Emotion showed in the twitch of his jaw and the line between his eyebrows—the smallest of movements showing a powerful undercurrent of feeling.

We both leaned in. The day had been long, but the heartbreak had been more exhausting. Our lips meeting was a haven. Gabe sighed and pulled me closer. We were both sweaty and worn, but none of that mattered when Gabe's lips, so gentle, brushed against mine. Lips I didn't know if I'd ever taste again. I gripped his damp hair, desperate to keep this moment, afraid he might change his mind. Or that this was all some sort of illusion my delirious brain had drawn up after hours of racing.

Gabe's kissing became more feverish, too, before he pulled back, gulping for air, forehead resting on mine. "I guess I should stop. You are in the middle of a race."

I wanted to tell him this race was a lost cause anyway, but disappointment churned in my stomach at the thought of DNFing another year. Especially after he'd sacrificed his own race to save mine. So, I let him release me. Gabe pulled a bottle of pickle juice out of his backpack and unscrewed the cap. "I need you to drink all of this."

"We were supposed to win together," I said glumly, thinking of Clay getting A-Team because of my cramps.

"Stop. Okay? Helping people is what I care about. Your win is my win."

"I don't know if I can make this a win."

"You can," Gabe said. "But you've got twenty-three miles to go and only six hours left. It's going to be brutal. And if you want to go home, I'll carry you off this course right now."

Home. I'd never hear a sweeter word. The offer swung so succulently in front of me. The promise of shower and sleep and cuddles with Gabe could have made me weep. When you put on so many miles, your brain starts turning animalistic. It's hard to remember your why. All you want to do is make the pain stop.

But I dug deep. I thought of Mom's letter. I thought about Gabe. Hell, I thought about me. I'd worked this hard. I could rally for a few miserable hours.

"I'm going to finish this," I said.

Gabe nodded. "I thought you'd say that." He nodded toward the bottle in my hand. "Get to drinking. When Trevor returns with the ice, I'm going to massage your thigh with it. Then we get you back on the course."

I did exactly as prescribed by my coach without whining or hesitation. I knew I'd have to rely on his wisdom if I had any hope of conquering the rest of the race. The stretch and the pickle juice chased away my cramps. However, I had to catch up on all the time I'd spent walking.

Gabe was there every step of the way—talking to distract me, offering encouragement when I felt doubtful, handing over water, giving me chews. I noticed he had the slightest limp to his gait. It was a miracle he was still upright. He'd completed his own one hundred thirty-four miles.

Now he'd tack on another twenty-three. It made me want to collapse just thinking about it. I tried to tell him he could rest, that he didn't have to run the entire thing with me, but he wouldn't hear it.

"Together," he said. "We finish this together." I liked the sound of that, so I dropped the issue.

At mile thirteen, the halfway point for the run, I felt well enough to see past my own pain, and I had this surge of gratitude. For once, it didn't feel like the universe was out to get me or even that it was a neutral observer, as I tried so hard to believe.

No. The universe had sent me Gabe—a guardian angel of a coach. The path to Ironman had been treacherous, but if the race hadn't gotten canceled because of a storm, and if I hadn't gotten the flu, and if I hadn't had a crash that knocked me unconscious, and if Clay hadn't dropped me, I never would have started a relationship with Gabe. We would have remained passing ships.

I wasn't cursed. I was lucky.

Even thinking about all the bumps in the road this training season: my knee problems, the group ride landing on Friday the Thirteenth, Clay taking my pedal—all of it brought us closer together.

The realization made me feel stronger with each step.

The spectators certainly helped the cause. Some were just out there ringing cowbells and offering high-fives. Others had food offerings: M&Ms, chips, peanuts, orange slices, and the occasional alcoholic beverage, which I politely refused. My stomach didn't need any help feeling queasy.

I'd seen every poster board message imaginable:

Your pace or mine?

You are stronger than you think!

The cool thing about hobbies: you don't have to do them.

Incoming: Certified Badass!

Smile if you peed in the lake.

Go, TEAM TROUBLE!—Because Emily and Beck made an appearance. The diamond on Emily's left hand winked in the setting sun, and as we ran on, I forced every detail Gabriel had to offer on the engagement, which was very limited being that he was a man.

Some spectators had been there from pre-sunrise to post-sunset. You would think the hype along the course would mellow out as the evening wore on, but it turned into a different kind of party.

I met Gabe's mom, and I didn't know it was possible to instantly adore someone by association, but there was this overwhelming sense of connection with her. I wondered if she felt it, too, because she pulled me in for an embrace, and even though it was brief, there was a lot of emotion in her grip.

Then she'd turned to Gabe and said something in Spanish, to which he replied with a kiss on her forehead before we took off jogging again.

At one tent, a group played music from a portable stereo. While the adults under the tent talked, a gathering of kids danced on a grassy slope, waving glow sticks. A little girl who looked about three or four had on a cape that flapped as she spun. It took me a moment to realize it was designed to look like butterfly wings. The little butterfly danced right next to the course, smiling and waving as we passed.

"Would you look at that?" Gabe said. "*Mariposa*."

"Magic," I panted. And through the pain, fear, and exhaustion, I glowed from the inside.

Look for me in the butterflies.

Mom wasn't here. But she was. She lived through me in the way I remembered her and did what she loved. I wasn't losing her. She was right here.

Hours later, with only ten minutes to spare, we heard the cheering, and the red carpet came into view.

Gabe put a hand on my shoulder.

"This is your moment," he said. "Go on ahead, and I'll meet you on the other side."

I nodded.

Mom, you are my why.

I journeyed down the red carpet, stadium lights paving the way, hardly seeing past the blur of tears.

As I crossed the finish line, the announcer boomed, "April Baird, you are an Ironman!" And I collapsed to my knees and just cried and cried. For the voyage. For my mom. For the mercy of the universe sending me Gabe.

Volunteers surrounded me, but it was my coach who got me back up. Gabriel held me. His arms were steady, but his voice shook as he said, "I'm so fucking proud of you, April."

Freshly adorned with medals, a volunteer walked us all the way to the end of the corral, where we found Trevor, Billie, Gabe's coach, and his mom.

Trevor pulled me in for a hug, and when I protested, saying I was too sweaty, he held me anyway. When we parted, Billie made like she meant to hug me too, then thought better of it, giving me a pat on the arm instead. I felt delirious looking at her. She had a beer in one hand and Mardi Gras beads around her neck. She followed my gaze.

"No one told me these races are pretty much a huge party. Hippie Hollow was hopping."

I laughed and shook my head, stopping when Gabe's coach stepped forward. He looked between Gabe and me before giving a crisp nod. Then he extended a hand for Gabe to shake. "You did good, kid."

Gabe found enough energy to radiate at that. His smile could have rivaled the stadium lights.

We sat on the concrete and ate our finisher pizza with our family and friends before finally calling it to make the trek to get our gear. Retrieving your bike from transition after seventeen hours of grueling fitness is borderline cruel and unusual, but we finally made it back to Gabe's truck. Bikes in the back, asses on towels, sinking in the seat, Gabe looked like he was ready to pass out right there.

"The only thing I'm dreading about getting home—" Gabe said, eyes closed. "Taking my shoe off."

I cocked my head, and he opened a single eye to peer at me.

"I think I'm going to find I have one less toenail."

I winced. "That's why you were limping."

"It's fine. It will probably grow back."

"The glamorous life of being an Ironman." We both laughed—loopy with exhaustion. "I just thought of something." Gabe looked over, concerned by how my tone took a serious dive. "Now that the race is over, do I have to stop calling you Coach?"

He reached across the center console, albeit woodenly, until his hands met my cheeks. "Baird, do you think helping you finish an Ironman is all I have to offer?"

I licked my bottom lip, and even exhausted as he was, his eyes tracked the movement. "No. I'm sure you can teach me other things." I laughed as the idea popped into my head. "Like Spanish."

His thumbs stroked my jaw for a moment, and he swallowed. "Do you know what my mom said to me after meeting you earlier?"

I shook my head.

"Elegiste el amor." Gabe brushed a loose strand of hair behind my ear before translating. "You chose love," he rasped.

I stopped breathing.

"And she's right. I love you, April Baird."

I had to fight to get my reply out, and when I did, I was crying again. "I love you, too, Gabe."

His eyes shined, and his long fingers slid to the back of my head, pulling me closer. We breathed each other in. I thought of all the pain that had led to this moment. Each hardship was a stepping stone to Gabe. It had been such a difficult path to journey, but I'd take it every time if it meant being with him.

As his lips pressed into mine, the butterflies were back, and they were, in fact, pure magic.

Epilogue

GABRIEL

Three months later

April lay face down on someone else's table, a tattoo gun buzzing relentlessly against her calf. I noticed April's grip tightening on her elbows.

"You still doing okay?" I asked. She'd been a trooper, but I'm sure her skin was starting to get raw after three hours.

She turned to look at me. Her face was flushed, but she smiled cheekily. "Yeah, after being on your table, this is like a vacation."

The buzzing stopped, and the tattoo artist quirked an eyebrow at me.

"She's kidding," I said.

April winked at me, but it turned into a wince as he wiped the area.

"Okay, all done," the artist said. "Wanna see it?"

April was off the table in a flash, standing in front of the mirror. Her hazel eyes met my reflection for a moment, and I saw all the nerves there. I gave her an encouraging nod. She was going to love the ink on her leg.

April rotated her body until the tattoo came into view. An intricate and delicate butterfly stretched her wings proudly across April's calf.

The tears were immediate. I knew they were mostly happy tears, but there was no mistaking the loss threaded beneath.

"Come here," I whispered, pulling her into a hug.

"I love it," she said wetly.

I looked at the butterfly in the mirror as I stroked her back. Instantly, I thought of the picture of her and her mom that hung at the shop. Her mom had her Ironman tattoo, and a young April had tried to draw it but had inadvertently made her own creation, which resembled a blotchy butterfly.

Seeing April stand there, an Ironman finisher with a more refined butterfly on her calf, felt like things had come full circle. Like this was the plan all along.

Hand-in-hand, we walked into what was once Just Tri—now Just Bikes. Chuck jumped up from his spot under April's workbench, and she greeted him with under-the-collar rubs. Hard to believe he was the same scared dog Trevor had introduced me to. Now, he welcomed customers with his wide, tongue-lolling smile and spent his days curled up at April's feet.

"Let's see the ink," Billie said, snaking between racks of refurbished bikes, which had replaced the shoe-trying-on area. Some triathlon customers had been sad to see the loss of the running and swimming sections, but the transition had attracted a new crowd of cycling enthusiasts. Things were still early, but April loved spending her days working on bikes without the interruptions of shoe sales.

April turned slowly as if showing off a ballgown.

Billie's hand flew to her mouth. "Oh, babe." She knelt to get a better look. "It's stunning."

April looked over at the picture of her and her mom, her eyes shining.

"She'd be proud," I said. And I wasn't sure if I was talking about the butterfly or the shop or what she'd overcome to become an Ironman. All of it, I supposed.

April's hazel eyes swung back to me, and her smile was so beautiful it made my heart pinch.

"Okay, you two got it from here?" Billie asked, going back to the counter to get her things. "Y'all got fuck eyes."

"What?" I asked with a surprised laugh. I didn't think I'd ever get used to Billie's lack of a filter.

"We do not," April said with an eye-roll, but when Billie bent down to pat Chuck, she gave me a suggestive look.

"Good night, Chuck." He tried to give Billie a parting lick, which she barely dodged.

"Night, lovebirds!" Billie called, switching the sign to closed as she exited.

April surveyed her shop, looking pleased with herself.

"Come on. I'll help you clean so we can get home faster." Home being her house—after spending every night there for three months straight, April convinced me to officially move in with her. Tomorrow was my last official day to have the apartment, but it had been empty for weeks. After helping April rip up old carpet and renovate the bathroom, the house was starting to feel like mine, too. It's something I didn't take for granted—being able to pull into the driveway of a storybook home after a long day.

"Yes, Coach," April said, grabbing a rag to start dusting. "Speaking of, did your newest athlete finish his FTP yet?"

"He did." I threw away Billie's empty bag of mushroom jerky before sweeping behind the counter. "He's got a lot of potential." All my athletes did because they were all new to the sport this year.

Word had gotten out about April's comeback during the race, and the board decided that showed more about my coaching ability than my actual race time. They offered me the spot on A-Team, coaching elite athletes, but I declined and parried with the idea that April led me to.

Under my advisement, Triple Threat opened a whole new branch at the company specifically for those new to the sport or at finishing a certain distance. I realized helping ordinary people become a better version of themselves was really all I wanted.

The only problem about not accepting A-Team was that it left the spot wide open for Clay, that is until someone made April's pedal theft known to the board. There were a lot of ears at Clay's party, but I had my money on Trevor. Regardless, Clay was no longer coaching at Triple Threat.

April hooked up her phone to the shop's speaker and started an audiobook. This one was in Spanish. She had to listen to it at half speed and paused a lot to ask questions, but she was a quick study, and she'd made leaps and bounds with her Spanish.

Not that I was in any hurry for her to become fluent. After meeting April, my mom started planning our wedding, and the other day, she broached the subject of becoming an *abuela*.

I always put a stop to the conversation, but the crazy thing was I could see it, getting married to April, having kids with her. Something I never would have dreamed imaginable for my life was now something I thought was possible. In fact, I craved it—everything with her.

When April stepped up on her tiptoes to dust a high shelf, I set the broom aside and placed myself right behind her, my palm at her navel to stop her from moving. She shivered under my touch, then relaxed into me as I pulled the rag from her hand and wiped the area. I handed the rag back to her, and she turned, her face angled towards mine. When my lips met hers, everything quieted—it was as though a blanket of snow fell on the rest of the world while I warmed up with April.

It turned out April hadn't been the only one who needed a curse lifted. She'd demolished a wall I hadn't even known was there. Now, a road stretched before us with endless possibilities, and I was ready to traverse each and every step with her by my side.

Before you go!

Thanks you for reading "The Trouble with Love and Coaches." It's a dream come true to have this story in readers' hands! I've already taken up a good chunk of your time, but would you consider submitting a review for this book? I wouldn't ask if it wasn't important. Reviews drive an author's career, and I very much like this job. If you don't know where to start, Goodreads and Amazon are great places for reader reviews!

Hearing from readers is always my favorite. If you want to connect, you can visit my website www.harrietashfordwriter.com or find me on Instagram/TikTok @harrietashfordwriter

And because I can't just leave without giving y'all a little something, here is the engagement from Beck's perspective! It's on the house. Just visit the QR code below.

Acknowledgements

I f I've learned anything about self-publishing, it's that it takes an entire team. First of all, thanks to my husband, Bryan, for encouraging me to follow my dreams and for being a sounding board for my crazy ideas. I'm convinced the banter is only easy for me because you are as sassy as you are sweet. Thanks also to my boys for being patient while Mommy navigates all of this. Ben, you are too little to really understand any of this now, but your smile always helps keep me anchored when the tasks seem impossible. John, I really didn't think you'd be interested in my romance author career, and I wouldn't have blamed you, but you've turned out to be a Team Trouble member through and through. You always act so interested in how many reviews I have along with how many books I sold. Those things don't really fall into the average seven-year-old's interests, but I get the feeling it matters to you because it matters to me, and that says a lot about your heart.

Thanks to my parents, both by blood and by marriage. You guys have always been so supportive in my endeavors, so it's really no surprise you've shown up for me in this way too, but I so appreciate it. You've watched the boys so I could go to author events, you've cracked open your address books and called everyone on the list to tell them about my novel, and you've listened to my endless chatter about author life. I love y'all so very much.

I need an entire separate paragraph for my bestie, Monica. You'll see her listed a few times below because she has just done so much for this novel. She's always so generous with her expertise and talents. Thank you for another killer cake for the reveal, for not unfriending me for my hyper-fixation on Spanish phrasing, and for helping me reshape the last third of the book. (If you enjoyed Clay getting his bell rung, you can give this girl right here a high-five)

Big round of applause for my Spanish experts: Monica, Christina, and Jenny. I'm sorry for sending you the most random questions at all hours. All three of you are proper Christian ladies, and I asked you some very scandalous ways to use your mother tongue. I think I speak for all my readers when I say thank you for your service.

Thanks to my bonus sister, Kyle-Ann, for being my farmer market selling buddy and for singing praises about my book to customers when I was too shy.

Thank you to my massage expert, Katelynn! It seems like fate that you stopped at my table at Ink and Indie and I just so happened to ask you what you were studying, only to find out you were about to become a massage therapist. Thank you for making sure Gabe isn't a walking, talking HIPAA violation. Your expertise helped me to write some of my favorite scenes.

Thanks to my alpha/beta readers: Bryan, Monica, Katelynn, Sarah, Jessie, Sarah, Christine, and Paige. You saw the novel in such a raw form—the good, the bad, and the ugly. Your encouragement helped drive me forward, and your feedback made my novel so much stronger. Some of you helped me tear down scenes and rebuild. My novel is a completely different beast after your suggestions. From the bottom of my heart, thank you!

Huge thanks to TEAM TROUBLE! Woot woot! You brought your A-game this publishing season. Thanks for giving my stories wings. You are the kindest, cutest, most encouraging street team a girl could ask for.

Thanks to Staci at RomanceLandia. You were the first bookshop owner to believe in me. I love you and all you do for indie authors. You deserve all the success and good karma.

Thanks to my editor, artist, and proofreader: Bryn, My Lan, and Ramona. I know I'm paying y'all, but you crushed it! Bryn, your ending comments on my novel will live rent-free in my head forever. Ramona, thanks for taking my novel early. You are always such a pleasure to work with. And My Lan, the day you become too busy and famous to create the cover for my novels, my tears will flood the streets.

Finally, thanks to you, dear reader. I absolutely adore hearing when a certain part of my writing resonates with you. You come with your own experiences and breathe new life into my stories. So thank you! I have the best readership on the planet, and I will die on that hill.

About the Author

Harriet Ashford is hopelessly addicted to the second-hand falling in love feeling from reading and writing romance novels. She lives right on the line between Houston and Pearland with her husband, two boys, and sassy blue heeler.

While she works on your next book boyfriend by night, she teaches by day. If she's not at her desk, she's probably reading or hanging with her favorite guys.

Made in the USA
Coppell, TX
14 June 2025

50736477R00174